FAMILY SPIRIT

A LANDON LEGACY SERIES

JULIE CAMERON

LANDON
LITERARY

CONTENTS

ACKNOWLEDGMENTS

My heartfelt love and appreciation to my family and friends who support me every step of the way through all my stories and endeavors. I would truly be lost without you!

As always, many thanks to my patient and insightful writing coach Doug Kurtz, to Cate Byers, the best line editor on the planet, and to Dan Ramia and Kevin Cameron for being so generous and welcoming to me every time I take over their home as my personal writing paradise and retreat.

Special thanks to my Thursday Night Critique Group, my Beta Readers, and most especially to Ryan Mick, for all the open and honest feedback.

DEDICATION

For my courageous brother, Kevin, who is an eagle that flies.

CHAPTER ONE

Harry Landon stepped off the elevator onto the fiftieth floor of the Republic Plaza building, which housed the offices of Landon Literary, the publishing house he owned with his brother, George. The building, located on the 16th Street Mall in the heart of downtown Denver, was a couple of blocks up from his favorite coffee shop, Stan & David's Cafe, and it had become his daily habit to stop in each morning for coffee and for updates – some would call it gossip – on whatever was going on in Denver.

He loved his ritual, and he loved Landon Literary, in spite of the fact he had only just started coming here more regularly in the last two years.

For the first time since he and George had started the company he was feeling like he was a part of the action, since landing their latest best-selling author. It gave him a sense of pride that the first thing everyone saw when the elevator doors opened was the Landon Literary logo above the reception desk.

He was part of that.

The reception waiting area reminded him of a Victorian study, complete with a deep-brown leather sofa and matching wingback chairs. The wooden bookshelves were filled with various titles from the works they'd published over the years, and he'd always imagined having a library like this in his own home one day.

He took a deep breath, enjoying the scent of worn leather, furniture polish, and printed paper. The hint of freshly-brewed coffee drew his attention to the front desk, where Sandy, Landon Literary's competent receptionist, was brewing the first pot of the day.

Sandy was a petite blonde who looked like she could be a young fifties-era housewife, but inside lurked an efficient drill sergeant who didn't put up with crap from anyone. Including Harry, which secretly made him the tiniest bit afraid of her.

"Harry? Are you still with me?" The woman's voice on the other end of his cell phone purred in his ear, and his attention snapped back to their conversation.

"I'm just getting off the elevator, and I don't always get the best reception here," he responded absently, as he waved to Sandy, on his way toward his office.

"I was thinking we could go away for the weekend." Sarah's nasal voice, which always sounded like she had a cold, was in sharp contrast to the comfort of his surroundings, and he was sorry he'd picked up her call. "I'm really looking forward to spending some alone time with you."

He knew she was going for a hot-and-sexy take-me-now tone, but all it brought up in his mind was cheap-nine-hundred-number and he resisted the urge to roll his eyes, even if she couldn't see him do it.

Not that Sarah wasn't hot and sexy – and she was definitely not cheap, considering the bill at dinner the other night – but he had known by their second date that she wasn't right for him, and he'd had been trying to untangle himself from her ever since. She had the speech and the attention span of a two-year old, and they both made him want to put her in a time-out until his ears stopped ringing.

"Sorry, can't," He replied, although he wasn't the least bit sorry. "I'm booked solid this weekend with work."

He needed to tell her it was over, but he was never any good at that part. He hated the break-up phase because they always took it so personally, and he didn't like hurting their feelings. It was easier just to stop calling them, and eventually they got the message.

"Okay, baby," She whined, "Don't work too hard. You're going to need all your strength for when I get my hands on you."

"I gotta go." Harry disconnected the call before he had to listen to whatever it was she thought she was going to do with him. He despised being called "baby." He was forty-two years old, for chrissake. He was nobody's baby.

How could he have been dating women for over twenty years, and still not have the hang of it? Why couldn't he find the right woman like his brother, George, had?

Before George married his spunky administrative assistant, Emma, Harry was convinced he and his older brother would both be bachelors the rest of their lives. He loved his brother, but he honestly couldn't imagine any woman putting up with the guy. He was a bit of a curmudgeon. Although, since Emma had come into his life, Harry had to admit that George was a much happier man.

As if realizing he was the topic of someone's internal conversation, George rounded the corner of the executive suites, and almost collided with Harry.

"Was that Anna?" George asked, as Harry pocketed his cell phone.

"Anna? Where?" Harry whipped his head around so fast he gave himself a kink in his neck. She wasn't supposed to be in the office today, or he wouldn't have risked coming in, even at George's summons.

"Wasn't that Anna you were making plans with on the phone just now?" George looked exasperated, but since he frequently did, Harry didn't think much of it.

"No, it was Sarah. Anna's out today though, right?" Harry asked, in a casual no-big-deal-just-wondering kind of way.

Anna was another woman Harry needed to end it with. He'd been trying to do just that for about two months, but for some reason she didn't seem to get the message. Every time he turned around, there she was.

Of course, as Landon Literary's newest editor, it was normal for her to drop by his office periodically during the day to ask him questions, and to get his opinion on the manuscripts she was reviewing. What wasn't normal was the inordinately high number of times she was stopping by, when an email, phone call, or even a text would suffice. It was as if she needed his validation, or approval, to make her day complete. Then, before he knew what hit him, he'd be having lunch, or drinks after work with her, and his resolve to break up with her was once again squashed under her shoe like a bug.

And that was why he'd been avoiding coming to the office.

He was such a chicken shit.

The problem was that he liked Anna. She was smart, beautiful, compassionate, and a great conversationalist. He enjoyed spending time with her. They always ended up having a nice time together, no matter what they did.

But he could tell she was looking for more in their relationship than he was, so he'd started his *Avoid Her At All Costs* campaign, and it was beginning to interfere with his job.

"Let's talk." George turned and headed to his office, as if he had no doubt Harry would follow.

Harry wondered what would happen if he ignored the command, and kept walking to his own office instead, but decided it would only put off the inevitable. He sighed, and followed George, feeling like a kid who'd been caught TP-ing the neighbor's house.

George's office was next to Harry's, and was decorated in the same warm earth tones as the rest of the company's suite. His office was accented with bright reds, while Harry's was accented in deep blues. George's large cherry wood desk was precisely centered at the floor-to-ceiling glass window that overlooked downtown Denver.

"Seriously, Harry, what's going on with you?" George headed for his desk, but Harry wasn't about to let his older brother have the upper hand by forcing him to sit in a guest chair and receive a lecture.

"Oh, not again." Harry sat down on the leather couch in George's sitting area, and propped his feet on the coffee table like he was in his own living room. "When are you going to stop playing helicopter older brother on me, George, and let me live my life? Why do you care if I sleep with one woman or five hundred? I'm having fun. Stop being such a fuddy-duddy. Just because you found the love of your life and settled down into mediocrity, doesn't mean I have to, too. I don't do commitment."

George stood in the middle of the room, his hands fisted on his hips, and stared at him. Harry knew he'd said the exact wrong thing.

"Who do you think you're talking to?" George joined him and sat in the matching armchair. He gave Harry a look that clearly showed he was calling bullshit. "I am not one of the women you're currently trying to dust. I'm your brother. I know you, remember? And that was a complete load of crap."

He was right.

Harry slumped further into the couch feeling like he'd just been caught lying to the pope. He wasn't sure why he'd spewed all that crap. It just came out. George knew him better than any other person in his life, and he never would have fallen for it.

"You have so much to offer." George leaned in, and rested his arms on his knees. "No matter what line you keep using to break up with your latest fling, it isn't that you 'don't do commitment'. You simply haven't found the right woman yet." George scrunched up his face, looking as if he was trying to solve some ancient mystery. "Why are you wasting your time with women who are half your age, and are only interested in you for the things you can buy them?"

"Wow, cliché much?" Harry knew George was right, but it still pissed him off to hear it. "You're one to talk. I seem to remember a crazy woman named Crystal who latched on to you, then me, then back to you, because she couldn't decide who had more money. And you've got at least twelve years on your wife, so don't throw me under that moral lesson either."

"You're right. That was hypocritical of me." George looked at Harry for a long moment, but Harry knew better than to believe the conversation was over. "I want you to be happy." George looked like he wanted to continue with, "like I am." But he seemed to change his mind at the last second.

"I want me to be happy, too. I just don't seem to know what that looks like yet."

George nodded, as if Harry's words explained everything. Then he said, "Believe it or not, I didn't drag you in here to complain about your love life. I wasn't originally planning to talk about your constant parade of women." George grinned, and Harry knew it was his way of saying *I'll always be here for you, not matter what.*

"What I really wanted to talk to you about is your recent – and very noticeable – absence from the office." George sat back in his chair and replaced his grin with his most official looking Publishing Executive face.

"What are you talking about?" Harry was stalling, and from the look on his brother's face, George knew it, too. "Fine." Harry dramatically threw up his hands in mock defeat. "I'm avoiding Anna. Are you happy now? I've just proved what you've been telling me for years: *Don't shit where you eat.*"

"I have never said that to you."

"Not in so many words, you would never be that crass." Harry grinned, unable to resist taking a stab at George's impeccable demeanor. "But you are not above gloating. So, let's have it."

Harry sat back and flapped his hand, indicating that George should get started. The sooner he got it out of his system, the sooner Harry could go to his own office and get some work done. Anna was only going to be out for a few days, and Harry had a ton of catch-up to do.

He wasn't proud of how little he'd actively participated in helping to run the company in the past, but he'd done a complete one-eighty recently, and he loved every minute of it. George's coma two years ago had scared the proverbial shit out of him, not just because he'd almost lost his brother, but because he'd almost lost his brother's legacy in the process.

If Emma hadn't given him the emotional equivalent of a boot to his ass, he might still be wallowing in self-pity and denial, wondering what to do with his life. Who knew he had such great instincts when it came to discovering new and talented authors?

"Tell me why you have been avoiding Anna." George asked, and Harry was thrown off balance. He'd expected George to tell him to sort it out with Anna, and get his head out of his ass.

"Because she thinks there's more to our relationship, and I can't get her to face reality. So, I'm hiding. I'm not proud of it, but—"

"What makes you think she wants more?" George leaned forward, and looked like he was getting ready to interrogate a suspect.

"You mean, other than trying to stick her tongue down my throat every time she sees me?" Harry was half joking, but she was always touching him, and hanging on him, as if they were a couple who'd been married for years. It was uncomfortable.

"You kiss her?" George exploded out of his chair so fast, it made Harry flinch.

"No, I don't. She kisses me. Because she keeps catching me off-guard."

"This has to end."

"That's what I'm saying. I've been trying to do that, but she isn't getting it."

George started pacing the room. He was running his hands through his hair, and Harry knew that was a sign that he was working through a particularly difficult issue. Harry had never seen his brother so freaked out. He was usually so unflappable.

"Don't get me wrong," Harry continued, because he felt the need to defend Anna, "I like her, and I like spending time with her. Just not every minute of the day."

"Look," George said as he sat back down in the chair next to Harry, "we need to talk. This is all my fault."

George looked at him with so much anguish, Harry was sure his next words were going to be, *Anna has inoperable brain cancer.* Instead he said, "Anna isn't who you think she is. Anna's—"

"Excuse me." Karla, George's new assistant, knocked on the open office door. "Sorry to interrupt, but I have a message for Mr. Landon from Legal. It's marked as urgent."

Harry knew from George's expression that he'd been about to say something important, but he couldn't help himself from snickering over the formality of Karla continuing to call George 'Mr. Landon.'

Apparently, George didn't find it nearly as entertaining, because he sat back in his chair, deflated, and groaned.

"Just 'George,' Karla," he said, and sighed. It was probably the tenth time Harry had heard him try to correct her since she'd started working there. "No need for 'Mr. Landon,' remember? Thank you, I'll take a look at it."

Harry could understand her confusion about what to call her boss. George was probably twice her age, and she must look at him like a father figure, which made Harry want to laugh.

Karla shook her head, and held out the envelope to Harry. "No, not you, Mr.— uhm, George. It's for Mr. Harry Landon."

Drat, now she was thinking of him as a father figure? That hurt.

Karla handed Harry the paper, then hurried out of the office.

"About Anna..." George persisted, but Harry was already focused on reading the note and ignored him. He read the words, "...urgent matter regarding your ex-fiancée," and almost stopped breathing.

"Something's happened to Jenny." Harry's stomach plummeted like the Tower of Doom ride at the amusement park. "I have to go."

He ran out of George's office without another word.

CHAPTER TWO

"May I get you something to drink, Mr. Landon?" Elaine, the law firm's long-time receptionist, asked Harry. "Coffee? Tea? Soda?"

He considered requesting a bourbon, neat, but figured it would probably throw the poor woman off her game, and he didn't want to offend her.

"No, thank you, Elaine. I'm good."

He had only been standing – okay, pacing – in the waiting area of the Starr and Schuster Law suite for about three minutes, but it seemed more like weeks. The waiting area was warm and inviting, with leather armchairs, and the current editions of *People* magazine stacked neatly on the glass coffee table that was so pristine a doctor could have performed surgery on it. But none of that was having its usual welcoming effect on him.

The scent of Elaine's too-liberally-applied Chanel No. 5 was giving him a headache.

"How much longer will—"

"Harry?"

The door behind the receptionist's desk opened, and Jason Starr, Esq., came out to shake Harry's hand. He was dressed in a charcoal gray Armani suit, and looked like he had just stepped out of a *GQ* magazine. The one for attorneys.

In his early forties, Jason was handsome, successful, and an all-around great guy; three qualities that Harry knew made women stab each other with their stilettos climbing all over each other to get to him. Sadly, for all the women of the world, Jason preferred men, and had recently celebrated his fifteen-year anniversary by taking his husband, Michael, to a secluded beach house in the Maldives.

"Sorry to keep you waiting. I had a minor complication I needed to resolve. Come on into my office, and let's get started." Jason smiled warmly at Harry and gestured him into the inner sanctum of the firm.

Jason had been best friends with Harry and George since childhood. Growing up, they had gotten into a lot of trouble together, some things that, to this day, only the three of them knew about. They had been inseparable. When Jason passed his bar exams, Harry talked him into being retained as the legal counsel for the brothers, which at the time was at their brand new publishing company.

The message was marked as urgent, which worried Harry, because Jason wasn't the type to push the panic button for nothing. Plus, it had something to do with Jenny, which automatically made it important to Harry.

The plush neutral-colored carpet muffled Jason's steps as he walked behind his antique oak desk and sat in his chair. He shuffled through some papers, as Harry chose one of the dark leather guest chairs in front of Jason's desk.

Harry knew that most attorneys had wall-to-wall book shelves filled with intimidating legal volumes, but Jason went a step further and added a whole wall of shelves filled with books he enjoyed reading, but had little or nothing to do with the law. He'd told Harry that he wanted people to know he was a skilled attorney, but that he was also human.

Jason had a reputation for being a fair but shrewd negotiator, and Harry recognized the *I'm in my lawyer mode, so don't mess with me* expression on his friend's face that indicated he was about to hear something he wasn't going to like.

"So, it's a serious meeting then. What's with all the formal lawyer routine?" Harry tried sounding unconcerned, but Jason was making him nervous. "Should I be worried? Your note said this has something to do with Jenny."

His friend raised his head, but didn't look him in the eye, and Harry knew he it was going to be bad.

"How often did you talk to Jenny after you two broke up?"

"We never kept in touch."

"So, you haven't spoken with her since that day?"

Over the years, Harry had considered checking in with her to see how she was doing, but he had never followed through. He felt that he owed her something after all the time they'd been together, and for how he'd ended it. He wanted to make sure she was happy, to be sure she was...

What?

Okay?

Financially secure?

Still in love with him?

Last year, he had almost asked his friend Blake, who was also a private investigator, to look into Jenny for him as well. But he'd chickened out at the last minute, too afraid to find out that she hated him and didn't want anything to do with him.

Or worse, to find out that she was happy and had moved on without him.

"What's going on, Jason? You already know everything about Jenny. You were there when we were dating, and you were there when I ended it. You didn't get me down here with an urgent message to reminisce. What's the real reason I'm here?"

"Harry, I'm sorry to be the one to tell you this." Jason finally looked Harry in the eye. "There was an accident, and Jenny was killed."

Jesus.

His whole world shifted, and he reached out instinctively to try to grab onto something.

"What?" He'd heard what Jason said, but it wasn't sinking in yet.

Jenny was dead.

He was going to be sick.

The room felt too warm, and the space around him seemed to be getting smaller. Jason sounded like he was far away – like he was talking from the opposite end of a very long tunnel – and it was a struggle to make sense out of his words.

Harry took a deep breath and made himself focus on what Jason was saying.

"We were contacted by her attorneys because this was the only way they knew to get in touch with you. I felt it might be easier for you if you heard the news from me."

His sweet Jenny. The one woman he'd ever truly loved.

She was dead? How could that be?

"What happened?" He wasn't sure he wanted to know the answer. He knew it wasn't rational, but he figured that if he didn't know any of the details, then maybe she wouldn't actually be dead.

"Car accident. The police are still investigating, because there are apparently some inconsistencies, but her car hit a tree. She was killed instantly. I'm so sorry Harry. I know this must be difficult for you."

"Jesus Christ, Jason." He was starting to return to his own head, and things were coming back into focus again. He was stunned. He hadn't seen her in...

Hell, ten years.

Not since the day he'd said he was sorry, and then left her, standing all alone at the altar.

"Her attorneys contacted us because she named you in her will," Jason continued.

"She named me in her will? Did she leave me money? Why would she do that?" None of this made any sense. They hadn't been in contact for years.

"She didn't leave you money." Jason paused, and he looked like he was wishing he'd stayed in the Maldives. "She left you her son."

"What the hell?" Harry couldn't believe what he was hearing. Jenny had a son, and he had no idea.

"*You* and Jenny had a son. According to her attorney, she claims you as the father, and has appointed you as his legal guardian."

"Are you shitting me?" Harry shouted as he bolted out of his chair.

"Keep your voice down. Max is in the next room."

"Who the hell is Max?" He was still shouting, but he couldn't seem to turn down his own volume. Harry had witnessed Jason dealing with irate clients before, so he wasn't surprised that the guy could sit there and remain calm and unflappable, while he was coming unglued, but it still pissed him off. This was not the time for any professionalism bullshit.

"Max is your son," Jason repeated the words, as if they hadn't sunk in the first time. Probably because they hadn't.

They stared at each other in silence, like they were kids again and trying not to be the one to blink first. He was waiting for Jason to say it was all a sick joke, and Jason was apparently waiting for him to get a grip.

"This is insane." Harry broke the stand-off and started pacing, as if that would somehow help rattle the thoughts in his head into some sort of meaning. "Do I have to take custody, or whatever it is? Can't I decline being his guardian?" He didn't know if the kid was even his. "Wait a second... How old is the kid?"

"The 'kid' has a name. It's Max." Jason sounded like he was losing patience with Harry.

Too bad. Let *him* wake up one morning to find out the woman he'd once loved had died, and left him a son he'd never known he had. See how well he could take it when he was on the receiving end.

"Fine. How old is Max?"

"He's nine."

Shit.

The kid – *Max* – could be his son. But that would mean that she had been pregnant when he'd left her, and that was too awful, even for him. He would never have let that happen. He was very careful about that.

No. There was no way Max was his.

"So, what happens if I politely decline?" He had to get out of this. He was not raising a kid, and definitely not a son. He had no idea how to raise a son. All he knew was how *not* to raise one, thanks to his own father's example.

"Max would become a ward of the state, and he would go into the system. Do you want that for him?" Jason raised his eyebrow, but Harry had seen that trick used on other clients, and he was not falling for it. He was not going to be manipulated into raising a son who wasn't even his.

"What about Jenny's family? Can't someone else take him?"

"Her attorneys informed me that no one else has come forward claiming guardianship." Jason glared at him like he thought he was some kind of evil villain, and he felt himself starting to crack under the pressure. "She might not have any family left, which would explain why she named you as his guardian."

"Don't look at me like that. You and I both know that I am not father material. Jenny had to have been out of her mind. I can't take him."

"I understand." Jason sighed, and massaged his left temple. Harry knew this meant that he was thinking through a difficult problem – which, at the moment, was Harry – so he waited for Jason to continue. "It will take some time to draw up the papers, and get everything settled. Will you at least be willing to take him in the interim so that he doesn't get shuttled around several times?"

"Are you serious? You've been to my loft. It's not a place for a nine-year old. Too much breakable stuff... too many sharp corners."

"He's nine, Harry. Not exactly a toddler. All I'm asking is for a few days while I sort through the paperwork to file with the Family Court. Can you give him that much?"

Harry felt like shit. He was acting like an ass. The kid was going into the foster system, and he was complaining about taking him on for a few days.

"Yes. Yes, I can. I'm sorry, this whole thing has taken me by surprise, and I overreacted. Yes, I can take him for however long you need." He had no idea what he was going to do with him, but he would figure that out later. Maybe George's wife, Emma, would have some ideas. She had buckets of nieces and nephews. She'd know what to do.

"Good for you, Harry. He's a sweet kid. You're going to like him."

"Christ, I hope not."

"I'll go get him." Jason got up from his chair, gave Harry a sympathetic look and an encouraging pat on the shoulder, then left through a side door.

"Shit." Harry braced his elbows on his knees, and massaged his aching head with his fingers. This day could not possibly get any worse.

"You will *not* abandon my son like you abandoned me, Harry Landon."

Harry bolted from his chair like vault gymnast, then cracked his shin on the edge of Jason's desk when he spun around to see who had spoken.

"Jenny?"

He was so relieved. It had all been some kind of horrible mistake, because Jenny was standing behind his chair. And from the look on her face, she was royally pissed off. He didn't care. Pissed was much better than dead.

She was so beautiful. He would have recognized her anywhere, despite not having seen her in ten years. The deep chocolate-colored eyes, the long auburn hair, and the tiny freckle just under her left eye (which seemed to be twitching; that was new), all seemed so familiar, like coming home. She was a few years older, and he could see small lines etched around her eyes and mouth that she'd never had before. But she was still his Jenny, and his heart skipped a beat seeing her again.

He was an idiot for not keeping in touch. He'd missed her.

"They told me you were dead," he said instead. "I'm so glad to see—"

"I am dead, dumb ass, or neither of us would be here right now."

"If you're dead, then… I'm hallucinating?" He couldn't seem to wrap his head around what he was seeing. She looked so real, but she couldn't be standing there. It was impossible.

"You haven't changed a bit, Harry Landon." She smiled, and spoke as if she hadn't heard him questioning his own sanity. "You're still the gorgeous, blond-haired, blue-eyed, captain-of-the-football-team heart-breaker you always were." She sighed, and Harry felt the years and the distance between them slip away as if they'd never existed.

"I was never on any football team, and you know it."

She snorted. "I'm stereotyping. Sue me."

The far-off look in her eyes disappeared, and she spoke firmly, as if remembering she had a job to do.

She crossed her arms, and she started tapping her foot. Not a good sign. She always did that when she was expecting answers from him. From previous experience, he remembered that she could do that for a very long time, and he'd learned it was best to just tell her what she wanted to know.

"I'm here to make sure you don't try to get out of taking Maxi. I appointed you his guardian, and you *will* be his guardian." That sounded ominous, even for Jenny. "You left, you jerk. You left me standing at the altar, buttoned-up in thousands of miles of white satin and tulle, clutching a three-hundred-dollar bouquet of lilies-of-the-valley – *long* before Kate Middleton made them popular, by the way – while two-hundred-and-fifty of our nearest and dearest sat in pews watching as you and your rapidly retreating ass ran out before the 'Dearly Beloveds' even started. You abandoned me. You left me behind without a backward glance. But you will *not* do the same to Maxi. I won't let you."

"But how—"

He was interrupted when the side door opened, and he saw Jason leading a small boy into the room. He turned back to Jenny to convince her that she'd made a huge mistake appointing him, but she wasn't there.

"Where did she go?"

"Where did who go?" Jason asked, as he tugged a reluctant Max closer to Harry.

Harry was losing it. That was the only explanation. The logical conclusion was that he had assumed Jenny would be upset with him, and he had imagined her showing up to yell at him about it. It was his brain's crazy way of dealing with the fact that he now had to make some major decisions that would change a kid's life.

"Max, this is Harry," Jason said, as if introducing a debutante to her first dance partner at her coming out party. "Harry, this is Max. Your son."

That last comment was hitting below the belt, which made him want to strangle Jason. They did not have any proof yet that the kid was his son, and Jason had no business stating it out loud. Christ, he was an attorney. He should know better.

Which was probably why he'd said it, as one last push to convince Harry to keep the kid.

He studied the nine-year-old boy standing in front of him. The poor kid didn't look any happier about the situation than Harry, and he never once took his eyes off the floor in front of him.

What must he be thinking right now? He's got to be scared shitless.

He looked like Jenny. He had the same auburn hair, which was badly in need of a cut, and he had her mouth, and her nose.

Harry's chest felt tight at the thought of how different his life would have been if he had only stuck it out. He had loved Jenny. He could have made it work. Had he missed his only chance for a loving relationship when he ran?

He didn't believe that Max was his son, but the poor kid was a casualty in all of this, and Harry's heart went out to him. He couldn't keep him long-term — he was never having kids — but he would still make it right for him. He would make sure he went to a good home with loving parents. A kid should have two parents who loved him.

He crouched down so that he was at eye level with Max. "Hi, Max. I'm sorry about your mom."

Max continued to stare at the floor as if he didn't hear him. "I know your mom wanted you to come and live with me," Harry continued, "But I'll bet you know someone else who you would rather—"

"No. There's no one. Okay? Happy now?" Max finally looked up from the floor.

And Harry found himself staring back into his own deep-blue eyes.

CHAPTER THREE

First thing on the agenda was a paternity test. He didn't care what color the kid's eyes were, Max wasn't his son, and he was going to prove it. Elaine had given him the contact information of a place near Cherry Creek that could do DNA tests.

Max hadn't said a word to him since his outburst denying anyone else would want him, and Harry was starting to worry there was something wrong with the kid. He just stared out the car window as if he was visualizing himself in a parallel universe. Not that Harry could blame him, he was wishing the same thing himself right now.

Harry pulled into a space in the lot outside the collection facility, cut the engine, then looked at Max.

"Look, ki— Max. I am really sorry about your mom. I knew her a long time ago, and I loved her very much." Harry felt his throat get tight, and he had to swallow several times before he could continue. "I know this must be really hard for you, so if you want to talk—" Harry was cut off when Max unbuckled his seat belt, got out, and slammed the car door shut.

So much for talking about it then. Fine. He really didn't know what else he could say .

Harry got out of the car, beeped his remote to lock it, then went around to Max's side to lead him into the facility. The kid was slower than molasses rolling uphill in January. He dragged his feet as he shuffled into the office, and the whole time, he never looked up from the space on the ground two inches in front of him. Harry felt a pang of guilt over what the kid must be going through, but this needed to be done. The sooner the better. Rip it off like a band-aid

He held the door open for Max to go inside, and tried to appear positive. "This is going to be really easy, and shouldn't take much time. When we're done, I'll take you out for ice cream. How's that sound?"

Nothing.

The facility looked like any other doctor's office Harry had visited. There were cheap, but cushioned, armchairs clustered around various laminated Ikea-looking end tables, and the room was painted in a pea-green colored paint. Harry wondered if the color was supposed to put people at ease, but all it made him think of was soup.

Max stopped at the reception counter, and stood there with his head tucked into his chest, not saying a word. Harry wasn't sure he had even heard him. Then it occurred to Harry that Max seemed to know the protocol when checking into a clinic. Should a nine-year old boy know how to stop at the counter and wait for an attendant?

"Hi, may I help you?" asked the bright young nurse behind the reception desk.

"Yes. Hi," Harry responded. "We need a paternity test."

"Sure. We can help you with that. Do you want the personal knowledge test or the legal paternity test?"

The which and the what now?

Already, Harry was feeling out of his element, and couldn't wait for this to be over. He was starting to want to hide his face in his chest like Max. But someone had to be the adult. And the sooner he got this done, the sooner he could pass Max on to someone else.

"What's the difference?"

"Well," the nurse explained, "the legal paternity test is a little more expensive, because it's more involved. But if you need the results for anything legal, that's the test you have to take. If it's only for your own personal knowledge, then the personal knowledge test is just fine."

He had no idea how far he would need to take this, but better safe than sorry. He did want to know for his own personal edification, but if the results couldn't be used legally, he didn't believe that would do him any good. Besides, he didn't want to have to come back here again with Max if it turned out he needed it to be more official.

"We'll do the legal one, please."

"Okay. Sure thing. Just take a seat over there, fill this out, and we'll get you in as quickly as possible." She handed Harry a clipboard containing several sheets of paper, and a pen with a bright plastic daisy attached to it. Apparently, these people didn't trust their clients not to walk off with their highly valuable drug company logoed pens.

"Come on, kid, let's sit over there." He pointed to a couple of chairs in the corner of the waiting room that faced a TV. At least Max could watch something while Harry pored through the forms.

Name, address, phone, date of birth, social security number. This was simple enough, and he was able to get through the forms quickly. At least for his own information.

Max's information was not as easy.

"What's your full name, Max?"

"Maximus Harold Fallon." Max sounded immensely proud of his full name, and Harry had to fight back a laugh.

Maximus? Seriously?

Did his mom *want* him to get the shit kicked out of him in grade school?

He must not have done a very good job at covering his amusement, because Max glared at him, then turned toward the TV in a deliberate move to block Harry out.

"What the hell are you doing here?" Jenny had popped back into existence, and scared Harry so much he jumped, which in turn startled Max enough that he looked up at him with a suspicious expression.

Great. The kid probably thought he suffered from seizures.

What he was really suffering from was hallucinations. At least, he hoped that's what she was. She was probably just a manifestation of his guilt, and she would go away soon.

"You are subjecting my son to needless stress right now," Jenny continued, "and I don't appreciate it one bit. I already told you he's your son, you don't need to have him tested."

"And I'm just supposed to—" Harry started to argue with her, then decided he would be much better off not giving in to whatever thoughts seemed to be conjuring up this Jenny apparition, and turned his attention back to Max.

"So, your middle name is Harold, huh?" he asked Max, instead. "Did you know that's my first name?" He looked at Max, hoping he could get him to open up, but he had already pulled the shutters back down over his face again. "My first name is Harold, but it's so awful, I only use Harry. You can call me Harry, if you want."

Still nothing.

"I'm serious, Harry." The Jenny thing, whatever the hell it was, continued to push her point, and she looked like she was about ready to blow a gasket, if her toe-tapping was any indication. "He just lost his mother. He's been through enough. What he needs right now is for you to show him some compassion and understanding. He doesn't need to be poked and prodded."

"What's your birth date?" Harry asked Max, turning so that his back was to Jenny in order to better ignore her.

"November 25th." Max spoke the words into his chest, so Harry could barely hear him. But at least he was speaking, which was progress.

"I wish he could see me like you can." Jenny sat in the chair next to Max, and tried to run her hands through his hair to straighten it. But they passed straight through Max's head, and he flinched slightly.

Could Max feel her? If so, she was something other than a thought in Harry's head.

"I wish I *couldn't* see you like he can't." Harry hadn't meant to respond to her, but he hadn't been able to stop the words from coming out of his mouth. Sure enough, Max was looking at him like he was a lunatic. Again. "Not you, Max, I was talking to someone else."

Max looked around the empty waiting room and obviously didn't see his mother, because his look passed right by her without any hesitation. Great, now the kid was going to be worried he would be staying with someone who, at the very least, talked to himself.

"You shouldn't be making him do this, he's just a small boy." Jenny was acting nervous, but Harry couldn't tell if she was concerned for the kid, or if she was worried because she knew the test results would prove Max wasn't Harry's. "He doesn't like hospitals. They upset him."

"Had a lot of experience in hospitals, has he?" Harry muttered under his breath, but he was only half paying attention while he finished filling out the forms. "This isn't a hospital, it's a clinic. He's not spending the night, they're only going to swab his cheek."

"Maxi, honey, come on." Jenny tried coaxing Max's attention in her direction by waving her hands at him. "You don't need to do this. Let's just walk away. Okay?" She clapped her hands a few times, but Max still didn't respond, so she slumped down in her chair in defeat.

He could tell that she was still worried about something, because her foot continued to tap in mid-air.

Was this wrong for him to do? Would he be permanently traumatizing a nine-year-old kid by forcing him to get a cheek swab?

Should he simply trust Jenny that Max was his son?

He couldn't do that. Too much depended on the result. He didn't want to be a father. He wasn't father material.

Harry had gotten as far on the forms as he could, and wanted to get this whole thing done and over with. He took the clipboard back up to the desk.

"Do you know how long this is going to take?"

"The test itself only takes about thirty minutes." The nurse took the forms and leafed through them, checking them. "I'm just going to need to make a copy of Max's birth certificate or his social security card." She glanced again through the forms. "You haven't finished answering all the questions on his form."

"You have everything I know right there." He pointed to the forms. "I'll have to get a copy of his birth certificate from my attorney, and send it over. Will that work? Or do you need that now for the tests?"

"No, we can do the tests now, but we will need the rest of his information, and his birth certificate, in order to complete the chain of custody sheet and finalize your results."

"Okay, one step at a time here. Let's get this done today, and I'll work on getting you the rest."

"Sure, Mr. Landon. But just so you know, we can't complete the results until we get—"

"Uh huh, yep, I got it. I'll get everything to you as soon as I get it myself. But, while we're already here, you can still do the swabs, right?" He glanced down at her name tag, and gave her the benefit of his full smile, as he turned on the charm for good measure. "Cindy."

"Of course, Mr. Landon." Cindy knocked over the pen container, and daisies exploded all over her counter. She smiled back at Harry. "Let me check and see if they're ready for you, and I'll be right back."

"Come on, Max. We're up, buddy."

Max slowly got up from his chair and death-shuffled toward Harry. He had to give it to the kid, though, he could certainly turn on the drama. Harry used to do that as a kid, too, whenever he was being forced – dragged – into doing something he didn't want to do.

"He gets that feet dragging thing from you," Jenny said in his ear, as if she could read his thoughts.

Shit. *Could* she read his thoughts?

And why the hell was she even still around?

"I'm not hallucinating, am I?" he asked her quietly. It was a rhetorical question. He already knew the answer.

"No, you're not."

Harry gave his head a good shake, but knew it wouldn't make her disappear. He was being haunted by his ex-fiancée, and he didn't have any idea how to get rid of her.

"Why are you here?" Harry figured the sooner he discovered what her purpose was, the sooner he could get her to move on, or pass over, or whatever she needed to do to go into the light. "Why are you here, instead of... wherever you should be, now that you're... you know?" Harry glanced around to see if Max was witnessing him talk to thin air, but he was still walking The Green Mile.

Jenny looked at Harry like she thought he was no smarter than a turnip. "I already told you, I'm here to make sure you take care of Max."

"Okay, well, I am taking care of him. So, why are you still here?"

"I'll go when I'm good and ready, Mr. Bossy-ass. How do I know you won't end up throwing him in some Dickensonian orphanage from hell as soon as I've left?"

"Dickensian. And I would never do that." Harry struggled to hold onto his temper. He wanted to throw something at her for believing him capable of locking her son in an institution. Did she really think so little of him? He wouldn't do that to someone he hated, let alone a nine-year-old boy.

He sighed. So much had changed over the last ten years.

The nurse opened the door between the waiting area and the exam rooms, and gestured them inside. "You and Max can come on back now, and we'll get you all done."

Harry started to follow her into the hallway, then noticed that Max had stopped at the front desk. He wasn't moving to follow Harry, and he looked as if he was about to lose his lunch.

Jenny, too, was looking genuinely afraid. Why would a ghost have anything to be afraid of? She stood close to Max, whispering urgently into his ear, but Harry could tell Max wasn't able to hear her, because he didn't react at all.

"Max?" Harry was starting to worry now, too. "Hey, kid. Are you okay?"

Max looked up at Harry with so much fear in his eyes, that Harry himself started to panic. His heart stopped beating and for a brief, infinitesimal moment, everything in the room stopped completely.

Harry stood alone staring into the eyes of a frightened nine-year-old boy. Except, the boy looking back through those eyes was a thirteen-year-old Harry, and his eyes were vacant.

"Please, Harry, he doesn't like hospitals." Jenny's voice snapped him back to reality, and Harry stumbled against the wall. His heart beat so loudly in his chest, he was sure people would be able to hear it all the way to Boulder.

What the hell had just happened?

He looked at Max, and saw a raw vulnerability take over the brave, even cocky, act he'd tried so hard to maintain. Harry knew he couldn't go through with this. He would have to find a different way to get the tests done, because he wasn't going to subject this poor kid to another trauma.

Jesus, he was an ass. The poor kid just lost his mother, and all Harry could think about was getting him out of his life as fast as possible. Why was he acting like such a dick? What the hell was wrong with him?

"Come on, kid, let's get out of here." Harry carefully reached out his hand, and waited for Max to take it. It felt like an entire year went by as he waited for Max to decide, and Harry realized that he needed the kid to take it. He needed Max to know that he would take care of him, for however long he was with him.

Max looked up at him, and Harry could see the caution in his expression. But there was something else in the kid's eyes, too.

Hope?

CHAPTER FOUR

After parking his car in the attached garage of his loft building, Harry wheeled Max's luggage and a couple of duffel bags through the back access door. He looked back to see that Max was doing his death march shuffle again, and sighed. He waited very patiently, and silently patted himself on the back for not yelling at the kid to hurry up. That was progress, right?

Except that Max was giving him the stink-eye, so something had given away his impatience. Probably the staccato beat he was tapping out on the handle of the door with his index finger?

There was a clumsy moment when, both bulked up by luggage, they banged into each other, the door, and the inside hallway, before they navigated the space around them and again settled into single file and headed toward the front. Harry felt a pang in his chest when it occurred to him that this could have been one of those moments that under different circumstances would have had them sharing a belly-aching laugh and ending up limp and gasping for breath in a heap on the floor together.

Jenny started laughing, and it sounded so bright and spontaneous that he smiled. It had been pretty comical.

Then he looked down and noticed the large scuff mark on his once meticulously polished black Ferragamos, and he sighed.

"Holy smokes, who's that?" Jenny asked, as she pointed down the hall.

Luke Stevens stood in the lobby of the building flipping through his mail, while his dog, Sheldon, sat patiently waiting by his side. Luke was Harry's neighbor, and lived in the only other condo in the building. He was somewhere in his late-thirties, and had those rugged good looks that always made women stop in their tracks, just exactly as Jenny had done. One of the women Harry had dated once told him that it had something with the combination of his thick, dark brown hair setting off his deep sea-green eyes, which made her do a double-take when she met Luke.

Harry had secretly looked at Luke as a George Clooney to his Brad Pitt, and figured that if they could do movies together they'd make a fortune. Except that neither of them could act.

"He's my neighbor."

"Your neighbor?" Jenny asked, as she ogled the unsuspecting man. "Well, invite him over for a cup of sugar."

Harry was about to tell her that you don't invite someone over for a cup of sugar, you go to their house and ask to borrow a cup of sugar, when he realized the ridiculousness of the entire situation.

First: She was a ghost. Why the hell would she care about flirting with a flesh-and-blood human, no matter how good-looking he was?

Second: What was he, last week's left-overs? She didn't have that reaction to seeing him.

And third: He was losing it.

His phone rang, and he pulled it out of his pocket to check the caller ID.

Anna Erickson calling.

Nope, not going to answer that. He silenced the phone, then stuffed it back in his pocket. He knew he'd have to call her eventually, or she'd probably end up at his front door, but he didn't have the time to deal with her. He'd have to talk to her at the office tomorrow.

"Do you need some help with all that?" Luke came up to him, and gestured to the pile of bags, then rescued a duffel that was leaning precariously off a suitcase.

"Hey, yeah that would be great, thanks." Harry was glad to see Luke, although he wasn't sure how he was going to explain Max to him. "Let me ask you something. Did you know that kids under the age of thirteen aren't allowed to sit in the front seat of a car?"

"No," Luke replied, looking slightly thrown off by the odd question. "But I guess I never really thought about it. I don't know any kids under thirteen."

"Well, I didn't know about it either, but I do now." Harry glanced at Max, who looked like he was bursting at the seams trying to keep from running over to pet Sheldon, but was working very hard to play it nonchalant.

As they all headed up the stairs to the second level of the building, Sheldon tentatively wandered over to sniff Max, who took that as his opening. They became fast friends. Sheldon fell all over himself (and almost tripped everyone in the process) to get more attention from Max, while Max buried his face in Sheldon's fur and hung on.

"Would you look at that," Luke said, while he watched in amazement as his dog licked Max's face.

"I thought that dog was afraid of everyone." Harry was as surprised to see the interaction as Luke was. In the year that Luke had lived there, he had never seen Sheldon so exuberant about another living being. It had taken Harry three months to get Sheldon to let him pet him.

"He is," Luke replied. "Who's this?"

"It's kind of a long story, but this is Max, and he's going to be staying with me for a few days."

Max stopped playing with Sheldon long enough to give Harry an angry glare.

What was that all about? The kid knew this was temporary.

"Huh. If looks could kill..." Obviously Luke had seen the look as well.

Harry shrugged it off, as he led Max down the hall and stopped at his front door to unlock it and head inside, then dumped everything inside the front entryway. Luke followed Harry inside and set the duffel bag he was carrying on the floor next to the other bags.

Harry looked back to see Max in the hall, holding onto Sheldon like a lifeline.

As children, Harry and George weren't allowed to have dogs inside the house – weren't allowed to have dogs at all, actually – so it was possible Max grew up with the same rule, and was reluctant to let Sheldon come in with him. "It's okay, Max, you can bring Sheldon in with you."

Max let go of Sheldon's collar, and Harry was glad to see the happy dog bound into the loft and immediately sit on the floor in front of the couch. He sat there, wagging his tail and waiting expectantly for them all to join him, which is what he and Luke usually did when they got together to hang out at Harry's.

Jenny wandered inside, too, but she wasn't checking out the condo as Harry expected her to do. Instead, she was watching Luke like he was her last meal, and Harry resisted the urge to roll his eyes. Apparently, Luke had the same stupefying effect on women, dead or alive.

Max was not as certain as Jenny or Sheldon, because he stayed in the hall, as if waiting to be given permission to come inside.

"So, Max, is it?" Luke asked, as he extended his hand to shake Max's. It was apparently all the invitation Max needed, because he took Luke's hand, and crossed the threshold.

"My name's, Luke, and that's Sheldon. We live next door. Tonight's pizza night for us. I was planning to bring some over here and hang with Harry. Do you like pizza?" At Max's hesitant nod, Luke clapped his hands together. "Okay, then. Sheldon and I will be back later. Does that work for you guys?"

"That would be great, Luke, thanks." Harry was relieved that he not only didn't have to figure out dinner, he wouldn't be alone with Max. He wasn't exactly winning the kid over so far, and he didn't have any idea how to entertain him.

"You can supply the beverages," Luke said, then grinned, "and the long story." He whistled for Sheldon, and they left, shutting the door behind them.

Jenny's eyes followed Luke until he disappeared out the front door, then she turned and grinned at Harry. "He's a really nice guy. Does he hang out here a lot?"

Harry could tell by her tone that there was some hidden meaning behind her question, and he was instantly suspicious. Unfortunately, he couldn't ask her about it in front of Max, so he glared at her instead. When she only winked back at him, he turned his attention to Max.

"Come on, I'll show you where you can sleep." Harry loaded his arms back up with the luggage and headed toward the back of the loft off the main area, hoping that Max would eventually get curious (or brave) enough to follow.

His loft was a three-bedroom with a deck off the master bedroom, and a large patio in the backyard. It might have seemed like overkill for a bachelor, but he was currently glad for the extra room, and he'd always loved the convenience and solitude of having an over-sized yard. His master bedroom was tucked behind the kitchen on the left side of the condo, which was split in the middle by a large and comfortable living space, complete with a seventy-two-inch flat screen TV over the fireplace, because Harry loved a good movie. The right side of the condo lead to the two extra bedrooms, and their shared bathroom.

"That's your bathroom," Harry said, pointing to a door between the two bedrooms. "And this is your bedroom."

Harry opened the door to the right of the bathroom, because the room to the left was his home office and the kid wouldn't be sleeping in there. His cleaning lady always kept the spare bedroom clean with fresh sheets, although he didn't get many visitors – at least not any who didn't sleep with him. It was more for show than anything, but Harry was glad she always kept him prepared.

There was a queen-sized bed, a short six-drawer dresser with matching mirror, and a small desk and chair next to the bed. It should be just fine for a kid who wasn't going to be here that long.

Emma had remarked once that the room looked more like something out of a hospital than a home, and she'd bought him a brightly colored quilt to compensate for the fact that he'd never painted over the builder's neutral colored walls.

"Why don't you have a dog, Harry?" Jenny asked, as she materialized in Max's bedroom.

"They're too much work, and I'm not around often enough." Harry realized that he had just spoken out loud, so he turned to Max to cover. "Uh, that's what you were thinking, right? Why don't I have a dog?"

Blank stare.

"Okay, well, unpack, and get settled in, and... whatever... and... uh..." Realizing that he'd been reduced to stammering, Harry decided it was time to leave and give the kid some space.

"He's nine, Harry," said his hallucination, which stopped him at the door. "He could use a little help figuring out where to put stuff. Besides, he's probably feeling weird being here. You could be a little more welcoming."

Welcoming? Was she serious? His whole life just went ass over tea kettle, and she had the nerve to complain that he wasn't more welcoming? The kid was staying with him, in his home. How much more welcoming does it get?

"I'm—" he started to say, then realized he was about to argue with her in front of Max, who couldn't see her, and stopped. He picked the suitcase up, set it on the bed, and opened it to start unpacking Max's things. "Uh, so, why don't we figure out where you want to put everything? We can get you all organized, and then maybe it will be time for pizza with Luke and Sheldon. How's that sound?"

No response.

"Jeans and t-shirts. We can put these in the drawers. Right?"

Feeling completely out of his element, Harry fumbled to unpack Max's bags and put clothing away, when Max finally started to help. Max pulled open a drawer to indicate where he wanted the jeans and t-shirts to go. Apparently, it mattered to a nine-year-old boy where his possessions should be placed.

CHAPTER FIVE

Harry was floating on an inflatable lounge chair, drinking some weird looking beverage with ice and a tiny umbrella. He didn't remember ordering such a sweet drink – normally his tastes leaned more toward bourbon or whiskey – but the brunette with the killer body in the red thong bikini drifting next to him had the same thing, so she must have given it to him.

"Harry, there's something wrong with Maxi."

Maxine? Was that her name? He couldn't even remember where he'd met her. Whose pool was this again? It didn't matter. He just wanted to lie here and continue to admire the view. But that damn bee was back...

"Harry! You need to help Maxi."

"Mmm... sure babe. Let yourself out. I'll call you later. I promise," Harry mumbled into his pillow, as he was just beginning to realize he was dreaming. He tried to return to the pool and the brunette, when a jolt of lightning shot through him, and he bolted upright. Definitely wide awake now.

"What the hell?" Harry asked, as he rubbed his shoulder. Jenny leaned over him, looking like she was getting ready to poke him with her finger, but she stepped back when she could see that he was awake. "What in God's name are you doing here?"

She had spent the entire night like a spectator at Wimbledon, first watching Luke, then Harry, then back to Luke again, all the while grinning like the Cheshire Cat. It made Harry anxious to get her alone and find out what was going on in that diabolical head of hers. But she'd disappeared, with a wink and another shit-eating grin, as soon as Max's head hit the pillow, and Harry had hoped that meant she was gone for good.

Apparently, she wasn't 'good and ready' to leave yet.

"You need to wake up and go help Maxi. Something is wrong."

He was about to argue with her, when he heard low moaning coming from Max's room.

"Okay, hang on." Harry started to get out of the bed, but remembered at the last second that he always slept naked. Incorporeal or not, he didn't feel comfortable just baring it all in front of her. "Uhh, Jenny, unless you'd like an eyeful, and I do mean 'full,' you might want to disappear while I put on some clothes."

"For heaven's sake, it isn't like I haven't seen it all before." But she turned around, and he grabbed his sweatpants from the foot of the bed, and put them on.

Max's moans grew louder, and he began shouting, "Stop! Stop! Please, No!"

What the hell was going on? With his heart speeding as fast as a NASCAR driver, and only half dressed, Harry bolted from his room and ran to check on Max.

Max was thrashing in the bed and screaming nonsensically at the top of his lungs. His eyes were closed, and he seemed to be caught up in a nightmare.

"Jesus Christ!"

"Help him, Harry. He's just a little boy." Jenny looked desperate, and he knew he should be doing something, but he was deathly afraid to even go near the kid.

"What the hell am I supposed to do?" What if, in trying to help, he did something wrong, and ended up breaking him instead?

Harry stood helpless as Jenny hurried over and sat on Max's bed. "Maxi, honey, it's okay. It's going to be okay." Harry watched in fascination as she tried to put her arms around Max, and he seemed to spasm from the experience of them passing right through him.

"Aren't you supposed to be careful not to wake someone up when they're having a nightmare?" Harry was in such a panic he had no idea if he even spoke out loud, and the pounding in his head was getting louder.

"Harry? What's going on? Harry? Open up." The pounding turned out to be on his front door, and Luke was shouting for him to open it. Sheldon must have been with him, because there was a short, but very commanding bark as well.

Harry rushed to the entry way, and was glad to discover that at least his legs were working again, albeit shakily. He opened the door to a concerned, sleep-rumpled Luke, who was also only wearing sweatpants. Sheldon streaked inside and ran straight to Max's room.

"What is going on? I could hear Max all the way—" Luke stopped short and they watched, dumbfounded, as Sheldon leapt onto the bed, and began licking Max's face.

Max immediately calmed down to hiccups, and pulled Sheldon to him like a stuffed animal. Within minutes he settled down, wrapped his arms around Sheldon, and fell into a deep, calm sleep using the dog as his security blanket.

"Oh, my God. My poor Maxi." Jenny rocked back and forth sitting next to Max on the bed. "I think I might be having a heart attack."

"You're a little bit beyond that now," Harry said, before he realized he'd spoken the crack out loud, and hoped that Luke hadn't heard it.

"What?" Luke asked, glancing a confused look at Harry.

Oops.

Jenny turned around to scowl at Harry, and he knew she was going to let him have it, but she stopped short, and her mouth dropped open.

"Holy Moses," she said, once again doing her tennis match head bob between Luke and Harry. "You two are positively stunning standing there together. You make a beautiful looking couple."

"Stop it," Harry demanded. Her mood changes were giving him whiplash. Did all ghosts do that? It was almost as if she'd lost touch with reality when she'd lost her anchor to the corporeal realm. "This is serious."

"Are you talking to me?" Luke asked.

"Sorry, no, I was just... talking to myself. This is a serious situation." Harry was worried that Luke would start wondering if he was living next to a head-case, but he had bigger things to think about. He was still reeling from the experience of being awakened by a boy who had caused an earthquake, and then calmly gone back to sleep. "What the hell was that? And what am I supposed to do now?"

Jenny didn't respond, which was probably a good thing since Harry didn't know how he would explain a conversation with her. Instead, she curled up on the bed next to Max like she'd become his personal sentinel, while Harry continued to stand in the doorway and gape for a moment longer.

Luke finally turned to look at him, and Harry caught the briefest flash of heat in Luke's eyes as they traveled from his chest up to his face.

Harry felt a frisson shoot through his system, but tamped it down instantly. Luke's look was more likely anger – pissed that he was now living next to a lunatic, and a kid who suffered from nightmares.

Shit. Harry was certain that the next words out of Luke's mouth were going to involve finding another place to live.

"Why doesn't Sheldon stay here with Max tonight?" Luke asked instead.

"I'd really appreciate that, thanks." Harry felt so lucky to have Luke for a neighbor and best friend, he almost hugged him. "I don't know about you, but I could use a drink. Care to join me?"

He didn't wait to give Luke the opportunity to decline, and led him out of Max's room, closing the door halfway. He went into the kitchen where he gathered two glasses and a bottle of Jameson. He glanced up at Luke only after he had poured healthy-sized shots into each glass. Luke grinned back at him, and took one of the glasses.

Harry shot his back in one swig, letting the dark-roasted caramel taste linger on his tongue for a moment before he swallowed. He stood with his eyes closed, letting the alcohol spread to his belly and warm him from the inside. Until that moment, he hadn't realized that he was shaking from the let-down of the adrenaline that had hit his bloodstream at the first scream. He poured himself a second glass, this one for savoring, as opposed to the first one, which was more for its medicinal effects.

"I am way out of my league," he finally said when he felt he could articulate some sort of coherent thought. "I have no idea what to do with a kid, let alone one who apparently suffers from nightmares. I was paralyzed. And he just kept screaming." He sipped his Jameson again, then continued, "Jesus. What would make a kid scream like that?"

"Some kind of trauma?"

Silence.

Harry stared at Luke as the cold once again crept back into his body. He wished that what Luke had just said could somehow be taken back, that it could somehow not be true. But Harry knew – he knew from personal experience – the kinds of things that go bump in the night, and can cause nightmares like the one Max had tonight.

"He just lost his mother," Harry said, hoping that was as bad as it got. But deep down, he knew there had to be something more. The loss of a parent would have him crying in the middle of the night, not screaming. Didn't screaming imply something... else?

"Do you know anything about his background?" Luke asked in a quiet voice, accurately guessing at the horror that must have been evident on Harry's face.

"No," Harry responded, and he wasn't surprised by the anger and animosity he could hear in his own tone. "But I'm sure as hell going to find out. Then I'm going to kill the bastard who's responsible for putting that kind of fear into a nine-year-old boy."

Did Jenny know what caused the nightmares? She seemed upset enough in the beginning while Max was screaming. But as soon as he was calm, she turned the attention to Harry and Luke pretty quickly.

Was that a distraction to keep Harry from asking questions she didn't want to answer?

No. That didn't seem like the Jenny he'd once known. He couldn't imagine her doing anything that might traumatize her own son.

Except die on him.

Harry shot the last of his whiskey, wondering if he would ever feel warm inside again.

CHAPTER SIX

arry paced his office feeling like a junkie waiting for his dealer. He'd confirmed with Karla that Anna was still out of town with her brother on a book tour, so at least he was safe coming in for a couple more days without having to worry about running into her.

His office had the same general layout as his brother's, with a large cherry wood desk positioned near the floor-to-ceiling window overlooking the same view of downtown Denver. Harry had placed his desk off to the side, so that he could both see the view while he worked at his desk, and still be able to see his office doorway.

Harry's sitting area had the same comfortable leather sofa and chairs as George's office, but Harry had chosen to accent his in deep blues and silvers instead of the reds and golds that George preferred.

Harry sat in the leather couch, and sipped the coffee he'd picked up from Stan & David's Cafe on his way in to the office. The deep, rich aroma filled his nostrils seconds before the elixir hit his tongue, and he sighed in bliss knowing it would soon flood his bloodstream and give him the kick-start he needed. He only wished he'd thought to buy a gallon of the stuff. One measly little cup wasn't going to be enough.

He didn't sleep at all last night, even after Max had finally settled with Sheldon. Luke was more than generous giving up his dog for the night, and Harry felt lucky to have found a friendship with a man who was turning out to be more than just a next-door neighbor.

He also knew that he was way out of his comfort zone with a nine-year-old boy, and things had just escalated now that it appeared there was more going on with the kid. But, at the same time, he was second-guessing his decision to get rid of Max as soon as possible. How could he trust someone else not to make matters worse?

Then again, how did he know that he wouldn't? It wasn't as if he'd been trained for taking care of a kid. Unless he counted his father. The best thing he learned from his asshole father was *Psycho Things You Should Never Do To Your Child.*

It sounded like the title of a national best-seller.

He figured, with his own father as an anti-role-model, he could probably do okay. But he would first have to find out what the hell happened last night. He needed answers, and he was damned well going to get them.

"Jenny, we need to talk about last night. What is up with the kid?" Harry felt stupid talking to the empty room, but he didn't know how else to go about getting the attention of a ghost. "You show up right now. I mean it. We need to talk about this."

He turned around in circles, searching for her, but nothing happened. Where was she? Shouldn't a ghost have to come when called?

"Goddamn it, Jenny, I'm serious. What the hell is going on?"

Still nothing, just the rhythmic "tick-tock, tick-tock, tick-tock" of the old desk clock George had given him for Christmas a few years ago – something to do with hoping it would help Harry show up on time more often. It didn't help, because he was still chronically late to pretty much everything, but he loved the clock anyway.

"I knew it. You don't really exist, do you? You're a figment of—"

"Uhhh, Harry?"

Harry whirled around to see George and Emma standing just

inside his office door. George stood, one hand resting on the knob, and looking perplexed, while Emma tried to see around his shoulder.

"Problem with one of your many girlfriends? It was bound to happen." George grinned, so Harry knew he wasn't serious, but he wasn't in the mood.

"Don't start with me, I mean it." Harry pointed a menacing finger at his brother for emphasis. "I'm not having a good day."

This was all he needed. He had one recalcitrant ghost, one snarky and condescending older brother, and one witness in the room to keep him from punching said snarky and condescending older brother. And he really wanted to hit something.

"You're right, I'm sorry." George's apology took Harry by surprise. Apparently, their conversation the other day had turned something around in his older brother, and this was his way of letting him know he was trying to understand.

Harry collapsed on his office couch in a heap of exhaustion. He was so frustrated with Jenny, he felt like he was a nuclear missile set to explode but didn't have the final coordinates yet.

"Have you ever thought you saw someone who you know can't possibly be there? But they are?"

Emma and George exchanged some kind of meaningful glance, like they shared a deep, dark secret. Christ, they were always doing that. It was annoying.

George sat in a nearby chair, while Emma, who was somewhere around seven months pregnant, but who, to Harry, looked like she was going to explode any minute, perched on its arm and held George's hand.

She looked uncomfortable, and Harry stood up to offer her the couch. "Wouldn't you be more comfortable sitting here?"

"No, but thanks." Emma smiled, and waved him off. "If I sit in that, I'll need a crane to help get me out of it again."

"I'm sure that between the two of us, Harry and I will be able to get you on your feet again." George's smile faded when Emma gave him a look that would scare a rattlesnake. "What did I say?"

Emma ignored George, and turned her attention to Harry.

"Where's Max?"

"He's at Luke's for the day." Harry still couldn't believe how nice Luke was being. When he volunteered to take Max for the day, Harry was so relieved he almost hugged him. "He's bonded with Sheldon, and Luke's been great about letting them hang out together. Last night was a nightmare. Literally. The kid woke up screaming. It woke Luke up next door, and when he came to find out what was going on, Sheldon was the only one who knew what to do. Calmed the kid instantly."

"Oh, poor Max," Emma said, then glowered at Harry. "As in, his name is *Max* not *the kid*."

"What am I going to do, Emma? Tell me what to do." It didn't escape his notice that he relied on her far too much. It was the same thing two years ago, when George was in a coma, and he'd left Emma holding the bag on everything. He was hopeless. How did he expect to take care of a kid who obviously needed more help than he knew how to give?

"He just lost his mother. It seems to me that maybe what he needs is to get back into as normal a life and routine as you can possibly make for him. Get him around other kids his age to hang out with."

Harry was confused. Was he supposed to enroll him in soccer? Swimming? What?

"School, Harry," Emma said, as if he was clueless. Which he was. "School would be a good idea."

"School? School?" Was she insane? "Why would I enroll him in school? I won't have him that long."

"You don't know that," George said, like he knew something Harry didn't. Did he? Had he been talking with Jason about all the legal stuff behind Harry's back? "We have no idea how long it will take to sort through the process of getting him placed somewhere. And maybe, just maybe, Max is exactly what you've been looking for."

George and Harry locked eyes, and Harry could clearly see the message George was sending. *I want you to be happy.*

"And for however long you do have him," Emma continued, "he

will be considered truant if you don't get him into a school some-where soon."

"I don't know the first thing about getting a kid into school. Where the hell—"

"You do remember that my sister is the principal of an elementary school, right?" Emma looked like she wanted to shake him.

"Well, yes, but—"

"I have all of his paperwork the attorneys sent over." George rose from the chair and tugged Emma along with him. "It has his birth certificate and all of the information on his previous school. You're going to need all of that."

"Go see Marlie," Emma said, then kissed Harry on the cheek as if to reassure him. "She'll get you sorted out, and Max can spend some time with Spencer while you're there. They're about the same age. It'll be good for all of you."

"You and I still need to talk about Anna," George said, but he didn't seem to be in any hurry to pick up where they'd left off on their conversation yesterday, because he followed his wife out as if he was afraid she might disappear on him.

When they left his office, Harry felt like he had things a little more under control, in spite of the ringing in his ears.

And Jenny still hadn't made an appearance.

HARRY KNOCKED on Luke's door and waited, realizing this was only about the second or third time he'd been here. For some reason, when they didn't go out, they usually got together at Harry's condo.

Jenny hadn't shown up all day, and that made Harry suspicious that she was avoiding him. Was she hiding from him on purpose? Or was he blowing it out of proportion, and this was merely a ghost thing, like she ran out of juice and could only be visible for a certain amount of time?

Max answered the door, and looked like he was happy to see

Harry. Even Sheldon, who stood next to Max with his tail wagging, seemed happy to see him.

"Hi." That was all Max said, but Harry took that one word as a positive sign, because there'd been some enthusiasm behind it, and it was accompanied by a bright smile.

"Hey, Max. Did you have a good day?" Too late, Harry remembered the advice Emma had given him about asking Max open-ended questions that he'd have to answer with more than just a "Yes" or a "No" response.

Sure enough, all Harry received was a shrug.

"Where's Luke?" Harry asked, going for the open-ended option this time, and hoping for more of a response.

"He's in the other room." Max pointed to a door off the living room. "He said I wasn't allowed in there."

"Huh. Really?" Harry wasn't sure if he should be worried. "Did he say why?"

"He said he's got stuff I'm not old enough to see yet."

Well, that sounded...

Actually, that sounded intriguing. Harry thought he should probably be more concerned, but he knew Luke well enough by now to know that he wouldn't do anything to harm Max. He never would have left Max with him if he'd had concerns.

Max, with Sheldon following, went back to the kitchen, off to the right, and sat at the counter island. From what Harry could see, he'd interrupted an afternoon of drawing.

There were large sheets of what looked like expensive paper spread out across the counter with a variety of colored pencils. Max had been busy. There were several pictures scattered around the kitchen. He was pretty good, too. That was a damned good Iron Man.

Harry picked up a pencil, and could tell it was high quality, like something from an art supply store, and not from a local Wal-Mart. He sure hoped Luke had given Max permission to use these.

"He said you could go in though." Max didn't even look up from his masterpiece as he waved Harry away.

Luke's loft was the reverse plan of Harry's, but it looked more lived-in. There were running shoes in the entryway, bananas and oranges in a bowl on the island, and various plants – actual live plants – scattered throughout the main room.

Harry didn't have plants.

He'd never been able to keep one alive. Several girlfriends had given them as gifts over the years, "to spruce the place up," but the damn things always committed suicide within a week of moving in – the plants, not the girlfriends – so he'd given up trying.

He knocked on Luke's guest room door. Luke must have been expecting it to be Max, because when he opened it, his gaze was somewhere in the area of Harry's belt buckle. Then his gaze traveled up to meet Harry's eyes, and his whole face lit up with his welcoming smile. Harry's heart warmed, and he felt his own smile answering in kind.

"Hey, Harry. I wasn't expecting you so soon." Luke was dressed in paint-splattered jeans and a t-shirt. His feet were bare, and he was holding an artist's paintbrush.

"It'll take you a year to paint this room with that," Harry commented, gesturing to the paintbrush.

"Tools of the trade," Luke responded, as he stepped aside to let Harry into the room – a room that was filled with easels and canvases in various stages of development.

"Wait." Harry was stunned. "You're an *artist* painter?"

"Yeeees..." Luke grinned, obviously amused by his revelation.

"Shit." Harry felt like an idiot. "So, when I asked you to help me paint my loft, why didn't you tell me you weren't that kind of painter?"

"I was happy to help." Luke shrugged, as if it had been no big deal. "Besides, I wanted to be sure you didn't paint your bedroom something tacky like Randy Red."

"Oh, my God. He's Sebastian Lucas." Jenny finally showed up. At the most inopportune time. As usual. And it was usually when Luke was around. Could she have a thing for Luke?

Harry opened his mouth to lay into her, and then realized what she'd said. "Hang on. You're Sebastian Lucas? As in *the* Sebastian

Lucas? The one who's the hot topic all over the art world for his erotic paintings? *That* Sebastian Lucas?"

Luke shrugged it off, as if uncomfortable by the notoriety, and began cleaning up his brushes and work area without making eye contact.

"I've never seen any of your work," Harry admitted to Luke. "But it's sure got people talking."

"I snuck away once to see his show," Jenny said, with awe in her voice. "It was the most incredible thing I'd ever seen. Totally worth the consequences."

Consequences? Harry was confused. What consequences were there for a grown adult going to see an art show? He almost asked the question out-loud, but stopped himself at the last second knowing Luke would think he was nuts.

His thoughts were scattered when it occurred to him that he'd had a world-renowned artist paint his condo.

"Holy shit! I bought you beer and pizza to paint my walls. I am such an idiot. You should have said something. Man, I am so sorry—"

"Stop." Luke put a hand out to stop him. "I had fun. It was a great weekend, and I enjoyed spending time with you."

Harry looked around the room, taking in all the works in various stages of development. He noticed several sketches sitting on a nearby table and picked them up to get a closer look. Each one was of Harry, like someone had snapped photos of him in different moods; serious, concerned, smiling, laughing, and one that looked like he had been caught with an absent thought.

"These are..." He couldn't describe what he was seeing. They were perfect, like looking into a mirror that reflected only in black and white.

"Just stuff that pops into my head." Luke hurriedly gathered the sketches and tucked them into a book, then turned abruptly and went back to his easel and began cleaning up.

Harry was confused. A famous artist, who had no limit to the gorgeous models he could paint, was drawing sketches of him. Of. Him.

"Ooo-oo, someone's got a cru-ush," Jenny sing-songed, and Harry gaped at her. "I knew there was something going on with him. I could tell by the way he looks at you whenever you aren't paying attention. Which is pretty much all the time, by the way. Now this is where you say something flirty to him. Something about offering private sessions." She waggled her eyebrows at him, and he stood there in stunned silence.

"Earth to Harry." She made the mocking gesture of knocking on his head with her fist. "Hello in there."

Harry turned away from her to watch Luke as he cleaned his brushes.

"Fine. If you're going to ignore me, and my brilliant relationship advice, I'm going to go hang with my son. At least he has an excuse for ignoring me." Through his peripheral vision, he saw her stomp her foot when she didn't get a reaction from him. Then she left the room, which was also fine with him. She was way out of line, and he couldn't argue with her about it in front of Luke.

Was she right though? Was Luke gay? His stomach danced a tiny beat, and then settled. He felt like he should have known that, and maybe he did at a subconscious level. But the truth was, he'd never thought about it. They were friends. It didn't matter one way or the other.

He didn't know how he felt about the sketches. He should probably be angry – wouldn't this be considered some kind of invasion of privacy? But he wasn't angry.

He was...

He was...

Flattered.

Even a little...

Shy?

His stomach flipped again.

He moved closer to look at the painting on the easel that Luke had been working on before he'd come in. It looked almost finished.

A surge of adrenaline shot through his entire body as if he'd been charged by an emotional battery. The painting was of two men, naked, intertwined and obviously in love. He was stunned. His whole world narrowed itself down and focused on the two men making love in the painting. It seemed so real. He felt like he could reach out and touch the heated flesh, smooth the silky hair.

How would it feel to care so deeply for another person – to love someone so much – that you blended like two halves of a whole?

"My God." He felt like he'd experienced something spiritual, down to his inner-self.

It brought back a flicker of a memory, when he had tried something. Once. Before. A long time ago. Just to see.

But it had all gone wrong. So. Very. Wrong.

And his father had been angry. So. Very. Angry.

He forced his way back to reality, and reminded himself that he was only seeing a painting – it wasn't real. He didn't even know the men who were in it, so it shouldn't have had such an impact.

But it did.

And it shouldn't have.

"Max," he called out. His voice sounded like he hadn't used it in years, and he had to clear his throat to continue. He had to put some distance between himself and the intense sense of longing that had surfaced. "Come on, let's go. We have to go see Emma's sister about getting you into school."

He knew, in some portion of his brain, that he should say something to Luke, reassure him somehow. But he was at a complete loss for words. He felt more naked than the men in the painting, and he had to get out of there.

"Hey! What happened with Luke?" Jenny asked, but Harry ignored her.

He hustled a protesting Max out of Luke's apartment, mumbling a quick, "see ya' later," and closed the door.

But not before he looked back and saw Sheldon poke his head into the hand of a very devastated-looking Luke.

CHAPTER SEVEN

Fortified with a travel mug full of coffee strong enough to stand up and walk on its own, Harry led Max up a sidewalk to a middle-class family home on the corner of a quiet street. There were still patches of snow on the ground, mostly under the trees, but the day was sunny and warm enough, and Harry figured they would be fine wearing light jackets.

Marlie and Bill's house was always a welcome place. They told him many times that he was family now that Emma and George were together, and he hoped he wasn't over-stepping the boundaries by asking for Marlie's help getting Max into a school. He didn't know why he should have to deal with this when the kid was only going to be staying a short time, but he also didn't want to be arrested for him being truant. He wasn't sure what the penalty for truancy was, and he didn't want to find out.

He rang the doorbell and looked at Max with concern. Max had his head tucked into his chest, doing his best imitation of a turtle, as if he was trying to be invisible.

"Hi, guys," Marlie said, after opening the door. She gave Harry a hug and kissed him on the cheek, which he hoped meant that she didn't mind him intruding. "And you must be Max. Emma told me all about you, I've been looking forward to meeting you." She stepped back and gestured for them to come inside.

Harry nudged Max inside the house, then followed him.

"Spencer is in the kitchen heating up some pasta for lunch. Are you hungry?" Marlie continued, as if hoping food and a kindred spirit would get Max to relax.

"Thank you so much for meeting me, Marlie."

"Harry, my sister is married to your brother. How many times do I have to keep reminding you that you're family now? I'm happy to help in any way that I can." Marlie put her arm around Max's shoulders and guided him toward the kitchen. "We're going to get you all set up at Spencer's school. You're going to love it there."

With a sigh of relief, Harry turned to shut the front door, and let out a squeak like he'd seen a ghost.

Because he had. Jenny stood on the front porch.

"She seems nice. She's the principal, huh?" Jenny acted as if this was all very normal. Because, what wasn't normal about the ghost of your ex-fiancée following you to her son's principal's house?

He looked quickly around to see if anyone else was close by, then called out.

"Uh, Marlie, I think I might have left something in the car, I'll be right back." He stepped back out onto the front porch and closed the door to be sure no one inside could see, then he turned on Jenny.

"Where the hell have you been?" he demanded, and he didn't care that he sounded like an indignant father who'd just caught his teenage daughter sneaking in after curfew.

"I just saw you at Luke's, remember?"

"Where were you in the morning when I was trying to get you to appear and talk to me? Is there some kind of summoning ritual I'm supposed to do? Or, do you just come and go whenever you feel like it?"

"I'm pretty sure I can come and go whenever I want. And right now, you aren't sounding all that happy to see me."

Harry gave her the full force of his *don't mess with me* glare, and spoke in a commanding voice that brought it home. "I'm starting to notice that you're showing up when there are other people around, especially Luke, and I can't talk to you without looking like a lunatic. Are you doing that on purpose? To avoid talking about the kid, maybe? Because we need to talk about the kid."

"Maxi. His name is Maxi." Jenny looked like she wasn't buying his glare or his tone.

"His name is not Maxi." Was she nuts? He hoped to God none of Max's friends had ever heard her call him that. "Stop calling him that. You make him sound like a feminine hygiene product. Christ, no wonder he has issues. And he does have issues. My heart is still spasming from last night when he started screaming. What is wrong with him?"

"There's nothing wrong with him." Jenny stomped her foot, but Harry could tell it was all bluster. "He's a sweet little boy who's just lost his mother." She started to cry, and Harry wanted to take back everything he'd said, especially his stern voice. "I wasn't there for him."

"Please don't cry," said a sweet voice from behind him. "It's okay. You aren't here for Max anyway."

Harry turned back to the front door, which was open again, and saw Jessica, Marlie's six-year-old daughter, standing there watching his interaction with Jenny.

Shit.

"Hi, Jessica." He had no idea how long she'd been standing there. She was going to think he was nuts, yelling at nothingness out on her front porch. How was he going to explain this one?

"Hi, Uncle Harry," Jessica continued, as if nothing unusual was going on. "Why are you yelling at Max's mom? It isn't her fault."

"You can see her?" Harry asked, at the exact same time that Jenny asked, "You can see me?"

"Sure." Jessica snorted, as if this sort of thing happened to her all the time.

Harry watched, feeling numb and more than a little confused, as Jessica moved outside and sat on the front step. He didn't understand how she was so easy with being able to see a ghost, but he sat next to her and put his arm around her.

"Jessica, honey, you can see Jenny?"

Jessica nodded, then waved to Jenny, as if to prove it to Harry.

"Sweetie," Jenny said, as she moved closer to them. "What did you mean when you said that I wasn't here for Maxi?"

"Uncle Harry's right." Jessica looked at Jenny and scowled. "You shouldn't call him Maxi anymore."

Harry knew it was petty, but he felt vindicated, and gave Jenny an *I told you so* grin. She rolled her eyes at him, conveying that she thought *he* was still a nine-year-old.

"Okay, fine." Jenny sat down on the step below Jessica. "Max. If I'm not here for him, why am I here?"

"Oh, you're here for Uncle Harry." Jessica stated this as if it was obvious, and they were just being obtuse.

"Why in the world would she be here for me?" Harry didn't like the idea of a ghost showing up to meddle in his life. "And how do I get rid of her?"

"Oh, very funny. And not at all helpful." Jenny turned her attention back to Jessica. "Can you be more specific? What does Harry need that I can help him with?"

"I don't know how you're supposed to help him. You just need to help him be happy." Jessica shrugged, and Harry could tell they were losing her attention.

"Well, that narrows the field," Jenny muttered.

"Happy how, honey?" Harry took her hand in his, hoping to get her to focus back on the conversation. If he wasn't happy, he wanted to know why, damn it.

"I don't know that part." Jessica shrugged, as if people asked her these kinds of crazy-assed questions on a daily basis. "I just know that if she can't help make you happy, she'll have to stay here forever."

"Jessica, sweetie," Harry said, as he wrapped his arms around her and hugged her tight, "you do understand that this is not shit a five-year old should be saying, right?" Jesus Christ, she sounded like a possessed psychic in a scary movie, and it was giving Harry the freaks. She shouldn't be seeing ghosts, and talking in cryptic messages.

"I'm six, Uncle Harry. And you said a bad word."

He snorted a laugh, and gave her another squeeze because he was crazy about her, whatever her age was.

"I'll stay here forever? I can't stay here forever."

Harry looked over at Jenny, who'd gone so transparent, he could see the house across the street through her. However it was that she was supposed to go about making sure he was happy, they'd figure it out. He wouldn't let her get stuck here forever.

Besides, he was pretty sure he'd never survive it.

"Did you get what you needed?" Marlie came out the front door, and almost walked into Harry sitting there with Jessica. "Jess, I know how much you love your Uncle Harry, but he and I have a lot of stuff to get done so that Max can start school after spring break."

Harry leaned into Jessica and whispered, "You might not want to tell your mom about Jenny. She might not understand."

"Nope, she doesn't understand." Jessica smiled with the confidence of a six-year-old who knows she's loved to her very soul. "But she still believes me, because I believe me."

Harry was struck by how amazing this little girl was. Life was going to be tough on a girl who could see and talk to ghosts like they were real people. Lucky for her, she'd been born to Marlie.

"Your mom is helping me get Max into her school," Harry explained to Jessica. "Will you help him when he gets there?"

"Sure, Uncle Harry!" Jessica jumped to her feet. "Are you guys coming to Field Day?"

"That's a good idea," Marlie agreed. "He can meet the kids, see the school, and get a little bit acclimated. It might take some of the stress off his first day."

"What's Field Day?" Harry was starting to get that overwhelmed feeling again, like his mother ship had crash-landed on a foreign planet and no one spoke his language.

"We like to have an outdoor field event in the spring for the kids." Marlie smiled reassuringly at him, as if she was worried he'd bolt at any second. "We invite all the parents to come to the school for a barbecue lunch with the kids."

"Uh, okay, then. Sure."

"Yay!" At least Jessica was thrilled. She bounced up and down, then ran into the house yelling for Max and Spencer.

"Don't worry," Marlie assured him. "She will make sure he's met everyone before the event is half over."

"I know he'll be in good hands." And strangely, Harry felt much better knowing that Jessica had Max's back.

He followed Marlie into the house, then turned to look for Jenny.

But she had vanished.

CHAPTER EIGHT

Harry finally got Max to bed at the end of a day that seemed like it had come straight from the mind of Stephen King, and he felt he deserved a few minutes of mindless TV time on the couch with his most expensive bourbon.

He put his feet up on the coffee table. One of the many great things about living alone was that you could put your feet wherever you wanted, without being yelled at about "proper behavior" from anyone. He flipped through channels on his big screen with the sound off. He wasn't paying much attention to what was on because that wasn't really the point. The point was to go completely zombie and pretend all the flashing images were just pretty pictures, while his mind worked through all the unknowns in his life.

Max's bedroom was dark, but Harry had left the door slightly ajar so that he'd be able to hear if Max had nightmares again.

Which brought him to unknown number one: What the hell was up with Max and those nightmares? Jenny had been no help in that area. She kept changing the subject every time Harry tried to get answers from her. She was dodging him on this. He could feel it.

The problem was why? What was she trying to keep him from finding out? He didn't like suspecting Jenny, but she was acting so strange. Did she have anything to do with Max's nightmares? Had she been abusive?

No, that wasn't possible. Sure, it had been years since he'd seen Jenny, but she wasn't the abusive type.

That didn't mean that circumstances hadn't changed. Had she somehow snapped?

He was making himself crazy thinking the worst about a woman he had once loved and had almost married. Sure, now she was driving him to drink – literally – but that didn't mean she was anything other than a terrific mom to Max.

Except for calling him *Maxi* all the time. That was just criminal.

He needed to know for sure what was going on. That meant he needed to know what happened to Max, and he sure wasn't getting any of that information out of Jenny. Whatever she was hiding he had to find out.

He felt guilty about going behind her back, but he needed to know what he was dealing with if he was going to be any help to Max. If Jenny wasn't going to tell him what he needed to know, he'd have to find out the only other way he could. It was time to bring in Blake to do some investigating for him.

Blake was an old high school friend who had gone into some kind of Special Forces or something after graduation, and had come back from it all muscled-up and just a little bit scary. Talk about secrets. But he didn't know of anyone else who could "fix" a problem like Blake could.

He'd called Blake a couple of years ago when George's ex-girl-friend, Crystal, had tried to blackmail Harry with phony abuse charges complete with fake photos. If not for Blake, and his special abilities in getting the electronic copies of the photos, Harry and George might still be dealing with that crazy bitch.

Yes, Blake was exactly the person Harry needed right now to do some digging into Jenny's past, and he made a mental note to contact him first thing tomorrow.

"Harry, you're an ass." As if thinking about her had made her appear, Harry turned his focus to the other side of the couch and saw Jenny sitting there glaring at him.

At least this time she hadn't scared the shit out of him. Good news. That had to mean he was making some sort of progress, right? Either that, or he was at the point where he was beyond caring.

"Because I've never heard a woman say that to me before." His sarcasm was showing, again, but she seemed to bring it out in him. "Can you be a little more specific?"

He didn't actually want her to give examples. He already knew he was an ass, and was pretty sure he knew the reason why. At least this time.

"I've been thinking about what your niece, Jessica, said. And I think for you to be happy, I need to help you find true love."

"Oh, Jesus, you sound like a worn-out movie cliché."

"Luke's a great guy," she continued, as if he hadn't spoken. "He's really sweet with Max, and he's a good friend to you. But you ran out on him like he'd told you he had some kind of contagious disease."

He did not need a lecture from her on his relationships. He and Luke had a solid friendship. At least, he hoped they did. Either way, he'd be damned if he'd let her get into his head and start second-guessing himself.

"And you know all this how?" he asked, trying to infuse as much snark into his voice as possible. "From your two-day adventure of popping in and out of my life whenever you feel like it, and making me look like I talk to imaginary friends?"

"I'm here to help you. Remember? So, I'm telling you. You need to go over there right now and tell him you're sorry." She glared at him, and he could swear her hair was... growing? He felt the hum of a low-voltage electrical current pulsing around him as she continued. "Go over there and tell him how you feel."

Except that he didn't have a clue how he felt.

"You're kidding, right? You want to talk relationships and how you can help me? Why don't you tell me why your kid wakes up screaming in the middle of the night?" He rubbed his arms, as if fighting off a swarm of crawling insects. The stupid thing was that he wanted nothing more than to do exactly as she'd said, but his feet seemed to be permanently attached to his coffee table.

He felt relief from the humming sensation, which stopped when his phone rang. As he dug his cell out of his pocket, he heard a knock on the door. Probably George with news about Max's transfer, or whatever. He peeled himself off the couch to go answer his door, while he answered his phone on the way.

"Harry?" Anna's voice greeted him on the other end.

Shit. Anna was the last person he wanted to talk to. He should have looked at the display before blindly answering his phone. But Jenny had gotten him so worked up and distracted, he hadn't been paying attention.

He knew he needed to break it off with Anna, but what with Max being dropped on him, and Jenny complicating things, he hadn't gotten around to it yet.

To make matters worse, she seemed to be under the impression that there was more to their relationship, and tried to get closer each time he pulled away. He was going to have to be honest with her, and let her know it wasn't working for him. She would understand.

He absent-mindedly opened his front door as he ran through various excuses to politely get rid of her.

Luke was standing in the hallway.

Holy shit.

Harry's stomach did a quick flip, and he was left feeling tongue-tied. He chalked it up to being nervous because of how he reacted to the painting, but he was so relieved to see Luke he couldn't seem to remember how to form words.

"Harry? Are you there?" Anna's voice on the phone snapped him back to reality.

"Yeah, Anna, I'm here. Hi, babe." Harry thought he saw Luke's eye twitch, but it must have been a shadow from the low lighting in the hallway. "Hey, I can't really chat right now. Can I call you later?"

"Oh, sure. I just haven't seen you in a while." She sounded hesitant, but it was hard to tell without seeing her in person. Besides,

Anna was never unsure about anything. "I thought we could meet for dinner or—"

"Yeah, you bet. Dinner sounds great." Was that another eye twitch from Luke? "I'll give you a call and we'll sort out the details. Sound good?" Harry didn't even know what he was saying, he just wanted to get her off the phone, before Luke changed his mind about stopping by.

Luke shifted on his feet, and Harry hurried to wrap up with Anna. "I'll call you soon." He ended the call, knowing that he'd probably been rude, but he didn't want Luke to go, and he could easily make it up to Anna later when he saw her.

He knew he needed to say something to Luke – to at least apologize for bolting the way he did – but it was the actual putting-together-of-the-right-words part that was going to be difficult.

Jenny was right about one thing though, he did need to explain. Somehow.

"Perfect timing." Jenny said from her position on the couch. "I couldn't have managed that better if I'd planned it myself." She grinned, but it looked more like gloating.

Had she planned that herself? No, that wasn't possible.

Was it?

"Hi," Luke said, in a quiet voice. "Is Max asleep?"

"Yeah. He crashed about an hour ago." Harry still didn't know how to start this conversation, and he stood there trying to come up with something... anything. Words had never failed him before. What was his problem?

"Invite him in, you dork." Jenny stood behind him now, coaching him on correct social protocol.

Jesus.

He was standing in his own front doorway acting like a teenager on his first date.

"I'm sorry," Luke said, as he handed Harry the sketches he'd drawn. "I didn't mean to over-step—"

"No. I'm sorry." He hadn't meant to interrupt Luke so abruptly, but he wouldn't let the guy take any blame for his faults. "I was just... surprised, I guess."

"I get it. Really." Luke nodded, as if this were an everyday thing for him. "You aren't comfortable with me being gay, and that's okay."

"Invite him in." Jenny must have poked him in the back as she spoke, because he felt a sharp pain zing through his shoulder.

"Will you stop it?" Harry yelled over his shoulder.

Shit.

Luke glanced briefly behind Harry, as if looking to find another person in the room, then shifted his gaze to the floor. The look in his eyes before he averted them registered so much hurt that Harry's heart felt the same jolt of pain that had just gone through his shoulder. He glared at Jenny, but she held her hands up as if to say, *don't look at me, I'm standing here minding my own business.*

"Guess I'll see you around then," Luke said, and he turned to go.

"No, wait!" Harry was desperate to stop him, to try to explain, and he reached out and placed a hand on Luke's arm. "Please. Don't go."

"Invite him in for a drink." Unfortunately, Jenny was still behind him, prompting. "Talk to him."

He wanted to kick her. He didn't need a goddamned pep-coach.

"Look, do you want to come in for a drink? This is all so complicated. It's just a..." A what? A misunderstanding? A joke? A truly horrible reality TV show? "Major cluster. Please, will you come in and at least let me try to explain?"

Harry held his breath. His heart stuttered rapidly in his chest and he waited what felt like several weeks for Luke to make up his mind.

Luke gave another glance around the room, as if still expecting Harry to have company, then finally came inside, and closed the door. Harry smiled to reassure him, but it felt strained because all of his concentration was focused on carefully letting the air seep out of his lungs so that it didn't whoosh out in one loud release.

He didn't know why he'd been so worried. Their friendship was solid. Wasn't it?

He never had these issues with women, probably because he'd

never been friends with any of them before. Not like what he had with Luke.

Except for Jenny. They had always been friends.

Speaking of Jenny...

He looked around the room, but she had disappeared again.

Thank God.

"So, uh... Thanks for letting Max hang out with you today." He led Luke to the couch picking up an extra glass from the bar on his way. He poured them each a healthy dose of bourbon. This was becoming a habit. A pleasant habit.

"Not a problem." Luke took a sip of his whiskey, then continued. "Sheldon's crazy about him."

"It won't be for much longer, he isn't staying permanently. My attorney friend, Jason, is handling the paperwork to get him transferred to a family."

Luke frowned. "Really? Does Max know that? He told me you were his father, and he was here to live with you."

"Well, yes. But no. Hell, I don't know. I do want to find out why he's having nightmares though, and maybe help him with that."

"So, you don't want him to stay. But you want him to stay long enough to help him?"

The way Luke put it did make Harry feel like a walking contradiction.

"It's all so complicated." Harry rubbed his face, as if that would somehow shake out the confusion, and sort everything into place.

"You said that already. How is it complicated? Do you want to help Max?"

Harry felt like he should be irate that Luke was getting in his face about this, but he wasn't feeling that way at all. Instead, he felt lucky that Luke was here with him, and that he was interested enough to talk to him about it.

"I do want to help him. But I also don't want to break him." Harry sipped his bourbon, and realized his hands were shaking slightly. "I don't want to be a father. I don't know how."

"Who does? It's not as if they have colleges where you can get advanced degrees in it."

"I don't want to turn out to be like my father. He's not a good man. Neither George nor I has anything to do with him, although we have different reasons for it. George always resented that Martin was never around, and I always hated it when he was."

Luke looked like he wanted to start asking a bunch of questions Harry wasn't prepared to answer, so he continued before Luke could get started. "My point is that I don't know anything about raising a son. I want to help him. He's just a kid, for chrissake. Isn't it natural that I want to protect him? But I only know how I *wouldn't* raise him."

"Sounds to me like you're already ahead." Luke commented.

Harry had thought it was all worked out in his head. Find out what was wrong, fix it, then send the kid on his way. It was a logical way to approach it all.

Except that Harry wasn't feeling logical. He was feeling frustrated that Jenny was avoiding him. He was feeling angry that someone might have done something to give Max nightmares. And he was feeling scared shitless that he might not be the right person to help Max.

"It's..." Harry started to say, but then couldn't put the right words together to continue. "I don't know."

"It's complicated." Luke said flatly. "Complicated, like me being gay." It was a statement, not a question, so Harry knew Luke must still be angry.

"No. Not like you being gay." Harry wanted to start all over. How had he managed to screw up this conversation so badly? "I don't have a problem with you being gay. I was just... overwhelmed."

"Overwhelmed." Luke repeated, then sipped his drink, but watched Harry over the rim, and Harry knew he was going to have to be honest and speak from his heart if he didn't want to lose Luke as a friend.

Normally, if he'd been talking to a woman, he would say something complimentary, or simply change the subject and offer to take her out for dinner, and all would be right with the world again.

But Luke wasn't that easily manipulated. And Harry knew that his relationship with Luke was much more important to him than any of the women he'd dated. He didn't understand why, but he could feel, deep inside, that losing Luke would hurt a hell of a lot more than any of the women who'd come and gone from his life.

He realized he was comparing Luke to the women as if he and Luke had been dating, instead of just hanging out as friends. He wasn't sure what to do with that revelation. Everything was getting all mixed up in his head.

"I've never felt like that before." He waited to see how Luke would react to that statement, but Luke sat there like one of the models in his paintings. He was calm, quiet, and unmoving, as if waiting for instructions from the artist.

Harry took a deep breath and thought, *in for a penny, in for a pound*, then continued. "I've never seen anything like that before. There was so much raw emotion between them, so much... Devotion. Adoration. Hell, I don't know. How can two people feel like that?"

He honestly didn't know. He'd never felt the mutual connection – the oneness – that the two men in the painting showed for each other.

"You mean two men," Luke said. Again, it was a statement, not a question.

"No," Harry quickly responded, because he didn't want Luke to believe he was some kind of homophobe, like his father. "No, I mean... Well, yes, it had more impact for me, that it was two men, but not *because* it *was* two men. I—" He tried to continue, but his mind was a complete jumble of words. "I've dated many women, and never felt that same... I don't know... I guess it was a visceral reaction."

"Have you considered the possibility that you might be attracted to men?"

"Did you miss it when I said I've dated many women." Harry flashed Luke a grin, but Luke merely looked back at him like he was still expecting an answer to his question. "No, I haven't considered the possibility. I like to date women."

Luke shrugged. "Doesn't mean you don't also like to date men. Have you ever tried it?"

"Well, no. I..." Harry didn't know how to continue, and took a gulp of his bourbon instead. He didn't want Luke to get the impression he was anti-gay, but dating men wasn't even fathomable to him.

"All I'm saying," Luke continued, although he seemed to be picking his words very carefully, like he was navigating his way through a mine field, "is that you never really know unless you try. You said yourself that you had a significant reaction to seeing the men in my painting. That seems to say to me that you may be more interested in men than you let yourself believe. Have you considered the possibility you're bi?"

Harry almost choked on his drink. He looked at Luke, half-expecting him to start laughing and say he was kidding, but he looked back at Harry with something close to yearning in his eyes.

"No. It isn't possible." Harry tried to find the words to explain, without having to actually explain anything, but he was distracted by the whimpering and scratching on his front door.

Luke must have heard the noise as well, because he was already heading for the door by the time the sound had started registering to Harry.

"Shit, I'm not making any sense." Harry growled, then shook his head like a dog coming out of a bath, as if it would help jar something coherent out of his brain. "Look," he tried again, "you have to understand. I was brought up to believe—"

But he was interrupted by Max screaming from his room, "Stop! Stop! Noooo! Stop it!"

As Luke opened the front door, Harry ran for Max's room, and almost tripped over Sheldon who streaked by him, running straight to Max. Harry came into the room right behind Sheldon, and saw Jenny watching the dog calm Max down enough to curl up with him and go back to sleep.

Jenny looked panicked, like she thought Harry was going to hit her, and she ran over to stand next to Max. "Don't hurt him. He doesn't know he's doing this. It isn't his fault."

What the hell was she talking about? Hurt Max? He would never hurt a kid. How could she think he would hurt Max?

He was more convinced than ever that she was hiding something from him, and he wanted answers. "Goddamn it," he growled at her, and she disappeared right before his eyes.

"We need to talk," he demanded of the empty space where she'd been standing.

Harry hadn't realized that Luke had followed him, until he heard him speak. "If what you have to say sounds anything like, *'Can I have your dog?'* then there's nothing to talk about. The answer is, *'No'.*"

After today, Harry couldn't blame Luke for wanting nothing more to do with him.

Fair enough, Harry thought. But his stomach felt like he'd eaten too much hot sauce on his Mexican food, and he wanted to curl up and pretend none of this was happening to him.

"But I will help you find one of your own." Luke grinned at Harry, and it felt like the sun had just come out after a long, hard, cold winter.

Harry wanted to weep with relief that he hadn't screwed up his relationship with Luke. Something had changed between them, and he still didn't know what that was exactly, but Luke was still there with him.

He just wished he knew what to do to help Max.

"Jesus. He's breaking my heart." Harry walked over to the bed, and gently stroked Max's hair away from his face. He didn't know the exact nightmares Max was having, but Harry knew nightmares. He'd had enough of his own when he wasn't that much older than Max, and he wanted to hold the small boy, and tell him he wasn't alone. Because life was too awful for a kid who believed he was all alone in his nightmares.

"Still believe it's complicated?" Luke asked quietly from the foot of the bed.

CHAPTER NINE

Harry felt like shit, like he was lugging around ten-pound bowling balls under both eyes. He hadn't slept at all last night, what with Max's nightmares, and Luke believing him to be a homophobe and all, so it was almost noon by the time he dragged his half-dead carcass through the Landon Literary lobby to his office.

Once again, Jenny was nowhere to be found, and wasn't responding to his calling out to her, no matter how much he threatened her. Yes, he knew that threatening a ghost was probably useless – it's not like he could make that worse for her – but he had given it a valiant effort anyway. She was avoiding him, that was all there was to it. The question was: Why? What was she not telling him? Something more was going on.

Max was screaming at night, and Jenny was hiding. Two plus two equaled something very wrong, and it was time to find out what that something was. If Jenny wasn't talking, then he needed to get Blake on it, and get some answers without her. He couldn't go through many more nights like last night, that was for damned sure.

He only wished it was as easy as hiring a private investigator to help him figure out a solution with Luke. He knew he'd done a crappy job of trying to explain his reactions to the painting, and he really needed to get his head sorted out before he tried that again. Truth was, he loved the painting. He'd never seen work done by Sebastian Lucas except in glossy brochures and magazines, and hadn't been prepared for the emotional pull he'd felt from seeing one 'in the flesh,' so to speak.

So, the second thing on his list was to call Luke. He'd invite him over for dinner, and do his best to tell him how much he'd appreciated their talk last night, but that he couldn't—

"Harry?" Anna stood in front of him, looking exasperated, and he wondered if that hadn't been the first time she'd said his name to get his attention.

Oh, shit, that's right. She'd called him last night, and he'd already forgotten. Women hated that.

"Hey, Anna." He knew he was about to start walking on glass without shoes, and needed to soothe her. No matter what, when a woman was pissed, the first thing to do was apologize. "Sorry about last night, it was a bit crazy."

It wasn't like him to forget to call. He wasn't usually this neglectful of the women he dated. At least, not while he was dating them. He really needed to end this with her soon. Then he was going to run away to his Aspen condo to hide out for a while.

Except that he had Max to consider now, too. He could take Max with him to the Aspen condo. Or not. That didn't sound like a good way to hide out. But what would he do with him?

"I thought we could do lunch together?" Anna may have made it sound like a question, but Harry could tell she wasn't taking, 'No thanks,' for an answer.

Anna was a beautiful woman, with thick black hair and deep amber eyes that reminded Harry of the roasted caramel color of his favorite bourbon. Maybe he hadn't given them enough of a chance. Maybe a little more time together was just what they needed.

Plus, she was also the sister to one of their current bestselling authors, Dean Erickson, so Harry knew he had to play this one with a little more finesse when he broke things off.

"Lunch sounds like a great idea." He didn't have time for lunch, especially since he hadn't even been in the office five minutes yet, but he couldn't bring himself to turn her down.

"Lunch?" Emma barreled into his office, and almost knocked him over pushing him aside to get between him and Anna. "Did I hear someone say lunch? I'm famished. Eating for two, you know. Harry, George needs to see you in his office. You can have lunch together in there. Anna, why don't we make it a girl thing, and do lunch together?"

What the hell was up with her? Emma had never horned in on his dates before. She grilled him about them after the fact, but never before.

"Anna and I were—" he started to say, but was again interrupted.

"George?" Emma practically shrieked over her shoulder in the direction of George's office. "Anna and I are headed to lunch. Harry's here to meet with you."

George came out of his office, obviously compelled by Emma's command, but also looking like he didn't know what was going on any more than Harry did. "I thought you and I were having a late lunch at home." George looked confused, but Harry could swear Emma blushed.

Nevertheless, she remained firm in her conviction to go with Anna. "No, dear, that's tomorrow. Today, you are going to meet with Harry to discuss that thing we talked about. Re-mem-ber?"

Harry was damned if he knew what she was going on about.

"I see. So, this is it then." George seemed to be the only one who understood it, because he sighed, and gestured for Harry to come into his office. "Come on in, Harry. I'll ask Kelly to order lunch for us."

Emma smiled at George as she took his hand, then kissed him on the cheek. He smiled fondly down at her, but Harry could see he was as excited about this meeting as he would be about having a root canal.

What was going on? Why had they just sabotaged his lunch with Anna?

Anna looked confused, but Harry knew that she liked both Emma and George, and was obviously caught up in protocol. She looked over at Harry, and shrugged.

It looked like she'd gotten a temporary stay of relationship execution.

"YOU WANNA RUN that by me again?" Harry very carefully set his coffee mug down on the table to avoid snapping off the handle, or worse yet, hurling it against the wall.

"You heard me the first time," George responded, apparently deciding against repeating himself.

The desire to bolt from the office was so strong Harry had to grip the arms of the chair in order to keep himself seated in it. The sound of the leather squeaking under his fingers was almost deafening.

He could not believe what he had just heard. His older brother had finally lost it. He knew George hated their father; well, no shit, who didn't? But how could this possibly be true? He had to be making it up.

As he reached again for his cup of java, he half-expected Emma to throw open the doors and yell, "April Fools!" But nothing like that happened.

And April first wasn't for two more weeks.

"So, let me get this straight," Harry said, and withdrew his hand from picking up the mug when he realized it was shaking. "You're telling me that Daddy Dearest had a second family he kept a secret from apparently everyone but you. And that was why he was never home for any of the important holidays, like Christmas. Do I have that right?"

He and George never talked about their father, so this was a huge surprise to say the least. Martin had been the antithesis of a nurturing parent. The bastard had left so much emotional and psychological devastation in his wake that even as a grown adult, Harry couldn't think of him without the risk of triggering a severe panic attack. Which was why he and George had long ago decided it was safest to pretend the man didn't exist.

So, what the hell was George thinking, bringing him up now? Harry wanted nothing to do with Martin. He'd relegated the man to the past, and that's where he wanted him to stay. He didn't want to have this discussion, as if speaking of the man might bring him back into their lives again like some spectral demon. He already had one too many specters in his life at the moment.

"This is serious, Harry. You know I wouldn't have brought it up if it wasn't important." George scowled, but Harry could tell there wasn't any real anger behind it. He glimpsed raw hurt and genuine compassion in his brother's eyes, and Harry realized that this was just as upsetting for George as it was for him.

So, why bring it up at all?

"How does this even matter anymore? We haven't had any contact with him in years. Why should I care about this now? Or ever, for that matter?" Harry knew that the sooner they got this done, the sooner they could put Martin back in the past where he belonged, and they could move on to more important things. He already had enough on his plate with a botched friendship, a frightened kid, a recalcitrant ex-fiancée ghost, and a girlfriend (or two, counting Sarah) to dump, thank you very much.

He sure as shit didn't need Martin messing with his head.

Not again.

"It impacts you, because his second family is the Erickson's. Anna is our half-sister."

Harry choked on the coffee he'd finally managed to pick up and sip.

Okay, yes, this was bad – especially considering that for a brief moment he'd had a major attraction going for someone who had abruptly become his half-sister – but luckily nothing important had happened between them. They had gone out several times, but he could tell after a few dates that the relationship wasn't going anywhere. He had already placed her firmly in the 'friend' column.

Had he known something was wrong on a subconscious level?

Even kissing her had felt like he was kissing his sister.

Jesus. Had he really just thought that?

This was messed up.

"You didn't think that might have been important information to share with me *before* I started dating her? How do you even know this?" Harry felt compelled to ask, even though he didn't give a flying crap about his father, or where he'd spent his Christmas Eves. All he'd known was that when Martin was gone, he and George had several days they didn't have to worry about what the bastard thought of them.

"I followed him once, when I was fifteen, and saw it with my own eyes. And then I recognized Dean's name when he submitted his manuscript two years ago." George ran his fingers through his hair, which Harry knew was his tell that he was stressing over something.

"That's why you were so adamant about us not publishing it?"

"I never wanted you to know. I didn't want you to feel the hurt I felt when I found out our father didn't love us as much as his other family."

Harry's heart ached for his brother. It couldn't have been easy, holding in a secret like that for so many years. Harry had never had to feel the agony of being ignored by his father as George had.

The agony Harry had felt was in *not* being ignored by the hypo-critical bastard. He would have changed places with George in a heartbeat. No, he wouldn't have. He never would have wanted his brother to go through what he'd had to endure.

"I never would have said anything if it hadn't become necessary because of Anna. I had hoped that it would all blow over, because I didn't figure she'd last longer than three weeks. But Emma was adamant. And you know how she gets when she's determined." A very subtle grin broke out on his brother's face, and Harry felt the tension in the room lessen dramatically at the mention of Emma.

Harry felt a pang of jealousy over the intimacy George and Emma had. It wasn't a jealousy about Emma specifically, it was that he wanted the kind of relationship they had together. He wanted shared secrets, knowing glances, and being able to read each other so easily because they knew each other so well.

Harry didn't know why he was acting so indignant about all of this. He'd already planned to break up with Anna, so none of it really mattered.

The real reason he was so angry was because George had kept this a secret from him his whole life. They never kept secrets from each other.

Except, that wasn't true.

George hadn't been home the year Harry had 'disappeared' for six weeks. And Harry sure as hell never told him about that.

CHAPTER TEN

Harry loved a good barbecue.

But not this one.

Marlie had suggested that he bring Max to the Spring Field Day event so that he could meet the other kids in his class, and so that Harry could meet their parents.

He was thankful he had been able to patch things up with Luke and convince him to come with them, because Max had taken off immediately with Marlie's son, Spencer, and Harry was left feeling like he'd gone through some alternate universe shift, and landed on the planet Parentville. He was usually so good with women, and could charm his way around any situation. But these weren't women, they were *moms*, and that was a whole different ball game.

He liked a juicy tidbit of gossip as much as anyone else, but this was a whole new world where mothers not only back-stabbed, they bitch-slapped at the same time.

Obviously, you did not mess around with a mom.

Soccer-Mom: "Did you hear that Carol is pregnant again? Honestly, what was she thinking? I have two words for her. *Global warming*. That's all I'm saying. *Global. Warming.*"

Trophy-Mom: "Oh, I know. And that Ricky of hers is a juvenile delinquent in the making. I heard he brought a knife to school."

PTA-Mom: "It was only a butter knife. Carol accidentally packed it in with his lunch."

Trophy Mom: "But still. A *knife*. What's next? An Uzi?"

PTA-Mom: "I'm just saying, she probably had a moment of *pregnancy brain* and missed the knife. It was an honest mistake. Give her a break. Ricky's a good kid."

Soccer-Mom: "Global. Warming."

Trophy-Mom: "Oh, hi, Carol. Don't you look all glowy and beautiful."

Soccer-Mom: "Pregnancy sure agrees with you, honey."

PTA-Mom: "Hi, Ricky. Jack's out on the field with Spencer, if you want to go play some soccer with them."

"What the hell is *pregnancy brain?*" Harry asked Luke, speaking quietly and out of the side of his mouth to avoid one of the moms overhearing him. "And what does it have to do with global warming? Do they think that pregnancy brain – whatever that is – causes global warming?"

Should he be worried about this Ricky kid being a threat to Max while he's with Spencer?

He was so out of his element.

"Now you know which crazy moms not to invite to any of Max's birthday parties." Luke looked at Harry and grinned. At least someone was enjoying himself.

He was damned lucky that Luke was there. By mutual, unspoken agreement, he and Luke had basically picked up their friendship again as if nothing had happened.

He would occasionally feel a bit giddy whenever he saw Luke, but he wanted to attribute that to him being worried about how close he'd come to ruining their friendship. He wanted to attribute it to that, but he suspected he was actually developing feelings for Luke. Romantic feelings. And that was just too scary for him to try. Not again.

He felt like everything was more balanced finally, on an even keel, when Luke was around, and he was afraid to risk upsetting that. The craziness that had become his life seemed to be more manageable.

Hell, even Max was fitting in here better than he was. Which was a good thing. Max seemed to be coming out of his shell, and acting more like a normal kid. Although Harry wasn't sure he was the best judge of 'normal' considering his own childhood – what with a mother who'd been a drunk, and a father who was a narcissistic asshole, it was hard to be objective.

"I'm not sure Max should be hanging with that Ricky kid," he blurted out to Luke. It sounded stupid, even to his own ears, but Luke smiled at him as if he thought it was the perfect thing to say.

"I like that you seem to be getting the hang of the protective father thing, but it *was* only a butter knife." Luke winked, then jogged off toward Max and the other boys on the field, and Harry couldn't stop himself from smiling.

Having Luke's approval, even when Harry was being ridiculous, somehow made the whole thing seem right – as if it was okay for him to make idiotic mistakes, because Luke would still have his back.

"I like him." Jenny made her usual unannounced appearance behind him, but this time he didn't flinch. Much.

"I like him, too," Harry agreed. "I don't know what I would have done these last couple of days if he hadn't been around to help me out with Max."

"He's good with Max." He waited for her to say more, as they watched Luke kick around a soccer ball with Max, Spencer, and a kid who must be the infamous Ricky, but she remained silent.

"That's it? That's all you have to say to me." He tried to keep his voice low so that he didn't end up being the next gossip topic as the-crazy-guy-who-talks-to-imaginary-people. That would be all Max needed, starting out at a new school. But she was really pissing him off. The stress of the last several days, not to mention the lack of sleep, had him feeling like a hibernating bear who'd just been poked. "You disappear for two days—"

"I've only been gone one day."

"Yeah? Well, down here in the real world, it felt more like a month." He noticed that he was starting to get curious looks from people around him, so he pulled out his cell phone and held it to his ear to have a pretend conversation.

He might look like an asshole for yelling on the phone, but he wouldn't look like a nut-job for talking to himself. "I want answers, Jenny. Why is Max having nightmares so intense he's screaming in the middle of the night?"

"He's going to be fine," she said, sounding like she was trying to convince herself. And her eye was twitching again, so Harry knew there was still something that had her worried. "He's safe with you, Harry, I'm sure of it. And he's safe with Luke, too, so don't worry about that."

"I know he's safe with me," he said, his voice even and calm. "And I know he's safe with Luke. What I don't know is why you felt you needed to point that out to me."

He was doing his best to remain calm to keep her from freaking out and disappearing on him again, but she was working on his last nerve. He took a deep breath, then let it out before he asked, "Was he not safe with you, Jenny? Tell me what's going on."

"Of course he was safe with me! He's my son. How can you even say something like that to me?" Jenny looked so outraged that Harry felt compelled to believe her. But she was still hiding something from him.

"Then why won't you talk to me about his nightmares? You aren't giving me much to go on here, and it's forcing me to jump to my own conclusions. You disappear on me whenever I push too hard, and you're evasive when I ask you pointed questions. Tell me what the hell is going on."

"He's had a tough childhood." Jenny looked down and around, anywhere but directly at Harry.

"Yeah, well, who didn't? Give me something I can work with, Jenny, or so help me—"

"Hi, Harry!" Anna was walking toward him, waving at him like she belonged there. "Marlie told me you were out here at the soccer field. Which one's Max?" She leaned in and gave him a quick peck on the lips, and Harry almost gagged. The thought of being kissed by his half-sister made him want to wipe it from his mouth, and run screaming like a six-year-old who'd just been given cooties.

What was she doing here anyway? He hadn't invited her. He hadn't even told her he'd be here.

Harry looked around, and once again, Jenny had slipped away from him. Every time he thought he might be able to get some answers from her, she vaporized.

Goddamn it. She had to stop doing that.

He contemplated pretending he was still on the phone, so that he could ignore Anna, but eventually he would have to end his fake conversation and talk to her. He tucked the phone back into his pocket and turned to Anna.

"What are you doing here?" He hadn't meant it to come out sounding like an accusation, but, well, it was sort of strange that she just showed up. She looked like she'd come straight from the office, because she was not dressed for a barbecue. She was wearing a black form-fitting pencil skirt, with a white poet's blouse, accented with cherry red spiked heels and a matching belt. How she'd made it across the open field without falling on her ass was beyond Harry.

"Emma mentioned that you were bringing Max to an event for his new school, and I thought you'd appreciate having someone with you to help fight off all the single moms." She looked around like she was taking inventory of the other women, and it crossed Harry's mind that she might feel threatened by the other women.

"I appreciate that, but you really didn't need to come. Luke's with me, and we have it all covered." He really needed to sit down with her soon and let her know they were related before she did something to embarrass herself.

"Oh, you're here with your artist friend?" Anna sounded none too pleased about that, and it made the small hairs on the back of his neck stand up. He rubbed his neck and wondered if she was jealous of his friendship with Luke.

"I did it! I did it!" Max came running up at ramming speed almost knocking Harry over in his excitement. Harry hugged him to steady him, and smiled when he saw how overjoyed Max was. "Did you see my goal? It went right by Luke and into the net."

"Sorry, Champ, I missed it." Harry ruffled Max's hair, and looked up to see Luke jogging toward them. Luke looked as thrilled as Max, and Harry continued to smile, basking in the rightness of the moment.

"Well, you must be Max." Anna's voice snapped Harry out of his thoughts. "I've heard so much about you. I'm Anna." She held her hand out for Max to shake it. He looked confused, but apparently good manners finally won out, and he shook with her. "I'm a special friend of Harry's."

Luke coughed and wrapped a protective arm over Max's shoulder like they were just two guys hanging out, shooting the shit. He grinned down at Max and said, "He's a natural."

Harry didn't particularly like the way Anna said, 'special.' He could tell Max wasn't too sure how to take her either, because he glanced over at Harry for some kind of explanation.

"Let's get back out on the field, and you can reenact your goal for me. Can I be on your team?" He said it without even thinking, then realized he was nervous waiting for Max's answer.

Max beamed at him, like he'd just been given an Olympic gold medal. "You wanna be on my team?"

"Aren't you the soccer star who just blew one by Bend It Like Luke? Heck yes I want to be on your team."

Harry's heart flipped seeing the happiness on Max's face. He hadn't been paying much attention to Max, and that made him feel like he was just another one of those deadbeat dads in the world.

He would change that, starting now.

The thought surprised him, because it meant that, on some level, he'd already made up his mind to keep Max with him. Apparently, his subconscious mind was moving along at a faster pace than his conscious mind.

"Come on. Let's go get 'em!" Luke shouted, as he turned and started running back out to the field. Max took off after him like he'd just heard the starting gun in a race.

Harry laughed, deciding Marlie's Field Day idea had been brilliant after all, and ran to join them.

"Hey, what about me?" Anna stood there in her five-inch spikes and shouted after him.

"You can come, too." Harry replied, without slowing down. He knew he wasn't being very polite, but it wasn't his fault. He hadn't invited her here.

CHAPTER ELEVEN

How had life become so complicated?

He had a nine-year-old boy living with him who deserved a real father, and he was worried he was going to be a failure in that role.

He had a ghost popping in and out of his life whenever she damn-well felt like it, and she wasn't giving him the information he needed to help him with said nine-year-old boy.

It was all getting to be too crazy. He wasn't sure how much more he'd be able to take before he erupted like Mount Vesuvius. He wasn't used to this kind of turmoil in his life.

And the icing on the cake was that Anna was coming over any minute for "the talk" – the weirdest talk he'd ever had to have with a woman.

How did you tell someone you've been sort of dating that you needed to break up with them because you'd just found out you're related to them.

Where do you go from there?

Hey, we can still be friends?

If not for living it personally, he would have thought his life was a plot straight out of a TV soap opera.

The funny thing was that he could picture himself staying friends with Anna. She was easy to be around, and didn't take shit from anyone, even Harry. Especially Harry.

She was a killer negotiator, who worked out an excellent contract with Landon Literary for her brother, Dean. Harry had been impressed. It was the reason they'd hired her for the company.

Now that he thought about it, Dean was his half-sibling, too. His family was growing by the second.

It was giving him a headache.

But Anna was also a walking contradiction: A killer, take-no-prisoners editor by day, and a *Cheetos for breakfast is not the way to start your day* tree-hugger by... well, all the time. And he loved that about her.

He honestly hoped they could stay friends, because he'd always wanted a little sister. There wasn't any reason they couldn't have a sibling relationship. It wouldn't compare with what he and George had, because they had grown up together, and were brothers of the heart as well as brothers of the blood. But he was willing to try with Anna.

When his doorbell rang, he took a deep breath to steady himself – his new sister would be proud of his Zen-like composure – and opened the door.

Except that it wasn't Anna.

It was Blake Hunter. Blake always showed up without notice, and sometimes at the oddest moments.

"Hey, man." Blake clapped Harry on the shoulder, then pushed inside the door. "Your message said you had a job for me?"

"Uhh... yes. But we could have done it over the phone. You didn't have to come in personally." It wasn't that Harry wasn't glad to see his friend, it was just a bit inconvenient what with Anna stopping by as well.

"It's not like Boulder is across the country. It was no big." Blake went to the fridge and helped himself to a beer. "What'cha need? It sounded important."

"It's kind of a long story, but I need you to look into someone for me."

"You got it. Who is it?"

"Like I said, it's a long story. I have a friend coming over any minute, and then I'm heading next-door for dinner with my neighbor. Come with me. You can meet Max."

"Max?" Blake looked confused for a moment, but then continued. "That's the kid you ended up with, but who you think belongs to someone else? You want me to find out for sure?"

"No, I'll handle that with a simple paternity test. Shit, I still haven't gotten that test yet." Harry felt like someone had just dumped a house on his shoulders. How could he have forgotten about the paternity test?

Maybe because there was that small voice inside his head telling him that he was Max's father, and to stop pretending he still wanted out of the relationship.

His doorbell rang again, mercifully breaking into his thoughts, and he knew it had to be Anna this time.

"Listen, Blake, stay and hang out for a bit," Harry said, as he headed to answer the door. "Then we can go next-door for dinner and I'll fill you in on everything."

Yep, this time it was Anna.

"Hi, Harry." She leaned in to kiss him, but this time he was prepared for it, and he turned his face just in time for it to land on his cheek.

"Hey, Anna, come on in." Harry gave her a brief hug, and patted her on the back, which was perfectly appropriate from an older brother.

Blake came out of the kitchen and gave Anna a not-so-subtle once over before his gaze finally stopped on her face. Harry could swear there had been a spark of interest in Blake's ice-blue eyes before he broke eye contact with her to drink his beer.

That was interesting. Harry couldn't remember the last time Blake had a long-term girlfriend, so it was nice to see some interest. Maybe he could get Blake and Anna together.

Unfortunately, Anna didn't appear to appreciate the appraisal because her eyes narrowed, and Harry could sense her going into her killer negotiator do-not-pull-your-macho-male-bullshit-with-me-buddy mode.

Harry always liked to watch the reactions of women when they first met Blake. There was something about his muscular build paired with the mocha-colored skin, dark hair trimmed close to his scalp in a military style, and those piercing blue eyes that attracted women like free, all-you-can-drink mimosas at Sunday brunch.

But for some reason, Anna seemed to be immune. Or she was at least trying very hard to be.

Harry watched like a spectator at a tennis match as Blake shut down. That was new. Usually Blake turned on the charm when he was presented with that kind of challenge. But he ignored her, went over to the couch, put his feet up on the coffee table, and turned on the TV.

What the hell? He'd never seen Blake shut down with a woman so fast before. Especially when she hadn't said anything to him yet – it was usually after they started to speak that he lost interest.

And he had seen interest in Blake's eyes.

"I'm sorry, Harry, I didn't know you would have... *company.*" The last word sounded like she was calling him an ax murderer. Except that she'd watched Blake's every movement as he walked to the couch.

That wasn't the look of someone who didn't like what she saw.

This was starting to get fun.

Anna had never shown so much animosity toward anyone before. Even in the short amount of time that he'd known her, she was always pleasant to people, like it was her civic duty to treat everyone with respect and compassion. This had to go against her mantra, or whatever the hell she called her code of conduct in Granolaland.

Bottom line: Anna and Blake were both going through some major conflict in their own minds, and Harry was damned if he understood any of it.

"Blake's an old friend. He does some investigative work for us when we need it. We can go into my office and talk." Harry guided her past the glowering gargoyle on the couch and closed the door to his study to give them some privacy.

"Where's Max? I was hoping I'd get to see him again." Anna casually sat down on the small sofa, oblivious to the bomb he was about to drop on her head.

"Max is over at Luke's playing with Sheldon. Blake and I are going over there in a bit to have dinner with them."

"Oh. I see."

That was what she'd said, but Harry knew she didn't mean it, because her eyebrows came together and her forehead creased like she was working out a particularly difficult philosophical debate. "I thought you and I were having dinner."

"No, I wanted to talk to you—"

"Oh, dear. Here we go." Anna stood up from the sofa, squaring off as if preparing for battle.

"No, Anna, please just sit down. I need to explain something that George told me yesterday."

"You talked to George about this first?" Her volume increased, but she slowly lowered herself back onto the sofa, and Harry knew that if he didn't spit it out, he would no longer be in control of the conversation, and he might never get it out at all.

"Anna, you and I are related."

Silence. She blinked at him several times, as if clearing her vision would somehow make sense of what she'd just heard.

"Related." She sounded confused, like she didn't understand the meaning of the word. "As in family-related."

"Yes, as in we're related as family."

"So, you know about Martin."

"Know about Martin?" It was Harry's turn to be confused. "Wait. You mean you *know* about Martin?" The gears were working again, and he didn't like how this was starting to look.

"Dean asked me not to tell you. And since it didn't matter to me, I told him I wouldn't."

"Dean knows, too?" Harry was beyond stunned, he was verging on incensed. "Did he know when you both pitched us his book?"

"Yes." Anna shrugged like it was no big deal. "That was the reason he came to Landon Literary. I think he was afraid if I told you about Martin, you wouldn't publish his manuscript."

"He was right. George was vehemently against it."

"Water under the bridge. And that's business. It doesn't have any impact on our relationship."

"It doesn't?" Harry vaulted from the sofa as if she'd just stuck him with a cattle prod. "How can you even say that? We don't have a relationship. We *can't* have a relationship. We're related!" He flapped his hand back and forth between them, hoping that would somehow help it sink in to her. "We're half-siblings."

"Well, no, not legally. At least I don't think so." She scrunched up her face again in concentration. "I don't believe Martin ever adopted me."

"The bastard didn't even give you his name?" Harry hated his father, but it was still a surprise to him that his father wouldn't claim his own offspring.

"Harry, what exactly did George tell you?"

"He told me that Martin had a second family, and that you and Dean were our half-siblings."

"Ahhh, I see the confusion now." Anna nodded her head, then patted the couch next to her for him to sit back down. When he did, she continued, "Martin isn't my biological father. I have no idea who my real father is, but it definitely isn't Martin. So, we have nothing to worry about."

Harry didn't know whether to be relieved, or depressed. The good news was that they weren't related, and he didn't have to feel so grossed out because they'd dated. The bad news was that he still wanted to break up with her, and he'd lost a perfectly good reason to do it.

"Okay, well, see... the thing is..." He was normally better with this, but he was stumbling over his words like gangly teenager. "I don't think you and I—"

"I'm so glad we got that all cleared up." Anna stood up from the couch, and started walking to the front door. "I can't imagine what you must have been going through, but you don't need to worry about it anymore. Now, I know you have plans tonight with Max, so I'll clear out." She turned back from the front door and looked at him hopefully. "Or you could leave Max with Luke, and you and I could still go out. There's this new—"

"No, no." Harry followed her, and opened the front door all but pushing her out. He suddenly understood what a rabbit must feel like when trapped by a fox. "Luke is expecting me, and already has everything ready."

"Okay, then." She wrapped her arms around his neck, and kissed him full on the lips. "See you later."

And she was gone.

This time Harry didn't resist the urge to wipe his mouth.

What the hell just happened to him?

Harry sat next to Blake on the couch, and waited a moment to see if Blake would share why he was acting so weird about Anna. When Blake continued to watch the TV, Harry decided to just ask.

"What's up with you?"

"What do you mean?" Blake didn't even glance his way, and Harry knew something was eating at him.

"Why'd you shut down with Anna earlier? I thought you'd be pouring on the charm when she scalded you with that look."

"I don't poach other men's women." Blake sipped his beer, like that was the end of the discussion.

"She's not my woman." Harry shuddered at the thought, being that they were practically related, no matter what she said. "Poach away, my friend."

Blake finally looked at Harry, and grinned. "It's not poaching, if she's fair game."

CHAPTER TWELVE

The next morning, as Harry chopped onions and peppers for the Denver omelet he was creating for breakfast, he thought about how last night had gone a little better with Max.

Luke and Sheldon had stayed with Harry, anticipating another nightmare from Max, and it had been nice spending time late into the evening talking with Luke. At first, Harry had worried Luke was going to want to pick up their conversation from the other night, but he must have sensed that Harry wasn't ready – or able – to go into it more deeply.

Instead, they'd talked about Luke's art, and how he'd chosen to use an alias instead of his real name in order to keep his personal life separate from his professional life. Harry had always seen Luke as a confident man who used as few words as possible to get his point across, but he was also discovering that he was a private man who didn't want to be in the limelight, in spite of his success as an artist.

Harry had enjoyed the time with Luke, hanging out on the couch, feet propped on the coffee table, sipping their bourbons, and getting to know each other better.

Until the screaming started around eleven, nearly giving Harry a heart attack. He shouldn't have been surprised – he'd known it was coming – but he'd been so comfortable with Luke, he hadn't been paying attention. Sheldon seemed to sense it before Harry and Luke heard it, because he was up and sprinting to Max's room before Harry'd even set his feet on the floor.

He wasn't sure how much longer he would be able to keep this up. Selfishly, he had enjoyed the time with Luke, but he knew that it was time to have a chat with Max, and see if he could figure out the root of the problem.

It was more than just the lost hours of sleep that was bothering Harry. He genuinely liked Max – Jason had been right about that – and he was feeling strange delusions of superhero grandeur about saving the kid by taking him in. He wanted to find out who had made Max so scared that the kid screamed in his dreams, and he wanted to beat the shit out of that guy.

He knew he was fooling himself. He didn't have it in him to beat the shit out of anyone for any reason, but he did want to see the guy pay. Assuming, of course, that it was a guy. What if Jenny... No, he couldn't go there.

And it might not be a person at all. He could have been traumatized by anything. Clowns usually did it for Harry. But then, clowns traumatized everyone. Why the hell did they even exist?

Harry looked up to see Max shuffle into the kitchen, and plop himself on one of the bar stools at the counter. He was discovering that Max was not a morning person. He chalked it up to the nightmares giving him some kind of hangover in the morning.

He must get his morning mood from his mother, because Harry was usually an early riser, which was turning out to be a good thing now that he had to get Max to school every day by eight.

"Hey buddy. Want some eggs?" Harry didn't wait for an answer. He poured the eggs into the pan knowing that Max would eat them. Max grunted, but that was it, so he took that for an affirmative.

As he maneuvered the eggs into a perfectly formed and fluffy breakfast – this second one came out better than the first, so he would give it to Max – he decided now was as good a time as any to try to get Max to open up. He plated the omelet, added a few strips of crispy bacon, and placed Max's breakfast in front of him.

"So, hey, Max, I have a question for you." Harry tried to sound like it was no big deal, as he poured a glass of OJ for each of them. "Do you know that you wake up in the middle of the night, screaming?"

Shit. That hadn't come out right at all. Too blunt.

Max froze, holding his fork in mid-air, and stared at Harry with eyes that seemed to cover half his face.

"Shit. I mean, shoot. I mean, damn it, that isn't what I meant to say. Not the cussing part, although I hadn't meant to say that either, but the part about your nightmares." He was screwing this up royally. He was only going to make it worse. "Look, Max—"

"Leave him alone." Jenny popped into existence, which was just what Harry needed – not at all. "He can't help the nightmares, he's just a little boy."

"I'm not talking to you right now." Harry looked over at Jenny, and glared at her. "Go away."

Max looked at Harry, then at his breakfast, then back at Harry before he sighed and stepped off the stool.

"No, Max, I'm sorry, I wasn't talking to you. I was just--" What? What was he supposed to say? *I'm just having this side conversation with the ghost of your dead mother, who's really pissing me off.* "Stay and eat breakfast with me, and we can chat for a bit. Okay?"

"Okay," Max said, and although he didn't look convinced, he picked up his fork and started in again. Apparently, his hunger was more important on his hierarchy of needs than avoiding the crazy man who talked to himself.

But what bothered Harry more was Max's reaction when he thought Harry had told him to go away. He hadn't been surprised, or even upset that someone would speak to him in such a tone. He had been resigned to it, and had blindly followed the command as if he heard it all the time.

Harry came around the counter to sit on the stool next to Max, so that he'd be more on eye-level with him to have this discussion. "What's going on with you?" When Max didn't respond, Harry pushed a little harder. "I'm worried about the nightmares you're having. Did someone hurt you?" He watched Max shovel eggs into his mouth like it was his last meal.

"You're scaring him. Stop grilling him." Jenny hovered next to Max, and she looked like she would jump out of her skin.

Except that she'd done that already.

That thought almost made Harry laugh.

He was starting to lose it.

He decided to ignore the ghost in the room.

"Okay, so, I know you don't have any reason to trust me – we barely know each other – but I really want to help you. Your mom trusted me to take care of you, but I can't do that if you won't tell me what's going on." Harry looked pointedly at Jenny so that she would know he meant those words for her as well as for Max.

Max looked at Harry with such longing, as if he wanted to spill his guts out, but knew it would be the end of the world if he did. Harry wanted to pull Max into his arms and tell him that he would take care of him, but he didn't think Max was there yet.

What surprised him was that *he* was there. He wanted to fight dragons for this kid, and prove that he could fix anything.

"Whatever it is, Max, we'll deal with it. I'm here now, and I'll help you. Your mom wanted me to be here for you, and I am."

He had no idea what he was saying, but he knew he meant it. Well holy shit. Where did that come from? When had he made that decision, and not discussed it with himself first? He'd already made up his mind, and he wasn't letting Max go. He'd talk to Jason, and tell him not to file the transfer papers. Or whatever the hell they were called.

"Please don't push him, Harry." Jenny had spoken so quietly, he almost hadn't heard her. He looked up and saw that she was silently crying.

Harry didn't know that ghosts *could* cry. There weren't any tears flowing, so apparently ghosts didn't have bodily fluids? Then again, he hadn't even known ghosts existed at all until this one had popped into his life, so it wasn't surprising that he didn't know the protocol.

He wouldn't push Max, but he would get answers. Since Jenny wasn't forthcoming, and could vaporize whenever she felt like it – not to mention, zap the crap out of him – he would have to get his information from Max. But he would take his time and be patient with him. He didn't want to scare him any more than he already was.

He turned his attention back to Max, and thought about the best way to help him feel comfortable enough to talk to him.

Maybe they should get away – have a guy's weekend to spend some time together.

"Hey, buddy. Do you like to fish?" Harry wasn't sure if he liked to fish himself, but he knew he had to start somewhere.

Max shrugged. But he also looked interested, so Harry continued.

"I have a condo in Aspen, which is really close to this great reservoir. We could go away for the weekend and do some fishing."

"Can Sheldon and Luke come?"

Harry thought for a second about having Luke along. He liked having Luke around. Something had shifted in their relationship since their talk. Luke was more attentive, more openly supportive, like he'd understood Harry's confusion – around Max, and around Luke – and was trying to help him work through it, without applying any pressure to force it. He was just... there. They had developed a stronger bond after clearing the air with each other. And Sheldon would be good for Max.

But Harry was worried he might not get the opportunity to bond with Max, and find out what was going on with him if there were too many other distractions.

"Let's just keep it the two of us this time. Get to know each other. Okay?" Harry held his breath waiting for the rejection. They hadn't spent much time together without Luke and Sheldon as a buffer, and Max might refuse to go without them.

"Okay."

Was that hope Harry saw in Max's eyes?

Harry let out his breath, and patted Max on the arm reassuringly. "Great. Finish your breakfast, or we'll be late. We can head out when I come pick you up after school."

Harry wasn't sure what made him think of fishing for an activity – he'd never been fishing in his life. He was going to have to swing by an outdoors shop sometime today for whatever paraphernalia a person needed to go fishing with a nine-year-old boy, but it sounded like a good bonding experience. At least it was in the movies.

Besides, it's fishing.

How hard could it be?

CHAPTER THIRTEEN

Fishing sucked.

Thank god they hadn't talked him into the "whole camping experience" at the store, or Harry would have thrown himself into Ruedi Reservoir, and let it carry his body out into oblivion, or the Fryingpan River, or wherever it was the reservoir went.

Luckily, they were only twenty minutes from his condo, and a bed with six hundred thread count Egyptian cotton sheets. And a hot shower.

The guy at the permit office said the reservoir had rainbow and yellow trout – not that Harry knew the difference between a trout and a carp, let alone their colors – and that they could catch up to four each day. He figured that was more than enough for the two of them, and they were only going to be up there for two days.

He'd pictured this as going differently in his head: they'd be drifting gently in a small boat, drinking beer – well, he'd be drinking beer, Max would be drinking some sugar-free organic soda – and the fish would pretty much snag the hook and jump into the boat.

Voila! Instant dinner.

Not so much.

It had started off so well, too.

Jenny made a brief appearance when he was driving to the school to pick up Max, but Harry asked her to give him some time and space to spend the weekend alone with Max. When he used the "male bonding" phrase, she eventually agreed and faded out. But not before Harry glimpsed the reluctance on her face that told him she agreed, but would still be keeping an eye on him.

They had gotten to the condo in the early evening, eaten the dinner Harry had packed, and headed straight for the hot tub; Harry with his beer, and Max with his organic soft drink. They dried off in front of the fireplace, and roasted marshmallows, while Harry told Max stories of all the trouble he, George, and Jason had gotten themselves into as kids.

He'd thought about telling traditional ghost stories, but didn't want to risk exacerbating Max's already very scary nightmares. Besides, it seemed somehow wrong, given that he already had more than enough of a ghost story going on in his life.

When Max finally fell asleep on the floor by the fire, Harry laid a blanket over him, then slept on the couch next to him so that he could say they'd officially camped out together. He woke up with a sore arm dangling off the side of the couch. Pins and needles shot all through his arm and blasted out his fingers. He looked down and saw that, at some point during the night, Max had taken his hand and was still holding onto it as he slept.

Harry was willing to sacrifice a stiff arm for a few minutes when he realized that Max had slept, soundly, through the entire night. No screaming.

He was glad that it was an unseasonably warm day for early April at the reservoir, in spite of the overcast sky. A fog had rolled in, and it made him feel like they were wrapped in their own little cocoon together, just the two of them. They'd been fishing – and he used that term loosely – on the dock since just after breakfast, and so far, their catch total for the day was zero.

He was pretty sure they would be ordering pizza for dinner.

"I think you drowned another worm." Max pointed to Harry's line in the water. "Do you need me to put one on your hook again?"

It was mortifying to Harry that he got squeamish when it came to impaling worms on a skewer, but he was happy that Max seemed to like being superior in that skill. So far, the kid seemed to be taking better care of Harry than the other way around.

But Max was also glowing. He was enjoying their excursion, if the smile on his face was any indication. It was wonderful to see him smile. And if that meant Harry had to put up with a slight hit to his masculinity because of worms, so be it. Besides, no one else had to know.

"You sure know a lot about fishing," Harry said, beginning a fishing expedition of his own. "Who taught you how to bait a hook?"

He hoped his question sounded casual, like two guys hanging out, swapping stories, but Max stiffened, and the smile left his face.

Shit.

"I have an idea," Harry said, as he reeled in his line. "Let's take a break from fishing and sit for a minute. We can eat our lunch. I made us ham and cheese sandwiches, and even packed extra chips." He placed his rod on the dock and began unpacking their lunch, not giving Max a chance to argue.

He was relieved when Max reeled in his line, set his rod next to Harry's, then sat down beside him. Harry passed him a sandwich, and they sat quietly for a few minutes enjoying the scenery and the quiet.

"So, here's my idea," Harry began, hoping he wasn't going to blow the moment, but knowing he needed to take a risk if he was going to get Max to trust him and open up. "I know you have some secrets you aren't sure you should tell, so why don't we do this together. I'll tell you a secret that I have, and you can tell me a secret that you have, and we'll just keep going until we've shared everything with each other. Does that work for you?"

Harry smiled as he looked down at Max who had gone still. He knew he would have to give Max a big secret to start this off, if he wanted the kid to trust him.

But Max nodded his agreement, so Harry took the plunge.

"I'll go first then, and it's a big one, so I'm trusting you here." Harry took a deep breath, and let it out with the words, "I have been able to see your mom's ghost since the day I met you."

There.

It was out there now, and Max was going to think he was a lunatic.

But when he looked at Max, all he saw in his face was wonder, as if he'd just told him that he was secretly the President of the United States.

"She calls you *Maxi*." He felt compelled to give Max some kind of proof. He glanced again at Max to judge his reaction to that statement, and was rewarded with an eye roll. Yep, he'd figured correctly that the kid hated that nickname. "I told her she had to stop calling you that."

Max laughed. Holy shit, he actually sputtered out a genuine laugh. It was the sweetest sound Harry had ever heard. He felt like he'd won a Pulitzer, winning a laugh out of Max. No, it was better than a Pulitzer. And he was going to make sure there were more laughs in Max's future.

They sat in companionable silence for another minute. Harry hated to break the mood, but he needed to push forward. He leaned down and nudged shoulders with Max.

"So, you believe me?"

"I guess." Max shrugged, as if people told him they saw ghosts all the time.

"It doesn't freak you out that she's a ghost?"

"Should it?" Max looked like he'd just been insulted.

"Lots of people don't believe in ghosts."

Max shrugged again. Apparently, he didn't care what other people believed, and Harry felt like he'd done the right thing in telling him about his mom.

"Do you know why my mom is here? Aren't ghosts here because they're supposed to do something for someone, or something?"

Harry was reluctant to answer that question. Jessica had told

Harry that Jenny was there for him, not for Max, and he didn't want to break Max's heart by telling him that.

"Why do you think she's here, Max?"

"She told me she would always make sure I was safe." He seemed to realize he'd given something away, because he went back to stuffing sandwich into his mouth.

"Safe from what?" Harry watched Max carefully, hoping for some indication that he would spill his secrets, but he continued to focus on his sandwich. "Come on, buddy, your turn. Tell me why she felt she needed to always keep you safe." When Max didn't respond, Harry pushed a bit more. "Was she keeping you safe from a person?"

It was a guess, but Harry felt pretty sure only another person could make a nine-year-old scream in the middle of the night.

He hated being suspicious of Jenny, but she had been so evasive whenever he brought up the subject. He knew in his heart that Jenny wouldn't hurt Max, but his brain needed to know for sure that she was clear.

"Did your mom tell you not to say anything?" Harry was worried he was pushing this too fast, because Max brought his knees up to his chest and started rocking back and forth. "I need to know who hurt you, so that I can help you."

He wasn't getting anywhere this way, Max was never going to tell him. He needed to come right out and ask the question, like ripping off a bandage.

"Did your mom hurt you?" Harry was so scared to hear the answer, that he almost didn't get the question out.

"No!" Max exploded to his feet and glared down at Harry. "My mom would never hurt me."

"Okay, okay. I'm sorry. You're right, your mom would never hurt you. I know that." He did know that, but he was still relieved, because he could stop feeling suspicious about Jenny. He took Max's hand, and coaxed him to sit back down next to him. He put his arm around Max, and could feel the poor kid shaking so much that he was amazed he couldn't hear teeth rattling.

"A deal's a deal, buddy. A secret for a secret, remember?" Harry pulled Max closer, and felt him relax just a bit. "Who hurt you, Max?"

Silence.

The only sound for several minutes was the lapping of the water against the pier.

"Nobody."

Damn it. Max wasn't going to tell him. He didn't feel safe enough with Harry. It was frustrating, but Harry wouldn't push.

Harry felt like a sumo wrestler was sitting on top of his chest, and his eyes were burning with the futility he felt over not being able to help this sweet boy. But he wouldn't force him to tell what he wasn't ready to say.

"Nobody hurt me. He hurt my mom." And then he burst into heartrending sobs.

JENNY WAS WAITING at the condo when they got back, and she didn't look happy: the toe-tapping was a pretty good clue. Harry was pretty sure that her mood indicated that, in spite of promising to give them some guy-time together, she had been eavesdropping on his afternoon fishing with Max, and she was slightly less than pleased that Harry had pushed her son to spill his secret.

Fine. He had a few things he needed to say to her, too. Now was as good a time as any. And since Max knew that she was there as a ghost, he didn't have to worry about trying to cover up talking to her.

"Before you start yelling at me for being here during your male bonding weekend, I asked you not to push—"

"Max, your mom is here, and she's mad at me for pushing you into telling me about Curtis." Harry decided that the best defense was a good offense.

Max's eyes went as wide as a child's in a Margaret Keane painting, and he turned around in circles trying to see her.

"Mom? Where are you?"

"He knows about me?" Jenny apparently forgot all about yelling at Harry, because she immediately moved to Max's side.

"She's standing right next to you, buddy, on your left." Harry sat down on the couch, and tugged Max down next to him. Jenny followed slowly, keeping her eyes on Max the whole time, like she was worried he would disappear. "Anything you want to say to her? I can tell you what she says back to you."

"Mom?" Max was tentative at first, but then he continued. "I'm really sorry I told him about Curtis. I know I wasn't supposed to say anything, that it was our secret, but I couldn't hold it in any longer."

"Oh, baby, it's okay. It was too big a secret for you to hold onto." She tried to take his hand, but stopped herself at the last second, and looked at Harry for guidance.

"She's not mad at you." Harry translated for her. "She's sorry she made you keep the secret in the first place. It was unfair of her to expect that from you." Harry glared at Jenny, daring her to deny that last part.

"I had my reasons, Harry Landon." Jenny glared back at him, giving as good as she got. "Curtis was a mean, evil man, who had mean, influential friends. He swore he would kill me before he ever let me go. We had to keep the shelter a secret, or he would have found us and dragged us back home again. Max had to know that he couldn't tell anyone, or bad things would happen."

"That was a lot to expect from a nine-year-old."

"I know it was. But what choice did I have? Please tell him that I love him, and I only wanted to keep him safe." Jenny's image glowed brighter, and Harry took that as a sign she was so upset she was going to blow. He didn't know what happened to ghosts if they exploded, but he didn't think he wanted to find out. At least not with Max sitting so close to her.

"Okay, Jenny, calm down. I know you had no other options. Max knows you loved him—"

"*Love* him," Jenny said, interrupting him. "Present tense, not past. I still love him. Tell him that." Again, she reached out, trying to connect with her son, but recognized that it was hopeless, and let her hand drop.

"She loves you, Max. She wanted me to make sure you know that she will always love you, no matter what." Harry wished there was something more that he could do to help Jenny connect with Max, but he didn't know the first thing about ghosts. "She also knows that you are safe with me, and you can tell me anything. I'm here for you, Max. You know that, right?"

Max had been staring at him intensely during his exchange with Jenny, and all he seemed to be able to manage in response was a nod.

"Do you have anything you want to say to your mom? She's still listening." Harry was starting to feel like a psychotherapist mediating a talk between clients, but he wanted Max to have this opportunity before it was gone. For all he knew, Jenny would disappear now that Harry knew the truth about why Max was having nightmares.

"Can you tell her that I love her, too?"

"You can tell her, yourself. She can hear you. She's sitting right next to you." She was crying her eyes out, too, still without any actual tears. But Harry didn't think Max needed to know any of that.

But maybe Max didn't quite believe Jenny was there, because he continued to speak directly to Harry. "Will you ask her why she left me?"

Jenny gasped then cried out, "I didn't leave you." She looked at Harry and pleaded with him. "Tell him I didn't leave him. Please tell him, I didn't leave him." Her words broke down into nonsensical sobs that seemed to drain all the energy from her, because she slowly faded away, disappearing completely.

"She didn't leave you, not on purpose." Harry wasn't sure he could explain this himself, and wished that he had the ability to fade away, too. Max looked at him, expecting the impossible from him, and Harry was afraid he would say the wrong thing.

"She got hurt, and she died." He knew that was inadequate, and tried again. "She didn't want to leave you, it was out of her control. But she made sure that, if the time came that she ever did have to leave, you would be taken care of. She made sure you would be safe.

With me. I know it feels like she left you all alone, but she didn't. She didn't leave you because she wanted to. She left because she was forced to. You understand that, right?"

Max nodded, and Harry could tell that he was struggling to hold back the tears, because his lower lip began to quiver with the strain.

"Do you also know that Curtis won't hurt you or your mom ever again? I won't let him."

Then the dam burst, and Max was crying full on. Harry wrapped him in his arms, and held onto him. "I'm here, Max. I'm here."

CHAPTER FOURTEEN

M ax eventually cried himself to sleep in Harry's arms, but Harry couldn't seem to let go of him long enough to put him to bed. He stayed on the couch holding Max, matching the rhythm of his breathing, because he'd heard some- where that it had a calming effect on children.

It must be true. He'd almost drifted off to sleep himself when he felt Jenny materialize in the room with them.

"Are you ready to tell me the whole story now?" He hadn't seen her yet, but he knew she was there.

She came around from the back side of the couch and sat beside them, lowering herself carefully, as if she wasn't sure he would let her stay.

Harry waited, not wanting to agitate her if she was finally ready to talk. He also didn't want to startle Max. He should put Max to bed, but he knew from their morning wake-up routine on school days that the kid slept like the dead – when he wasn't screaming.

"I'm sorry, Harry." Jenny must have also been trying to keep from waking Max, because her voice was barely above a whisper. "I haven't been trying to make things difficult for you. But I'm scared. Not for me anymore, obviously, but for my son. I was all he had, and I don't know how to protect him now when I can't even touch him."

"Keeping secrets is only making it harder for me, you know." Harry understood what she said, but she had still made things more difficult for him by not telling him in the first place. "How am I supposed to help him if I don't know what I'm up against?"

She nodded, and he hoped that meant that she'd heard his words, but she didn't speak for several minutes. "He has friends, big friends, mean friends. They all work in the Bear Forest Sheriff's Department, but they used their power to intimidate. Indiscriminately. Mostly because they could."

"Jenny, honey," Harry reached but remembered he couldn't soothe her by touch, so he spoke softly to her. "Start at the beginning."

"I met Curtis the night after you left me." She glanced sideways at him, and gave him a glare. "You know, on our wedding day? That day that was supposed to be the happiest day of my life. Standing at the altar. You remember that day, right?"

"Yeeess... I remember. Go on." He couldn't help it, he wanted to laugh. She could still dish out the sarcasm, even in a crisis.

"Well, I was pretty pissed off. Did I mention the two-hundred and fifty guests I had to make excuses to because my groom dissed me?"

"Jenny..." Harry warned, but he knew there hadn't been any real anger behind her words. She was poking him, and that made him chuckle. Just like old times.

"Okay, fine." She sat back in the couch getting comfortable, although why a ghost would need to get comfortable was beyond him. For that matter, how did she keep from misting through the furniture?

This wasn't the first time he'd noticed that she still had very human mannerisms. Was it possible ghosts needed time to acclimate to being non-corporeal? Or was it normal for ghosts to continue acting like they had when they'd had bodies?

"I met Curtis at a bar. I was steadily working my way toward oblivion with my friend Mr. Jack Daniels. Great guy, Jack, he'd never leave a person hangin'. Oh, wait, I guess he would." Jenny started to laugh, and Harry grunted a chuckle, but he knew this was her coping mechanism when she was nervous. She'd always been big on sarcasm, and lame jokes.

"Yeah, right, going serious now." She reached over to pick up a throw pillow, but her hand passed through it, and she gave up. "He was a really nice guy. In the beginning. And I had pretty much reached oblivi-nirvana by the time he showed up, so I was fairly impressionable. He was a good-looking guy, buying me rounds of drinks, and he was very, very attentive. At least, that's how I remember it. I was half in love with him by the time the bar closed at three in the morning. Plus, you had crushed me, and I was more than a little bit susceptible to his charms. All of his charms." She looked sheepishly up at Harry.

"Jesus, you didn't." Harry was torn between the guilt he felt for having left her like that, and angry with her for letting herself be so taken in by such an asshole.

"Yeah, I did. I slept with him. Not my proudest moment. I know that. Turned out, he was a good Catholic boy, so he decided we would get married. And we did. A month later. One month after that, I discovered I was pregnant with Max."

"Wait a second. You slept with Curtis the night after our wedding?" Something she'd said didn't make sense to him.

"There was no wedding, remember?"

"You know what I mean." Harry was beginning to do the math. "You and I slept together the night *before* our wedding. I was careful. We used a condom. If you and Curtis had sex two nights later, then Max isn't mine."

"Of course he's yours. Curtis used a condom, too." She crossed her arms and glowered at Harry, as if that said it all. "Remember how you and I always talked about waiting on kids so that I could finish my degree? Well, my mind didn't change when I met Curtis."

Harry felt the stir of doubt in the pit of his stomach, and it burned like acid. He didn't miss the irony, either; a few short weeks ago, he was telling everyone who would listen that Max couldn't be his son, and now that it was a possibility, he wanted to take Max and run away with him.

"Harry, he has your eyes, and he has your mannerisms. He *is* your son." She sounded as desperate as he felt.

"It doesn't matter. He's mine now, and that's all that counts." He needed to get those adoption papers signed with Jason as soon as they got back. "Did you finish your degree?"

She had always wanted to be a teacher. She was going to educate the world, one student at a time, and Harry had been so proud of her.

"No."

He waited for her to elaborate, but he knew better than to push her. He also figured that Curtis was most likely the reason behind her unfinished degree, and Harry wanted to scream at her. *How could you let that bastard steal your dream?*

But Harry knew the he had also played a big part in the demise of her dream, so he couldn't say a word.

Jenny stared at him for a moment, like she was trying to read his soul, and then continued with her story. "When I told Curtis I was having a baby, he was not exactly over-the-moon about it. To say the least. He wasn't ready to 'settle down with kids yet.' But he didn't have a problem with getting married."

She paused, and picked at the edge of her sweater. Apparently, anything she'd taken with her to the other side was fair game for her to manipulate.

"Was that the first time he hit you?" Harry kept his voice low and calm so that she didn't misunderstand, and think he was judging her.

"Yes. It started with a back-handed slap across the face. But he was *so sorry*, and he begged me not to leave him. He added that it was my fault I'd gotten pregnant, and that I wouldn't be able to survive without him. So, I let him talk me into staying. The first time." She sighed heavily, as if reliving it was exhausting, and Harry almost told her to stop.

But she continued. "The second time, I went to the police. Which turned out to be a big mistake. His friends at the Bear Forest Sheriff's Department were his good ol' boys, and they dragged me home to 'face the music." They left me there in handcuffs while he taught me how to be a dutiful wife."

Jenny stood up and began pacing the room. Even being a ghost, with nothing more to fear for herself, it was still a difficult story for her to get out. "But you know how I am. I don't particularly like being told what to do, or how to act." She grinned a self-deprecating smile. "And each time, he added something new to his repertoire, a kick to the kidneys, a belt across my back… I never knew what was coming or when. And he always managed to convince me that I'd asked for it, that everything was my fault. I must have tried to run away about a million different times, and each time his buddies in the sheriff's department found me, like they had eyes in the backs of their heads."

"Jesus." Harry wanted to strangle the bastard.

"There's something going on there, Harry, I know there is. A few men, even amoral ones like those guys, can't be omniscient like that without having some really extensive spy network."

"What do you think was going on?"

"I don't know, but it was something big and intricate, because it seemed they had everyone in their pocket. And Curtis was smack in the middle of it."

"It wasn't until Max was six that I finally had enough money stashed away. Curtis never let me have any money, so I became very frugal with the grocery fund, and saved as much as I could. I hid it in my tampon box." She gave Harry an impish look. "You guys never go near a tampon box."

"That's not true," Harry protested. "I bought tampons for you when you asked me to."

"Sure, but you're one of the few exceptions to the rule. Curtis never bought them for me, so it was a perfect hiding place." She looked proud of her cunning, and Harry had to admit that it was a brilliant idea. "When I finally had a decent stash of cash, I made a contact, a safe contact, with a women's shelter in Denver. They were good to us. They helped me plan, and finally escape with Max. And we were safe for two and a half years. We started a new life, as new people, and Max was starting to come out of his shell. But Curtis found me."

"Shit."

"I let my guard down. We were moving out of the shelter to be on our own. I went to the store to stock up on groceries, and he found me. He was drunk. I mean out-of-his-mind-crazy drunk. I'd never seen him so far gone. He was screaming at me that it was all my fault, that I'd screwed up everything for him. He blamed me for getting him in trouble with his buddies at the sheriff's department, and that he was behind on shipments because he'd been using all their resources to track me down."

"Did he tell you what kind of shipments?"

"No. I don't know." She looked confused for a moment, as if trying to remember what he'd said, and then continued. "He dragged me into my car and beat the crap out of me. He bashed my head against the dash as he threatened me, and I'm pretty sure he broke a couple of ribs because it hurt to breathe. I managed to convince him that I would come home with him but that I needed to pick up Max first. He'd told me he didn't give a shit about Max, and that he was taking me home without him, and I started to panic. I tried fighting him off, and I ended up elbowing him in the nose. Luckily, he was so drunk, that was all it took, and he finally passed out. That's when I ran. I shoved him out of the car, and drove off. Part of me hoped he'd choke on his own vomit."

She sat there, staring into space like she was remembering being back in the car with Curtis.

"I was driving to get Max to run and move to another shelter, when I blacked out at the wheel, and crashed the car. When I came to, I was standing by the side of the road, watching the paramedics load my body into an ambulance. And that when I knew I had died."

"Oh, Christ..." He had left her to a madman. How could he have been so selfish? He had cared about her, had loved her deeply. But he'd known then, as he did now, that he didn't love her in the same way that she loved him, and he'd left her to fend for herself. "Why didn't you go to your mom?"

"She died a year after I married Curtis. Cancer." Her voice cracked on the "C" word, and she dropped her head.

"I'm so sorry." It was such an inadequate thing to say, but he couldn't begin to put into words how much he wished he'd been there for her. "I should have checked in with you. I could have helped. I—"

"Don't." She put up a hand to stop his words. "Curtis was my choice, and all the choices after that. You can't blame yourself for doing what you thought you needed to do. I could have reached out to you, too. But I didn't."

"I should have been there for you."

"Please don't do that to yourself. You are here for me now. You will keep Max safe." She reached out to touch Max, then stopped, inches from his face, as if remembering it wasn't something she could do without causing sparks.

"Safe from what, Jenny? Is Curtis a threat to Max? Do I need to worry about him?" Harry felt like he wanted to throw a shield around Max, and protect him from anything and everything that might want to hurt him.

"No. Curtis told me that last time that he didn't care about Max. Max holds no value for him." Jenny looked as though she couldn't understand that, and Harry agreed with her. "Max is in a good place now, and that's what matters." Her voice broke, but she took a deep breath and seemed to pull herself together.

"What's this guy Curtis's last name?"

"Matthews. His name is Curtis Matthews. But don't worry, he won't come looking for you or for Max. Just to be safe I filed everything with an attorney he never knew about, so he doesn't know you even exist."

Harry didn't feel nearly as confident, but he let it go for now. He hugged Max tighter to feel the solidness of him, and was sorry that Jenny couldn't feel the same.

"I'm glad you told me. I'm so sorry for what you went through, but you should have been straight with me from the beginning."

"You were already against taking him. If I had told you all the trouble connected with him, you never would have agreed to it."

"Fair enough." He felt like she'd stabbed him in the heart with a butcher knife, but he couldn't say she was wrong. "I get it. You were probably right."

"You're a good man, Harry Landon."

Was he?

Hell, he hadn't agreed, not in the beginning. And that was before hearing everything else that was involved.

But it was also possible that he would have felt an obligation to help, to make restitution for his part in what had happened to Jenny, and he might have taken Max without an argument.

None of it mattered anyway. As soon as he got back to Denver, he would file the adoption papers with Jason first thing.

CHAPTER FIFTEEN

They had gotten back so late last night from Aspen that Harry overslept, and had to hustle to get Max to school on time. He was a few minutes late getting to the office, but it didn't really matter, since he owned the company, and no one was going to fire him over it. George might bitch at him, but George always grumbled at Harry about being late. It was kind of their thing.

He and Max hadn't yet gotten into their groove as far as the whole school concept. They were still working on their morning routine and getting their schedule down, so there were bound to be glitches. They'd get the hang of it eventually.

After his talk with Jenny in Aspen Saturday night, she had drifted away, with the promise to leave her menfolk alone for the rest of the weekend, and not even eavesdrop. Harry had fallen asleep on the couch still holding Max, who had miraculously slept through the night. That made two in a row. Harry chose to believe that was progress.

"Hi, Harry. Got a minute?" Anna knocked on the open door of his office, and took a cautious step inside. "Am I interrupting anything?"

"No, come on in. I'm glad you're here." Harry stood up from behind his desk, but didn't know what else to do. Normally, he would give her a hug, which is what friends do, but he was trying to figure out how he was still dating her when he kept trying to break it off.

She closed the door – okay, so this was a serious visit – then took a seat in one of the chairs in front of his desk.

"I'm really sorry for how things went the other night—" he started to say, but was interrupted by Anna.

"Don't be, it's perfectly understandable that you were confused, and that's why you were holding back with us."

"Uh, right. Thanks?" He was still confused. How did she continue to believe there was an "us" in the equation? "So, about us—"

"It sounds so much like a soap opera, doesn't it?" She shook her head as if she couldn't quite believe it, and laughed a warm and easy chuckle.

"It does." He grinned, and was relieved to hear her laugh about it. He hoped it meant that she was finally realizing that they were going to get to the "let's be friends" conversation. "It's even more of a soap opera when you think about the fact that George and I both avoid Martin like the plague. I don't know what your relationship is like with Martin, but I never have contact with him. So, don't feel obligated to invite me over for any family dinners."

He grinned at her to lessen the severity of his message, but he sincerely hoped she understood that Martin was a non-entity in his life.

"I'm not sure what happened to cause that rift between the two of you, but I can respect that. Maybe someday you will be able to resolve your issues, and reconcile." She sounded hopeful, and Harry couldn't understand why it seemed to matter to her so much. He didn't particularly care if she had a relationship with Martin or not, he just didn't want to be involved in it.

"Never going to happen. But I appreciate the sentiment."

"We have a good thing going here," Anna continued, and he sighed, because that didn't sound like the start of the *I like you, but I just want to be friends* speech. "I don't usually feel very... uh... comfortable around men. But I did with you." She shifted in her chair, her body unconsciously contradicting her statement. "I mean, I *do* with you."

"You don't have to explain yourself, I understand." He didn't really understand, but he didn't know what else to say to her, because he was feeling awkward and out of his depth.

"Yeah, no... you probably don't," she said, but she grinned, and he knew he hadn't been as covert with his response as he'd thought. "Trust is not an easy thing for me, especially when it comes to men." Anna looked up in surprise, as if realizing she'd said the wrong thing. "Don't get me wrong, I like men. I like them a lot. They just scare the proverbial crap out of me." She smiled, letting him know that she was only half serious. "You were just so easy to be with, and I love that about you."

"I'm flattered." He got up from behind his desk and sat in the chair next to Anna to take her hand. He genuinely cared about this woman, and he wanted them to continue to be in each other's lives. "I hope you hang onto those feelings. You can trust me. I know that's an easy thing for someone to say, but I will do my best never to give you a reason to feel otherwise."

He was so relieved that she was coming around to the same conclusion that he'd reached. They would be friends, and everything would be fine.

"I'd like that. Really good relationships can be hard to find. I'm so glad you feel the same way."

"Absolutely." He was relieved that they had worked things out, and could remain friends. "Jason's coming over tonight with the adoption papers for me to sign to make it all official. I was thinking of having a party this weekend to celebrate Max being a new member of the Landon family. Can you come? You could meet the rest of the extended Landon clan."

"I'd love that. Can I bring Dean?"

"Of course. Bring anyone you like." Maybe she would bring a date, and they could get over this still awkward bump in the road. "But especially bring Dean. We're family now."

Harry rolled that thought around in his head, and decided he liked the idea. He didn't know Dean as well as he knew Anna, and he was certain that he could never feel as close to him as he did his full-brother, George, but he was okay with that.

"Kind of a strange way to go about getting more family, but whatever." Anna laughed, and Harry knew they were going to be fine.

Then she kissed him.

Full on the lips.

Open-mouthed.

And he wasn't so sure they were on the same page anymore.

***

HARRY TRIED NOT to think about how strange it was that the first person he'd thought of to help him plan Max's adoption party was his neighbor. Emma would have been a much better choice. Even George would have been the logical first person to think of. But instead, he found himself knocking on Luke's door.

The more he thought about it though, the more it made sense. Luke had been with him almost every step of the way since Max had shown up on his doorstep. He'd been there for every screaming night-mare, had gone with them to the school barbecue – also a screaming nightmare, in Harry's opinion.

Luke had been there to hang out with Max on the afternoons when Harry couldn't. And most of all, he'd been there for Harry while he grappled with his inadequacies and fears over becoming a father.

Harry's heart jumped in excitement when the door swung open. But it wasn't Luke standing in front of him. Instead, Harry found himself looking at a half-naked man he'd never met before. A very beautiful, half-naked man, and Harry's heart plummeted into his leather Louboutin loafers.

"Who the hell are you?" Harry asked before he could stop himself.

"I'm sure I could ask the same of you," replied the Greek god, who had a hint of an accent. Shit, maybe the guy really was a Greek god. Hell, ghosts turned out to be real, why not—-

Luke came to the door, and shoved the god aside like he was nothing more than a mere mortal, and Harry mentally shook himself for being ridiculous. "Sam, I've asked you to stop answering the door like you live here."

"But it always turns out to be so much fun when I do." Sam slowly looked Harry up and down, then once again for good measure, and apparently liked what he saw because he said, "Nice. Can I have him?"

"Jesus," Luke responded then gestured Harry inside. "Come on in Harry. Ignore Sam, he was just leaving."

Luke stood to the side, holding the door open, obviously waiting for the guy to leave. Sam picked up a shirt from the nearby chair, draped it over his shoulder instead of putting it on, and stepped so close to Harry their chests brushed.

What the hell?

"Sam." Luke barely raised his voice, but his intention was menacing, and Sam left without saying another word. Luke closed the door and turned to Harry. He narrowed his eyes, as if trying to judge how Harry was going to react.

Harry wished him luck with that, because even he wasn't sure what his reaction would be.

"Who was that guy?" Pissed. Apparently, his reaction was pissed. It wasn't his first choice. He'd been hoping more for: *This kind of thing happens to me all the time, no big.* But instead it came out as more of an accusation.

Holy shit, he was jealous. Full-blown, green-eyed monster, jealous. He didn't like a gorgeous god being in Luke's condo with him.

What did that even mean? Why did he feel like he wanted to call that Sam-guy back, and rip out his lungs?

Jesus Christ, what the hell was wrong with him?

"That guy was Sam." Luke said, as he headed to the kitchen and opened the fridge. "Want one?" he asked Harry.

Harry didn't know how to answer that question. *Was he serious?*

Then his haze of jealousy cleared enough that he finally saw the water bottle Luke was waving at him, and realized they weren't still talking about Sam. He could feel his face growing warm. He took the bottle from Luke, and resisted the urge to roll it across his forehead.

"Are you seeing this Sam guy?" He had meant the question to sound casual, like two guys checking in with each other on their dating life. But it had come out sounding more hostile, like he was giving Luke the third degree. He noticed that his throat had gone dry, and took a swig of his water.

It felt like an eternity ticked by while he waited for an answer, but Luke didn't seem to be in any hurry to respond. He hated the idea of Luke seeing that guy. Sam looked like someone who messed with people just because he could. And Luke deserved better than that.

Plus, he was jealous. There was that, too. He felt like a kid who was being forced to share his favorite toy without his permission.

"He's one of my models," Luke finally said, after Harry had almost forgotten he'd asked the question. "I don't date my models."

He stared at Harry, and a slow smile spread across his face making him look like the cat that had swallowed the canary.

Luke just stood there, leaning against the counter with his arms crossed over his chest, wearing that smug look on his face. He continued to stare, like he was waiting for something, and it was making Harry antsy.

"That's it?" Harry asked. "You're just going to stand there without elaborating?" He waited, but Luke didn't say anything else. He had always been a man of few words, but this was starting to get to Harry in a big way.

"What are you doing here?" Luke asked, abruptly changing the subject. "You don't usually stop by in the middle of the day."

"I came by to see if you're busy this weekend."

"Nope. What did you have in mind?" Luke's smile was back, and Harry felt like the only kid on the playground who didn't get the dirty joke the older kids were telling. He was also getting that fluttery feeling in his chest again, and was beginning to realize he had a slight crush on his neighbor.

"I want to throw an adoption party for Max." He stopped and took a sip of his water, because his throat had gone dry again. "Just a barbecue in the back yard, with family and friends, nothing too elaborate. But I was hoping you would help me host it." Harry knew it was ridiculous, but he felt like he'd just asked the Prom King to the school dance.

"Yeah. I'd be honored."

Harry let out the breath he didn't know he'd been holding, and took another swig of his water before launching into his acceptance speech.

"You've really been there for me, Luke. And for Max. You helped me sort through my mixed-up head, and figure out that it wasn't as complicated as I kept trying to make it. In a way, I owe you for finally realizing I wanted Max in my life. So, I was hoping you would help me – us – celebrate." Harry felt like he was rambling incoherently, but Luke was making him nervous. "I really want to thank you for everything. I don't think I could have gotten through any of it without you."

"I'm glad for you, Harry. I'm happy I was able to help you, but I knew you would work it out on your own eventually."

Luke smiled warmly at him, and before he could second-guess himself, Harry set down his water, leaned in and gave him a hug. He was sure he held on too long for the appropriate male hug time limit, but when Luke wrapped his arms around him, he felt like he'd come home, and he couldn't seem to let go. He closed his eyes and let the feeling of safety and comfort wash over him.

Luke smelled like paint with a hint of turpentine, but underneath it he smelled like cinnamon and oranges. Luke's hand moved up Harry's back, as he stepped in closer and tightened his hold. He felt Luke's erection against his own, and a buzz of excitement fluttered through his belly. It felt like that first second when the roller coaster reaches the summit, and hangs there for a moment. You know you're going to plunge, and it's going to be a thrilling ride.

Then the nausea set in.

Harry jumped away as if he'd been burned.

The horrible voice inside his head shouted, *This is wrong. Boys do not love other boys.*

His mind kept repeating the words *wrong, wrong, wrong.*

It had been years since he'd heard that awful voice. But he still recognized it. He would always recognize it.

His heart and his body were in a completely opposite world from his brain, and he was going to be sick from the conflict.

"Harry?" Luke asked, and moved as if to take Harry back into his arms. "Are you okay?" He looked more concerned than horny, and Harry wanted to cry.

"I'm... I..." He wouldn't. He couldn't.

We don't talk about it. We never talk about it.

The nausea rolled through him again, at the mere thought of touching Luke. He reached for his water and took several gulps to force back the bile, and try to calm his stomach. "I'm sorry. I shouldn't have done that. I'm sorry. Please, don't be angry with me. I don't know what happened just then, but it shouldn't have."

"I'm not mad at you. I get it." Luke stuffed his hands into the pockets of his jeans, as if he didn't trust himself not to touch Harry. "We can take it slow."

Harry tried to imagine what "slow" would look like with Luke, but the nausea reared its ugly head again, and he shut the image down fast.

"I need to go pick up Max." Harry looked around the kitchen feeling like he'd forgotten something, or left something behind. "Can we talk about this later?"

"Big points for at least not running out this time." Luke smiled, and Harry knew that by some miracle he hadn't screwed everything up entirely.

The problem was that a part of him liked the possibility of trying to take it slow. With Luke.

"Jason is coming over tonight with the adoption papers." Harry hesitated, then looked Luke in the eye and asked, "will you come over for dinner? Help us celebrate?"

Luke smiled and said, "I would like that."

CHAPTER SIXTEEN

H arry was nervous. He checked his watch for what had to be the nine-hundredth time in the last five minutes, and it still wasn't six o'clock yet. He had fifteen minutes to fill.

He had never been anxious about Luke coming over before, but this time, things were different. He couldn't deny that he had feelings for Luke, because he had liked how he felt holding him earlier. At least until the moment when he thought he'd throw up all over the man.

He knew part of his nerves were also because he was officially adopting Max tonight with the papers Jason was bringing. He hadn't even considered the possibility that Max might not like the idea, but he hadn't asked him directly yet.

How could he have been so self-centered to assume that Max would be on the same page? He'd been so wrapped up in trying to sort out his feelings for Luke, that he'd completely neglected Max. What if Max didn't want to be adopted?

Jesus, he was already acting like his father. He was planning to sign the papers without even asking Max, as if Max's feelings didn't matter. He was already doing everything wrong.

Except...

He hadn't signed the papers yet. And he was considering Max. He was not like his father. He would do this the right way, and talk to Max about it first. It didn't matter that Jason was bringing the papers. Harry didn't have to sign them if Max didn't agree.

He would never force *his* son to do something against his will.

He would always talk to Max.

He didn't know if Max would want him, officially, considering the rocky first impression Harry had presented. Harry felt like he was a bad-bet in the nurturing father department, given his own lack of healthy role models. He was nervous about Max's reaction to the idea. But no matter what Max said, Harry wouldn't bulldoze him, like Martin had always done when he didn't get the response he wanted.

Max was in his room sitting at the small desk doing his homework. What kind of homework did a fourth grader have?

"Hey, buddy, what are you working on?"

Max looked up from his book, and had the blurry-eyed look of a kid who was deep into his subject. "We're studying Colorado in Mr. Peter's class. We get to go on an expedition later to study the rocks, and soil and stuff, in a bunch of different places." He was more excited than Harry had ever seen him, and that gave him hope that Max would be happy here with him.

"Do you remember Jason, the lawyer who helped us get everything figured out when you first got here?" Harry wasn't sure how to approach this. It wasn't as if he could just blurt out, *So, I want to adopt you, what do you think?* That would probably scare the kid senseless.

"Yeah." Max slanted a suspicious look in his direction, as if he still didn't trust their arrangement to have a happy ending.

"Well, he's coming over tonight to help me with some paperwork that concerns you. I was thinking we should probably talk about this together. What do you think?"

"Okay," Max replied, but Harry thought he looked more like he was already shutting the blinds on his emotional house. "Talk about what?"

"Do you like living here?" Harry asked, trying to lead into the topic, but he was stopped at that point by a knock on the door.

"Luke and Sheldon are here!" Max jumped out of his chair and ran to let them in.

Harry joined them just as Sheldon came barreling inside, and jumped up to lick Harry's face.

"Well, that's new." Harry laughed as he wiped dog spit from his face with an extra show of drama to make Max laugh. "Thanks for that, Sheldon, but I'm not sure I want to make a habit out of it. Max, why don't you take Sheldon to your room to finish your homework while Luke and I get dinner ready."

"Cool. Come on, Sheldon." Max clapped his hands to get Sheldon's attention, and the two of them bounded back into his room.

"That was subtle." Luke grinned at Harry. "Just so I'm on the same page. You only want to talk. Right?"

Harry tripped over the shoes Max had left when he'd taken them off after school. The kid was always dropping things everywhere. His shoes always looked like they had simply come off his feet while he was walking. But Harry knew he couldn't blame his clumsiness on Max. Not this time.

Luke threw him off his game. Part of him was enjoying the euphoric feeling he was experiencing. But the bigger part of him was waiting for the nausea to return, and that was not nearly as fun.

He wasn't lying to himself. He did have feelings for Luke, but they weren't feelings he was supposed to be having. He didn't want to lose Luke, but it wouldn't be fair to let him think they could be anything more. He couldn't control the nausea, it was conditioned. And that meant he would never be able to have any type of an intimate relationship with Luke.

"Where'd you go on me?" Luke waved his hand in front of Harry's face.

"Sorry. Yes, I was thinking we should talk." The reaction on Luke's face looked like Harry'd just told him he and Max were moving to Alaska. "I value your friendship, and I don't want to jeopardize that relationship. I don't know what happened earlier with us, but I just don't see us going there."

"Right. Friends. Got it." He could see that Luke wasn't happy but he didn't know how to fix it. What else could he say?

Little boys who kiss other little boys are freaks against nature. Do you want to be an abomination? Do you want your father to hate you?

No, sir. I'll be good.

There was a tension between them now that he wasn't sure they could ever resolve, so he tried again to put it into words. "Luke, I wish—"

"Don't beat yourself up," Luke interrupted, and he sounded resigned. "You aren't there, and I get it. Don't let this cause a strain between us."

"I was thinking the same thing." Harry wasn't sure if he felt profound relief, or bitter disappointment. "Can we go back to the way things were before?"

"Sure. No problem." Luke waved a bag at Harry, then said, "Let's throw some steaks on the barbie now, huh?" He grinned, but Harry could tell that it wasn't his usual easy-going, self-assured expression. There was something missing.

"Tonight's the big night, huh?" Jason smiled as Harry led him into the living room where he, Luke and Max had paused their hot game of Uno. Sheldon let out a "Woof" when he saw Jason, but it was a friendly greeting, and he went back to lounging between Max and Luke.

"Luke, this is Jason," Harry said, by way of introduction. "He's a good friend, and the head of our legal department at Landon Literary. Jason, this is my neighbor Luke. He's been a huge help for me while Max has been here." Luke flinched slightly, and Harry wondered if he'd said something wrong. In spite of their casual evening, and their reassurances to each other that nothing had changed, there was still a tinge of awkwardness in the air. "Max, you remember Jason, don't you?"

Max was white as a sheet, like he had eaten something bad and was about to throw it up. Not five minutes ago, they were playing cards and Max was laughing, but as soon as he saw Jason, he retreated back to the shy kid he'd been when he first arrived.

Maybe Harry was jumping the gun. What if he'd misread Max's excitement in his room earlier?

"Hi, Max. Nice to see you again." Jason smiled at Max, but Harry could see that it had only made matters worse, because Max tucked his head into his chest and didn't respond.

"Max? Buddy, what's wrong?" What was that all about? Max knew Jason from before. He even liked Jason.

Was Max afraid of people in authority, like attorneys? Maybe something had happened with one of the dickhead friends of Curtis, and now Max was afraid of people in the law? He was going to have to talk to him about it after Jason and Luke left. He knew Max still considered his past to be a secret, so he'd have to get his permission before talking even to Luke about it.

Jason must have noticed Max's reaction as well, because he said, "Harry, maybe you and I should go into another room to review these documents?"

Or maybe Max didn't want to be adopted by Harry. He obviously couldn't make any long-lasting decision like that for Max without making sure he understood everything first.

"Yeah, sure. You guys keep playing. Max, don't let Luke cheat. He'll try to mess you up with those reverse cards." He winked to let Max know he wasn't serious, and to hopefully snap him out of his fear.

He led Jason into his office, and closed the door so they could talk privately.

"First, let me say how glad I am that everything has worked out for you, Harry. I know this wasn't what you had planned, but I also know that you are making the right decision." Jason opened his leather satchel and pulled out files as he spoke.

"Is it crazy that I'm more excited than I am nervous? I mean, this is a huge change for me. I know you know that, considering what a dick I was about it in the beginning, and it's a huge change for Max, too. But it feels so right."

"What did Max say when you told him?"

"I didn't get a chance to talk to him. We were interrupted before he could give me an answer." He had a moment of panic, like the floor shifted and he lost his balance. "I really appreciate you bringing these over, but I don't think I can sign anything until I've talked to Max about it first. He needs to know that he has choices. What if he doesn't want to be adopted by me? Hell, maybe he would rather have Luke adopt him. He'd get Sheldon as a bonus in the process. Let's face it, I wasn't exactly hiding the fact that I hated the idea of taking him on in the beginning."

"I think you're selling yourself short. I'm sure he's going to be thrilled when he finds out you want to adopt him." Jason smiled reassuringly at him, but Harry still had his doubts.

It was hard not to fall into the habit of doubting the outcome when he'd faced nothing but rejection his entire life from his own father.

"You don't have to sign these tonight." Jason's words brought Harry back to the present. "Keep them, look them over, and take the time to talk to Max before you sign them. They can wait a couple of days."

MAX DECLARED he was ready for bed the minute Harry shut the door after saying good-bye to Jason. That was new. He usually had to put significant effort into getting Max to bed on time. But tonight, he wanted to go to bed early?

He'd hoped he would be able to talk to Max before he went to bed, but Max practically sprinted to his room and closed the door before Harry got a sound out. Was Max trying to avoid discussing it with him? Unfortunately, it looked like it would have to wait until the morning. He was disappointed, but he was determined not to force Max.

He was determined not to be anything like Martin when it came to raising Max.

He joined Luke on the couch after checking in on Max, who had fallen asleep the minute his head hit the pillow.

He handed Luke a glass of bourbon, and was glad that they seemed to have settled back into their usual routine together. He liked his evenings with Luke.

"Do you think Max will need Sheldon tonight?" Luke asked, as he sipped his bourbon.

"He hasn't had a nightmare in four nights. I'm hoping that's over, or at least calmed to a more manageable level, whatever that might be." He was starting to get used to everyone sleeping through the night again, and hoped that they had seen the last of the midnight screaming. "Did Max seem off to you after Jason got here?"

"Off? Like how?"

"Did he seem subdued? Like he was when he first came to stay with me?"

"Not that I noticed. We played more Uno – he creamed me, by the way – and then you and Jason were finished. He did keep glancing at the door, like he was waiting for you to come back out."

"Huh, okay. I wonder what's going on with him."

Luke swallowed the remainder of his bourbon, and stood up. "Come on, Sheldon. Time to go home." Sheldon perked up at his name, and followed Luke to the door.

"Luke?" He wanted to ask if they were still friends, but didn't know how to phrase it that didn't make him sound like he was being a dick.

"We're good." Luke clapped him on the back, whistled for his dog, and left.

Harry knew she was there before she spoke. He could feel the small hairs on the back of his neck rise like a static shock.

"He's a good guy." Jenny stood by the front door, as if she had been waiting for Luke to leave before making an appearance.

"I thought you were gone." He hadn't seen her since their talk on Saturday in the Aspen condo, and was starting to believe she'd moved on, or whatever it is that ghosts are supposed to do when their job here is complete.

"Honestly? I thought I would be, too, now that I know my son is safe. But I don't feel any different. Maybe the papers have to be official before I can feel *complete*."

"I'm going to talk to Max in the morning and make sure this is what he wants, too. If he agrees, then we sign the papers." He leaned his head back and closed his eyes, relishing the quiet of the evening, and trying to make sense of his feelings around Luke.

"Maybe it's like Jessica said, and I'm not here for Max." She sounded confused, which wasn't very encouraging. If she didn't have the answers they were both screwed.

He lifted his head and opened one eye. "What are you getting at with that cryptic remark?"

"She said I was here for you, not for Max. Maybe that's really why I'm still here." Jenny sat down on the couch next to him, and leaned in to study his face.

"What are you doing?" He was starting to feel uncomfortable with her scrutiny. Could she hear what he was thinking?

"You really like him, don't you?"

"Max? Of course I do. I probably wouldn't be adopting him if I didn't." She would probably snap at him about the sarcasm, but he couldn't seem to help himself.

"No, Luke. You really like him."

"It's complicated." No way was he going there with her. How does one explain to their ex-fiancée that they have confused feelings toward another man; one minute he wants to kiss him, and the next minute he wants to puke?

"You use that word a lot. How is it complicated? It actually makes a ton of sense to me." She counted off on her fingers. "Your commitment issues with women. Your inability to stay in a relationship with a woman for more than ten minutes. Oh, wait, that's the same thing."

"Leave it alone, Jenny, it's none of your business."

"I think this is why I'm still here. I think I'm supposed to help you find true love, and I'm pretty sure that means Luke."

"I mean it. Drop it." She was way out of line, and he wasn't going to sit there and be psycho-analyzed by a ghost. He finished his bourbon, picked up Luke's glass, and carried them both into the kitchen, hoping that would give her the hint to stop talking.

But she followed him. "I'm thinking the shoe is on the other foot now, and you have a secret you don't want to share with me. I bet you're wishing you had the ability to vanish right now. Am I right?" Jenny crossed her arms and stood blocking his exit from the kitchen. Did she forget that he could walk right through her?

Then again, he wasn't sure how great an idea that was, given the unpleasantness of the feeling he got each time she'd poked him. He wasn't willing to risk it. Yet.

"No, I don't want to vanish, I just want to go to bed." He tried to walk around her, but she moved, and he ended up brushing against her. Yep, he'd been right, more unpleasantness. His arm felt like he'd stuck his finger into a light socket.

"Let me ask you this." She held up a finger in a threatening gesture that told him she would poke him. He stepped back.

"Oh, please, dear God, can we not do this?"

"How do you feel about Luke?"

"Seriously, if I knew that, don't you think I would have told him?"

"Except that I think you *do* know, but are *afraid* to tell him. Even more than that, I think you're afraid to tell yourself."

"Just kill me now." He was too tired to argue, so he leaned against the counter to wait her out.

"Okay, let's approach this logically." He didn't like the sound of that. When a woman decided to approach something 'logically' that was usually when things got confusing. "How do you feel about the last woman you dated? What was her name? Anna? No wait, Anna doesn't count, those were unusual circumstances."

"How the hell do you know about Anna and our *unusual circumstances*?" He was really starting to worry about her being able to read his mind. "Can you read my mind?"

"No. Focus here. Who is the last woman you fell in love with."

"That would be you." As soon as he'd said it, he knew his mistake.

"Honey, I don't know how to break this to you, but you were never in love with me." She smiled as she said it, but her tone was laced with sadness and a hint of pity.

"How can you say that? I wanted to marry you." It pissed him off that she was acting so condescending and self-righteous.

"And then you didn't. Old news." She began pacing the kitchen, and he figured, if he timed it just right, he'd be able to sneak by her without too much collateral damage to his insides. "Even then I could tell that you loved me, but that you weren't *in* love with me."

He watched her move, back and forth, back and forth, and waited for the exact moment when she was next to the fridge, and he could--

"Harry, you're gay. Or, at the very least, you're bi."

Say *what*?

His stomach flipped, and his heart began to beat so fast he felt as if he'd run the Boston Marathon. He couldn't seem to catch his breath, and he knew he was about to throw up all that good bourbon.

You don't want to be a freak of nature, do you Harry? Do you want me to tell your father?

No, sir. I'll be good.

"That isn't possible." He had to put an end to this discussion. There was no way he was going down that memory lane, not even with Jenny, who probably deserved an explanation more than anyone why he couldn't admit – could not physically give in – to being interested in men.

"Sure, it's possible. Your innate sense of fashion. I'd swear you have more shoes than Imelda Marcos. You cook and clean better than the average guy. Your days aren't constantly organized around some sports program or event. And, even though you like women, you have a mad crush on your incredibly hot next-door neighbor. Who. Is. A. Man." She grinned and moved closer. "Admit it, you do. I can tell."

He was in a panic, but he could also feel the anger and resentment beginning to build inside, and he no longer felt like he would vomit. "I can't be gay. I like women."

"Okay, you're bi."

"No. That's not possible."

"Honey, it's genetic, so you absolutely can be. You get it from your father. He's definitely gay, but he's so pissed off about it he treats women like shit. Unlike you, who makes friends with them."

"Martin is *not* gay."

"Oh, I beg to differ, my friend. Did you forget, I was around all those years when we were dating?"

He was beyond reason now. Who did she think she was that she could come back into his life to play Dr. Phil and make blanket accusations?

"No. My father can't be gay."

"Maybe not entirely. He might be bi, too."

He lost his composure, and started shouting at her. "He would never have allowed it. Why else would he have worked so hard to make sure it was conditioned out of his thirteen-year-old son."

Harry was so surprised he'd blurted that out, that for a moment he stood there staring at her, waiting for her reaction.

"What did he do to you?" She whispered the words as if she didn't really want to hear the answer. She looked like she had become more transparent, but he couldn't tell if that was really happening or if he was suffering from some kind of tunnel vision. Everything seemed to be closing in on him.

"He didn't do anything." Harry sighed and felt like the weight of his secrets were finally just too heavy to hang onto anymore. "He never did anything himself. He was probably too afraid of being contaminated by me. He sent me away to a 'counselor' and paid them make sure I was the proper hetero son he'd always expected."

"The bastard." She was becoming harder to see, which probably meant she was upset.

But the room was also getting smaller.

And hotter.

Collateral damage to his body be damned, he was leaving the kitchen even if she lit him up like a session of electro-shock treatment. Not like he hadn't survived that before.

He stormed toward her like a linebacker heading for the wide receiver, and miraculously she stepped aside. Then she vanished like a puff of stale air.

CHAPTER SEVENTEEN

Harry couldn't have picked a better day if he'd called the universe and asked for it made up specifically for them. The sun was warm on his face, and there wasn't a cloud in the sky. He hadn't flown a kite in years, so he jumped at the chance when Luke suggested they take Max and Sheldon for an outing.

Luke was holding Max's kite, and giving him lessons on the best method for success, but Harry decided to wing it himself and just take off. He could smell the freshly mowed grass, as he ran across the field and let his kite float up toward the sun. It flowed through the air, getting higher and higher, as he let out more string for it to soar. He felt free as he watched the rainbow-colored kite drift higher and higher into the clear blue sky.

"Harry!" Max pointed at Harry's kite, and laughed, the joy on his face beaming almost as bright as the sun.

"Watch out behind you!" Luke shouted to get his attention. "There's a big, black coyote running up on your left..."

Harry smiled at Luke, and felt the now familiar flip-flop of his stomach. He didn't know how he would have gotten through all of this without Luke, his constant, his rock.

"Harry, wake up." Luke looked disappointed, as if he knew their time together wasn't going to last.

But that wasn't Luke's voice coming out of his mouth. It was a woman's voice. Why was there a woman's voice coming out of Luke's mouth?

It sounded like...

He felt a sharp pain in his chest, and the beautiful day shattered into shards of glass.

Was he having a heart attack? That would be just his luck, to finally have everything he'd ever wanted, and then croak from heart failure.

"Wake. Up. Harry."

Definitely not Luke's voice.

Harry opened his eyes, and saw Jenny standing over him.

Awww, God, not again.

Well, at least now he knew he wasn't having a heart attack.

"What the hell, woman?" He rubbed the aching spot on his chest where she'd obviously poked him, then glanced at the alarm clock on his nightstand and groaned. "It's two thirty-six in the morning. You have got to stop doing that." He rolled over and covered his head with the pillow to try to get back to his dream, which was much nicer than a ghost who packed a taser in her pointer finger, and wasn't afraid to use it. Often.

"Max is gone."

"What?" That got his attention. Was she serious? Or was this some kind of paternal test?

"Max is in trouble." She was turning up her wattage, so he knew this was serious.

Fear ignited in his chest, flaring up to clear out any lingering remnants of sleep and incoherence from his previously fuzzy head.

"How can he be gone?" He knew that was a stupid thing to say, but he was in panic mode. His heart was beating so loud and fast, he thought his chest might explode. He nearly fell on his face as he tried to leap from the bed before untangling himself from the sheets.

He pulled on whatever clothes he found on the floor, and raced to Max's room.

"Max?" He knew that Jenny wouldn't lie to him about this, but instinct still had him calling out. "Buddy, are you here?"

He switched on the light to Max's room, and stopped dead in his tracks. The room was immaculate, as if Max had never been there. No clothes strewn around, no shoes on the floor, and his backpack was missing.

Had he packed everything and left? Had he actually run away from home?

"We don't have time for this. I told you he's gone. We need to go get him." Jenny was in full-shriek mode, but Harry couldn't hear her. It was as if she stood at the end of a long tunnel, and nothing she said registered to him.

His chest was too tight, and he struggled for breath. He was sure his heart was going to shatter into thousands of tiny fragments that would never be put back together again. Did Max want to leave? Was it so bad living here? Was this his answer to the adoption question? Was Harry's initial reluctance in the beginning still getting in the way, and Max didn't believe he was wanted?

He had to get out of his own head. It was two thirty in the morning, and Max was out there somewhere. All alone.

He had to find him.

"Damn it, snap out of it. We have to hurry." Jenny's words echoed his own thoughts.

The tunnel disappeared, and he saw Jenny standing in front of him again.

"Do you know where he is? Can you find him?"

"Yes, but you have to hurry." She must have been torn between staying here with him, and getting back to Max, because her image faltered like a candle flame flickering in a breeze.

He grabbed his keys, and raced out to his car. He didn't waste time buckling himself in as he started the engine and reversed out of his spot. Luckily, at this time of the morning, there weren't any other cars on the road, because he didn't bother to look, as he squealed the tires and gunned it out onto the street.

His heart was racing faster than the car engine. Maybe Max had been kidnapped? Harry was a wealthy man, from a wealthy family, so it was possible. If so, he'd pay whatever they asked.

Then he would kill them.

No, it wasn't a kidnapping.

Maybe it was Matthews and his cronies? Had they found Max, even though Jenny didn't believe they would?

He was letting his mind race along with his panic, and that wasn't going to help. He needed to get a grip. Max had run away from home, because he didn't want to live with him. That was the only explanation.

Hell, Harry'd wanted to run away when he was about Max's age. Why wouldn't Max want to do that, too?

And he would have to let Max go, if he was so desperate to get out that he would run away.

It would rip him apart, but he would do whatever Max wanted.

Right now, though, he had to focus, because Max was out there somewhere. All alone. And probably scared out of his mind.

"Where, Jenny? Where is he?"

"Over there. Hurry." Jenny pointed to the empty parking lot of the church on the corner, where he could see two figures. One of them was Max, and he was gesturing to the taller figure.

Harry turned the wheel hard, and the car went barreling into the parking lot. He slammed on the brakes, and threw the car into park a nanosecond before he was out of the driver's seat and running toward Max.

The man had a hand on Max's shoulder, and Harry knew in that one instant that he was entirely capable of killing another human being.

"Let go of him." Harry's voice was low and menacing, and he fisted his hands at his sides in preparation to start swinging. His blood was pumping so furiously, his head was pounding from it. If this was his natural "fight or flight" instinct kicking in, it apparently meant he was a fighter.

"Take your hands off my son, or I swear to god, I will break every bone in your body, and you will be eating through a feeding tube for the rest of your natural-born life."

"Sir, calm down." The man held up his hands, palms out, in a gesture to placate Harry. "I was only trying to ascertain if he needed any help. It's very late for him to be out here alone."

"Max, come here." Harry gestured for Max. He held out his hand, and could see that it was shaking slightly, either from panic at discovering Max gone, or anger at this bastard, he wasn't sure. Maybe a generous helping of both.

Max ran to Harry, throwing his arms around him and burying his face in Harry's chest.

Harry wanted nothing more than to hold him and tell him he was safe, but he still had to deal with the asshole in front of him. He gently pushed Max behind him, to shield him as well as to free up his own hands in case he needed them.

"The longer you stand here, asshole, the more detail I get of your face to provide to a police sketch artist." He was shaking with so much rage, he knew he was fully capable of carrying out his original threat of beating the shit out of the guy. But his first priority was getting Max home where he was safe, and that meant that this guy had to go. Now.

"I am the police. Detective Ryan Jackson, with Denver Police, District 2." Jackson slowly reached into his back pocket, pulled out a wallet, and opened it up to reveal a badge and ID. It was too dark for Harry to read the name, but the badge looked legit.

"I'm sorry," Harry said, after taking a long look at the guy. Was it possible that he truly was worried about Max's safety, and Harry was being a dick? "I woke up, and he was gone. He scared the shit out of me, and I over-reacted assuming you were—" He broke off, not wanting to scare Max any more than he already was. "I'm sorry."

"Max?" Jackson came closer, and tapped Max on the shoulder to get his attention. "Is that your name, son?" He waited for Max to nod, then asked, "Is this man really your father?"

Max nodded, but it was uncertain, and that made Harry flinch. Harry couldn't tell if Max was resistant to the idea of having Harry for a father, or if he was worried Harry would deny it. Either way, he was breaking Harry's heart.

"Are you okay to go home with him, Max?"

"Hey. What the hell?" Harry didn't like being on the receiving end of the same suspicion he himself had just thrown at this guy.

"I just want to be sure—"

"It's okay, sir." Max probably felt the tension radiating through Harry, because he squeezed his arms tighter around Harry's waist. "I wanna go home now."

"Me, too, buddy." Harry felt an immense sense of relief flood through him at the sound of Max saying, "home," and almost wept right there in front of the cop. "Let's go home."

"Thanks, Mister." Max looked shyly at the man.

"Ryan. My name is Detective Ryan Jackson."

Detective Jackson held his hand out and waited patiently until Max shook with him. Max looked like he had just met a super hero. Maybe he had.

Jesus.

Harry couldn't have been more wrong about the guy if he'd said his name was Mahatma Gandhi.

"Look, I'm sorry—" Harry started, but then didn't know what to say. *Sorry I thought you were a child molester? Sorry I almost ripped your fingers off your hand and stuffed them down your throat because you touched my kid?* He had never in his life felt such a visceral reaction. He would have protected Max from the devil himself if he'd needed to.

"It's okay, I get it." Jackson turned to speak to Harry. "I understand how things might have looked to you. I just got off duty, and saw him sitting on the steps of the church. To be blunt, he's real lucky he found me instead of someone else at this time of the night."

Harry felt like an ass. He'd come close to punching an off-duty detective who'd only been trying to help Max.

"That was pretty much why I came out swinging in the first place." Harry held out his own hand to the detective. "Thank you for being the one who found him."

"As a police detective, I am obligated to at least follow up to make sure Max is in a safe environment. Okay if I stop by in the morning, just to check things out? That way, if it all looks good, I won't have to make a formal report."

Jackson's words made it sound like Harry had a choice. But his tone didn't match his words. Harry understood, Jackson wasn't asking.

"Got it. Yes, tomorrow morning would be just fine." Harry wasn't thrilled to have an officer checking up on him, but he figured it could have been worse. He was pretty sure Jackson was letting him off easy by stopping by himself instead of calling Social Services to do it.

"Can I have your license so I can get your address?"

"Shit." Harry patted himself down, then looked back in the direction of his car, as if his wallet would miraculously appear out of thin air. "I ran out of the house in a panic, and seemed to have left my wallet..."

Jackson chuckled, and shook his head. "I get it, don't worry." He reached into the pocket of his jacket, pulled out a small notebook and pen, and handed them to Harry.

Harry couldn't believe how understanding the guy was being, especially considering he'd probably broken about a dozen laws in the span of about twenty minutes. He scribbled his address on the page, and handed the notebook back.

Jackson shook hands with Harry, and smiled. "Take Max home."

Harry watched as Jackson walked away, then he put his arm around Max and guided him to the car. His adrenaline rush was finally starting to crash, and he was shaking so hard he felt like a yellow fever victim. That had been the scariest moment in his life. He'd been ready to kill a man for even coming near Max. Was this how fathers felt about their kids all the time?

Or, at least the normal fathers? His father had never had a loving thought toward his sons his entire life. Martin wasn't prone to the warm and fuzzies.

He buckled Max into the passenger seat, and noticed tear tracks all down Max's face, which made Harry want to cry. Poor Max must have been scared shitless.

"Are you okay?" Harry's heart was in his throat, and before he could stop and think of the ramifications, he wiped Max's face with the end of his own shirt. Then he wrapped Max in his arms and hugged him to his chest. "Jesus Christ, you scared fifty years off my life."

"I'm..." Max's voice was muffled in Harry's chest, but he sounded like he was fighting back tears. Harry pulled back enough to look at Max. "I... I wanted..." Max tried again, but he hiccupped, and tears filled his eyes.

Harry felt his own throat tighten up as he watched Max struggle to get the words out. "It's okay now, buddy." Harry smoothed Max's hair out of his face, trying to soothe him. He wanted to wipe away the last couple of hours from Max's life. He wanted to put Max back to bed, and clear away this whole night as if it never happened.

"I thought—-" Max started to say, but then he swallowed several times as if trying to gulp down a tidal wave. Harry was in agony watching the poor, brave, guy wipe frantically at his eyes to keep the tears from spilling over.

Harry unbuckled Max, and held him tight so that he knew he was safe. He rocked and soothed him until he eventually calmed down to a sniffle. He would prove to Max that he could be a good father, because he wanted Max to stay with him.

Harry used his shirt again to wipe even more fluids from Max's face. "Let's go home. Huh? Let's go home, and we can really talk about this. Okay?"

"Okay." It was nothing more than a squeak, but Harry would take it.

He buckled Max back into the seat before closing the passenger door and going around to the driver's side.

He had completely forgotten about Jenny, until he almost walked right through her standing by the car. Her face was a mask of agony, and she was sobbing in gasps as if she couldn't catch the breath that was no longer necessary for her. She held out her arms, silently begging to hold her son, but they both knew that she couldn't, and Harry's heart went out to her.

"Your mom's here, too," he told Max, as he climbed into the driver's seat and started the engine. A tortured Jenny materialized in the backseat, still staring at her son. She flickered, wavering off and on as if she no longer had the energy to maintain her image.

"She loves you very much, and wishes she could hold you." He leaned over and gave Max one more hug, holding him for a moment, then whispered in his ear, "That was from your mom."

———

HARRY POURED hot cocoa into a mug, and added marshmallows on top before sliding it across the counter to Max. Jenny was pacing the kitchen, which was making Harry edgy.

The adrenaline rush had worn off, and the fear was kicking back in, so it was killing him not to start shouting about how dangerous it had been for Max to run away. But he knew he would have to approach this more delicately, so that he didn't scare him into silence.

Jenny wasn't helping the situation. She stood so close to Max that the poor kid kept bumping into her, jumping whenever they connected.

"Jenny, you're going to need to step back. You keep jolting Max. You're going to give him a seizure."

"Oh, baby, I'm so sorry." Her form went nearly transparent.

"It's okay, Mom," Max said immediately, as if he knew she would be upset, even though Harry knew he couldn't have heard her. "It didn't hurt that bad." Max looked hard at the same spot Harry had been looking, but Jenny had already jumped back about a foot.

"As promised. Cocoa with marshmallows." Harry tried to think of the best way to broach the subject without freaking Max out.

Max hadn't had a nightmare since Aspen, when he'd finally opened up about Jenny's abusive husband, and he didn't want to send Max spiraling back into that all over again. He would need to be gentle, and coax the answers out of him.

"Did you mean it?" Max asked, out of the blue. He sipped his cocoa, and glanced over the rim of his mug as if the answer was no big deal, but Harry could tell the question was important, because Max's voice shook when he asked it.

"Mean what?" Harry stirred his own cocoa, which he'd heavily dosed with bourbon when Max wasn't looking. It didn't taste nearly as awful as he'd thought it would, but it was still a sacrilege to bourbon – even the cheap stuff.

"When you said I was your son."

He set down his mug, and looked Max in the eye. He hadn't registered what he'd said in the heat of the moment in that dark parking lot, but he knew that whatever he said next would impact Max for a long time.

"Yes. I meant it with my whole heart."

"But that lawyer guy brought you papers so you could get rid of me."

Harry was so stunned, that he stood there with his cup poised at his lips, unable to remember what he was supposed to do with it. He decided to put it down.

"They weren't papers to get rid of you, they were papers to keep you." Get rid of *him*? What the holy hell? Harry came around the counter and sat on the stool next to Max.

Max looked so much like the dejected, dead-boy-walking Harry had first met, that he wanted to weep all over again.

"I'm not going to lie to you. In the very beginning, I didn't think I could handle you."

"No, don't say that to him. He won't understand." Jenny looked frantic, and her image was getting brighter, as if she was going manic.

"I'm not going to lie to him, Jenny." Max had been lied to enough, living with Curtis, and Harry didn't want his relationship with Max to be anything but honest.

"I didn't think I could keep you in the beginning, Max." Christ, he was making him sound like a puppy that he would have sent back to the pound. How could he have been such a jerk? "I was wrong. Look at me." He gently lifted Max's chin until they made eye contact. "You. Are. My. Son. I didn't know how lucky I was when you walked into my life. You are the greatest thing to happen to me, and I am never giving you up."

Max stared at him in silence, as if he wasn't yet convinced.

"Remember earlier today, when I asked if you liked living here? But we got interrupted when Luke and Sheldon got here?"

"Yeah."

"Well, I was asking you that, because I wanted to know if you would be willing to stay here."

No response from Max.

"With me."

Still nothing.

"Forever."

More nothing.

Was Max worried about Harry's reaction in the church parking lot? Was he afraid Harry was as violent as Curtis?

Harry's heart began to race, as he imagined all sorts of horrible scenarios that involved walking Max into the home of some happy, non-violent, couple and letting him go.

"Max, honey, tell him you want that, too." Jenny continued to get brighter, and Harry could barely see the details of her image anymore.

His heart was beating faster than a cocaine addict who'd over-dosed. Why wasn't Max answering him?

"Please answer me. I want to adopt you. But only if that's what you want, too. I'm sorry if I scared you out there tonight, when I threatened to beat up Detective Jackson. I thought he was a going to hurt you, and I only wanted to protect you." Maybe Max had heard these same words as excuses from Curtis, and he wasn't buying any of it.

He didn't know how he was going to be able to make himself do it, but if Max wanted out, Harry would give that to him. It would kill him, but he'd do it

"Look, it's okay—"

"You want to adopt *me*?" Max's voice sounded like a cat's squeaky toy, and he looked like he was on the verge of tears again.

"Yes. Please. Look, I know I messed up in the beginning, but I will make it up to you, I promise. Please tell me this is okay with you." He would make it okay. He had to make it okay.

Max's eyes filled with tears, and Harry wanted to curl up into a ball and weep. How could he have been so foolish to let himself believe this sweet boy would want such a broken man to be his father?

He had to think of what was best for Max, even if it broke his own heart to let him go. Max deserved a whole family to love him.

"It's okay, buddy. You don't have to." Harry felt his throat close up, and his eyes burned, but he would do right by Max if it killed him. "Don't worry. I promise I will find the right family for you."

"I don't want the right family. I want you!" Max threw his arms around Harry, and burst into tears.

Then Harry burst into tears. Again.

And Jenny exploded into pure light.

DETECTIVE RYAN JACKSON arrived the next morning as Harry was making pancakes and more hot cocoa for Max. Harry had decided this was a good sick day for both of them, and had called Max's school to let them know he wouldn't be coming in.

He sincerely hoped that didn't give the Detective the wrong impression, like he was a frivolous father who kept his kid home from school on a whim. But Max had been through an ordeal the night before, and deserved a day to recuperate.

He'd even called George, to tell him he wouldn't be in the office, and was fully prepared for a lecture from his older brother about work ethics. But George didn't object at all, didn't even make one snide comment. Instead, he'd told Harry that he was proud of him, and was glad he was focusing on Max as his first priority.

Harry was so surprised, he'd thought about asking Jenny if she could sneak a peek down in hell, and see if it had frozen over. Maybe he was finally growing up a bit in his big brother's eyes?

"Max, you remember the detective from last night." Harry led Detective Jackson into the kitchen, and hoped he didn't sound as nervous as he felt. "Detective, would you like some pancakes?"

"I'm good, but thank you, Mr. Landon."

"Please, call me Harry."

Harry went back to the griddle and flipped pancakes while Max sat wide-eyed, staring at Detective Jackson.

"How's it going, Max?" Jackson stuck his hand out, and Max looked at it for a second before shaking hands with him. "I just wanted to stop by and see how you're doing. Last night must have been pretty scary for you, so I wanted to be sure you're okay."

"I kept Max home from school today, because I thought he needed some time to process, and in case he needed to talk about it more." Harry looked at Jackson, daring him to find fault with his decision.

"Makes perfect sense, Mr... err, Harry." Jackson smiled, and Harry could see the kindness in the man's eyes.

It had been dark last night, so Harry didn't get a good look at the detective, but now he could see that Jackson was a handsome man, with dark hair trimmed close to his scalp, and a five-o'clock shadow that was probably intentional, considering it was only nine-thirty in the morning. But it was the deep brown eyes that really caught Harry's attention. For a hard-core detective, his eyes gave away an inner understanding and kindness that Harry found soothing.

"He should be okay to go back to school on Monday, but since it's Friday I thought today would be okay—"

"Please relax, I'm not here to judge you on keeping Max out of school for one day, especially considering the night you both had." Jackson put up his hands to emphasize that he meant this to be a friendly visit. "Basically, I do these visits to be sure the environment looks safe and stable for the child, and that he, or she, looks comfortable. I won't stay long, and don't want to interrupt your breakfast."

"Do you want some pancakes, Mister... uhmm.... Officer?" Max stuttered over how to address Jackson.

"I... uhhh..." Jackson sounded conflicted, so Harry decided to intervene.

"There's plenty, and we would be happy to have you join us. Unless you're on duty, and need to get going." Harry wasn't sure if it was even proper protocol to invite a detective for breakfast, but figured everyone had to eat.

"That would be nice, thank you." Jackson seemed almost as confused as Harry on what to do.

"Come on, sit here." Max patted the stool next to him, and that decided it for everyone.

CHAPTER EIGHTEEN

It had been far too long since Harry had thrown a summer bash. Sure, it was only the beginning of May, so technically not summer, but it was a perfect day for a barbecue. It was Max's adoption day, and even the weather was declaring it a huge success. He stood alone in his kitchen, assembling a tray of buns, while he watched the scene through the window overlooking the backyard.

All the important people in his life were strewn across his lawn. Emma was organizing the festivities with her two sisters, Marlie and Laura, while George, holding his new son, Charlie, watched with an amused expression on his face. He had never seen his brother so... content. George had finally grown into his own skin when he married Emma. Sure, he was still a fuddy-duddy, but he was a happier fuddy-duddy, cooing over his infant son.

All of Marlie and Laura's kids were there, crowding around Max, including him in games, and in their lives like he had been naturally born to them.

Even Blake had made one of his rare appearances, and Harry had to wonder if Anna had something to do with that. It would be entertaining to watch, if the preview he got the other day was any indication. And Blake would be just the guy to get Anna's attention away from Harry.

The day was perfect. It reminded Harry of the one in his kite-flying dream from the other night. That day had been gorgeous, too. He decided to take it as a good sign.

It sounded cliché, even to him, but everything he'd ever wanted had been in that dream. They'd been happy, the three of them. Well, four actually, since Sheldon was there, too. They were a family, doing normal family things like flying kites in the park, and he'd felt like the luckiest man on the planet. He didn't need a dream interpreter to point out the significance of the rainbow kites, especially given the inordinate amount of time he was spending lately thinking of Luke.

He was finally coming to grips with the fact that, although he wasn't sure he liked men exclusively, he certainly had deep feelings for this one.

All day yesterday, he found himself coming up with lame excuses to stop by Luke's, to ask him stupid questions like: Should they have games during the barbecue, and if so, what games? Wouldn't it be boring for Max to just sit around and watch grown-ups drink? Should they invite Max's friends from school, and if so, which ones? They weren't required to invite any of the moms, were they?

Like a heat-seeking missile, his eyes were automatically drawn across the yard to find Luke manning the grill like a professional chef. Harry watched him flipping burgers and brats while he chatted with various members of Harry's family. Technically, they were Emma's family, but they had all taken Harry in like an extension of George.

Luke blended right in, laughing and joking with everyone, as if he'd known them all forever. And damn if that wasn't a huge turn-on. The guy fit into his life so effortlessly, it made caring about him feel... normal.

He couldn't deny it any longer, he was seriously falling for Luke. He was feeling more than a casual bromance for his neighbor who painted emotional art, and it made him feel as if someone had reached into the darkest recesses of his soul and lit a bonfire in the middle of an icy tundra.

What would it be like to actually date Luke? What would it be like to kiss Luke?

You don't want to upset your father, do you son?

No, sir.

He took a deep breath, and waited for the nausea to come. He shouldn't be thinking about how much he wanted to kiss Luke. And there was no denying it any longer, he did want to kiss Luke. But he was going to ruin Max's adoption party if he ended up vomiting all over the guests.

Except that the nausea wasn't as bad. He was only a bit queasy.

His heart fluttered, and he felt hopeful that maybe he was getting used to the idea. He felt like a giddy schoolboy with his first real crush.

"You might want to wipe that drool from your chin before someone sees it." Jenny stood next to him, grinning like the Cheshire Cat. "Not that I blame you, of course. He certainly gets my blood pumping." She looked over at Luke and sighed dramatically.

"How is that even possible?" Harry was still on the low end of the learning curve when it came to ghosts, but he would lay good money on the fact that they no longer have pumping blood.

"It's just a figure of speech." She flapped a hand at him in dismissal. "I only meant that I think he's gorgeous, and wish I were still alive – well, and a man – to give you a little bit of competition."

"What competition? There's no competition." Jesus Christ. He sounded like he was in junior high and was too embarrassed to admit he had a crush.

He felt it in the excited flutter of his heart every time he looked at Luke, thought about Luke, was in the presence of Luke.

"Really? 'The lady doth protest too much, methinks.' It's okay." Jenny turned to look at him, her eyes sparkling. "You can admit you have a thing for Luke. I'd say you have excellent taste."

"It goes against everything I've had drilled into me." Harry didn't know why he was still trying to argue with her. Apparently, old habits really do die hard. She was right, of course. But he was still uncertain.

Forty-two years old, and he was still haunted by his thirteen-year-old self. "You don't think that's wrong, somehow?"

"You are what you are. How is liking other men any different from saying you like... oh, I don't know, brussels sprouts? Or that you're a vegetarian?"

Harry was baffled. "But I'm not a vegetarian. And how does my eating meat have anything to do with my feelings for Luke?"

"Ah, ha!" Jenny threw her arm up and pointed toward Harry's chest. "So you admit to liking Luke."

"I—"

"My point is that no one goes around demanding – or trying to *recondition* – you to eating meat, if your preference is to be vegetarian. In fact, restaurants go out of their way to offer you meat-free options. You, Harry Landon, are just not into eating meat."

Jenny looked so proud of herself, he didn't have the heart to tell her that her analogy had a vague sexual innuendo he could have done without hearing from her. "I understand what it is you're trying to say – however awkward it makes me feel at the moment – but the reality is that it isn't as simple as that. Too many biases get in the way with too many people, and those of us on the receiving end of it just wind up as expendable pawns in a bigger war. My father—"

He was interrupted by the sound of barking outside, and raised voices. He looked through the window to find Sheldon, standing in front of Max as if guarding him from some evil threat.

Then he saw the evil threat.

"My father..." he whispered. All the blood drained from his body, and emptied into his feet leaving him so light-headed he almost dropped the plate of buns he'd been holding.

The bastard was standing in Harry's backyard. Anna must have brought him, because she was standing there with him. What had she been thinking? He thought he'd been very clear with her that Martin wasn't a part of his life.

Harry hadn't had any contact with the man in almost twenty years. What the hell was he doing here? Was Anna playing mediator, trying to get Harry to reconcile with Martin?

She was never going to succeed with that.

Harry dumped the plate of buns on the counter, and ran as fast as he could out of the kitchen and downstairs to the backyard. He was in a panic to defend his son from whatever horrible shit was going down, now that Martin was around. Sheldon was a sensitive dog. If he was feeling compelled to protect Max, then Martin had already said or done something to upset Max.

"What did you say to him?" Harry demanded, before he'd even come to a complete stop.

"Ah, there you are, son. I wondered where you were." Harry's father spoke as if he owned the house, the yard, the party, and everyone in attendance.

Harry couldn't even look at the man. He turned his anger on Anna instead.

"What the hell, Anna?" Harry was so angry, he was starting to see stars. But he was very gentle when he pulled Max away from Martin.

Sheldon had stopped barking, but he continued to stand guard while Max petted him. Harry could see that Max was scared, because his whole body was shaking, and he wouldn't take his eyes off Sheldon.

"Don't be mad, Harry." Anna was wearing a placating smile, but Harry could see that she was uncertain. "When I told your dad that you were having an adoption party for Max, he naturally wanted to come and meet his new grandson."

Harry cringed at the words, "your dad," but he knew the real reason Martin was there was because she had told him about Luke. Martin didn't give a rat's ass about meeting Max. He'd never cared about his sons, why would he start taking an interest in grandchildren?

Martin showed up because of Luke.

Well, Harry wasn't a thirteen-year-old kid anymore, and he had to keep reminding himself that Martin had no power over him.

Out of the corner of his eye, Harry saw Luke come up to stand beside him, wielding a metal grill spatula as if he wanted to hit Martin over the head with it. Luke must have also understood that

Sheldon didn't bark at just anyone. Even though he'd never met Martin, Luke was there with his support. In spite of the charged energy in the air, Harry almost laughed from the thrill he got in his heart watching Luke come to his and Max's rescue with a kitchen utensil.

"How could you, Anna?" Harry was pissed that Martin was there, but he was most angry with Anna for bringing him. "I told you he wasn't a part of my life. I even told you I didn't want to be included when you got together with him. What part of that translated to you believing you had the right to bring him to my home?"

"Everyone deserves to have a relationship with their father. I thought this would be a good occasion to—" Anna started on a whisper.

"I don't give a damn what you thought." Harry was incensed, and didn't want to hear her explanations. "You were wrong."

Anna blanched, and Harry was glad that something had finally gotten through to her. Every time he tried to break up with her, she manipulated the conversation, and managed to hang onto him. He should have been more clear with her instead of trying to spare her feelings. But he never thought she would over-step herself so much as to go completely against him like this. He had been weak, and now he was paying for it.

"Now, Harry, Anna was just trying to help." Martin's voice was a jarring reminder that Harry still needed to deal with getting rid of him as soon as possible. He would have to think about Anna, and her betrayal, later. "She was concerned about how your relationship with this Luke person was confusing your relationship with her."

"There is no relationship with her." Harry glanced back at Anna, and saw the surprise on her face, which told him that she really had believed they were still dating. "What the hell are you doing here, Martin?"

"I'd like to know the answer to that question, too." George had come up, and was also standing at Harry's side. He didn't have a 'weapon' like Luke, but Harry saw that he wasn't any happier with their father's presence, if his stiff body language was any indication.

Then Harry saw Blake nonchalantly walk up to stand next to George, as if he was joining a group for a concert that was about to begin. But Harry knew better. He could see that Blake was tensed, alert, and ready for anything.

Harry looked around and saw that Emma was next to George, and her whole, wonderful, family was standing with her. Harry felt a warm rush of gratitude. They didn't know anything about Martin, but they knew whose side they were on, and it gave him the courage to stand his ground.

Even Jenny was there, he noticed. She stood on the fringe, looking a little awestruck by the amount of people and support around Harry, but she had built in tasers and wasn't afraid to use them.

Martin gestured to Anna, and his lips twitched in a loose imitation of a smile. "A sweet little butterfly told me I have a grandson, and she thought I should be here."

"Really." Harry glared at Martin, and crossed his arms over his chest. He knew Martin was full of shit. The real reason Martin was there was because of Luke. "And what about the grandson that was born a month ago? You didn't feel the need to come rushing over to George's house and welcome Charlie into the fold. So, tell us. Why are you really here?"

Anna blanched, and rushed to say, "He is Max's grandfather. I thought this might be a good time for the two of you to mend some fences. Start fresh with each other. Martin misses you, Harry, and—"

"You had no right to bring him." Harry didn't want to hear any more lies. "Luke isn't a threat to my relationship with you, because the only relationship you and I have is friends. And even that is in question at the moment." Harry glared at Anna, and she flinched as if she felt guilty. "Your father believes the world revolves around him, and he can do whatever he pleases." Harry didn't even try to hide the bitterness in his tone. He didn't care what the man thought of him anymore.

Anna looked from Martin back to Harry, as if she was confused by their long-standing animosity toward each other.

"Well, it's a good thing she did tell me about all the time you're spending with Luke. That's why I'm here." Martin spoke as if he'd just been paid a compliment. "You're reverting back to old habits, son, and it has to stop. You need to consider the *friends* you are making. Some people are not a good influence on impressionable young boys." He gestured vaguely in the direction of where Luke was standing.

Harry's head was pounding from his father's words, and the voices in his head.

You don't want to be a freak, do you son?

Do you son?

"Consider the friends you're making, son." Martin gave Harry a look of such condescension that Harry wanted to hit him.

You're an abomination.

Harry wasn't going to listen to either of them anymore.

"Shut up, you bastard." He was a grown man standing in front of his father this time, and he was done letting anyone tell him his feelings were wrong. Especially when everything he felt for Luke seemed so right. If he wanted a relationship with Luke, he would damn well have one.

Harry turned to Luke, wrapped one hand around the back of his neck, and the other around his waist as he pulled him in close. Then he kissed him before the voice in his head tried to talk him out of it.

He felt Luke's surprise, and was worried he'd made a terrible mistake when he didn't kiss him back. Harry knew he would have a lot of explaining to do later. It had been an impulse, and he hadn't meant for it to last longer than a quick touching of lips. He only wanted to bring his father down a peg.

He heard several gasps from the crowd, and knew that the angry-sounding one had come from his father. And he was pretty sure the one that sounded surprised, came from Anna, but the other gasps sounded pleased.

Then Luke was kissing him back, and his world tipped on its axis. He lost track of everyone around him. Everything narrowed down to him, and this man in his arms, and the feel of Luke's lips on his own.

Nothing had ever felt this right to him before. This was the feeling that had never been there with all the women he'd tried to date. This is what he'd been waiting his whole life to feel. Connected. Like the last piece of a puzzle that had been missing since he'd first opened the box.

And sweet Jesus, the man could kiss. Nothing this amazing could possibly be wrong. Luke put his hands on Harry's chest, and gently nudged him, signaling that the kiss should end.

Harry lifted his head and reluctantly pulled back. He was afraid to look at Luke -- afraid he'd be pissed that Harry had used him as a tool to strike out at his father. He wasn't sure how he was going to explain that it had started out that way, but then had turned into something entirely different.

He searched Luke's face for his reaction, but he couldn't quite read it. Luke looked contentedly startled, as if someone had just told him the ice cream cake was made out of tofu, but he was willing to try it anyway.

Then the nausea set in.

He wasn't sure what had taken it so long to make an appearance – maybe because this had all happened so fast, and he hadn't thought about it first – but it was making itself known with a vengeance. He swallowed several times, and tried taking in deep breaths, but he didn't think he'd be able to contain it.

He was just deciding he would aim for Martin, when Luke handed him a bottle of water, and twisted off the cap for him. Harry had no idea where Luke managed to get his hands on the bottle. Maybe he had been a Boy Scout, and had learned to always be prepared.

Or maybe Luke was just that tuned-in to him that he'd seen it coming.

Harry swallowed the water and was able to stem the nausea tide, although a part of him regretted not taking the opportunity to vomit all over Martin when he'd had the chance.

"Harry?" Max's quiet voice broke into his thoughts.

Now that the threat of being sick was contained, it was time to return to the real world and face whatever consequences his action had produced. He took another deep, cleansing, breath, and looked at Max.

"Yeah, buddy, what's up?" He had no idea how he was going to explain this to his brand new son, but he sure as shit knew he wouldn't handle it like his father had when he'd been Max's age.

"Are you and Luke, like, dating now?" Max sounded curious, like he was confirming something he already knew, but just wanted to be sure.

Harry looked into Luke's eyes, and took the biggest leap of his life. "Yeah, buddy. If he'll have me."

Luke smiled, and took Harry's hand. Harry felt like the cement truck he'd never known he'd been carrying was lifted off his shoulders.

"Cool." Max beamed, as if he'd just been told they were heading to Disneyland.

"You are an abomination." Martin was, unfortunately, still in attendance, and he looked like he was about to explode. His face was red, his hands were fisted at his sides, and his mouth spat saliva with each word that exploded from his lips. "If you think I'm going to allow my grandson to be raised by two—"

George spun Martin around, and punched him in the face. Martin went down like a worn-out prize fighter in his last round.

"I've been waiting thirty years for an excuse to do that, and you finally gave it to me." George's tone was low and menacing as he loomed over Martin. "You will keep your bigoted opinions to yourself, because no one here wants to listen to that bullshit. If you plan to leave this party – a party to which you were not even welcome – with only a split lip, you'd better not say another word."

George fisted his hand again, and looked like he might punch Martin just for the fun of it, but Harry grabbed his arm and stepped forward.

Harry heard Blake mutter from behind him, "Aw, damn it, George. I wanted to do that."

"Martin, you have a choice to make." Harry wasn't putting up with any more of Martin's bullshit. He kept his voice steady and deliberate as he continued. "You can either accept me for who I am, and enjoy a relationship – however limited it will be – with your grandson. Or you can remove your hypocritical ass from my lawn, and my sight, and never darken my life again. I am no longer a scared thirteen-year-old kid without any power. So, make up your mind."

"Those are not my only choices, son." Martin rose from the lawn as if sitting there had been his choice from the beginning. "You might believe you are in control, but you are not. I will not stand by and allow my grandson to be subjected to your—" He stopped when George raised his fist, and Blake growled, then continued, "lifestyle choices."

"Let George hit him again, Harry. You can be vegetarian if you want to be." Jenny's voice roared across the yard like she was a basket-ball cheerleader, and Harry wanted to laugh.

"Leave now, Martin. You aren't welcome here." Harry looked over at Anna, and he felt a rush of sadness. He'd wanted them to be close. But he felt betrayed by her for letting Martin in without first talking to him about it. "And take your Benedict Arnold step-daughter with you."

Anna gasped as if he'd struck her. "Harry—"

Martin roared. "She isn't my step-daughter. I didn't adopt her."

Anna looked so shocked that Harry almost felt sorry for her. Apparently, Martin's cruelty could still catch her off guard. Her shock instantly morphed into a look of so much hate, Harry was surprised Martin wasn't knocked to the ground again. Then she turned and left without another word.

Harry glanced over at Blake, and could see confusion struggling with definite interest in the bounty hunter's eyes.

"You're a hateful bastard," Harry said to Martin, and he was starting to feel pity for Anna. No one deserved the toxic shit Martin could dish out, and Harry couldn't begin to understand why she put up with it. He wouldn't. Not. Ever. Again. "I don't want you anywhere near my son." With one hand still holding Luke's, Harry put his other arm around Max and held him close.

"Your lifestyle is hateful to me." Martin pontificated, even though no one was paying any attention to him anymore. "I will not allow my grandson to be tainted by you. No law is above God's law." Martin looked around as if seeking support, but the group had already turned their backs on him and had begun drifting off.

Harry couldn't stand the sight of the man. He turned away with Max as George and Emma's brothers-in-law calmly, but very deliberately, escorted Martin out of the yard.

Harry knew he was going to have to come clean with Luke about what happened when he was thirteen if he had any hope of a lasting relationship with him. He still thought of himself as broken, and he owed Luke an explanation, at least, for using him to get back at his father. It was going to be a brutal conversation, one he'd never intended to have with anyone, but he needed to be honest. He cared too much about Luke to be anything but open and honest.

He would include George. His brother deserved to know, too, and George would have his back. Even more important, George would be there to pick up the pieces in case Luke decided Harry wasn't worth sticking around for.

"Uncle Harry?" Jessica came up to them as if nothing out of the ordinary had just happened to spoil the mood. "You don't have to worry. Jenny will help you, and it will be fine."

"How sweetie?" Jenny asked. She seemed desperate for answers as she crouched down next to the little girl.

"Uh, Luke, why don't you and Max head up to the food table, and start without me." Harry had a really big soft spot for Jessica, and wanted to be sure he and Jenny had a quiet moment with her.

Max ran off to meet up with Spencer, who was calling for him. But Luke gave Harry one last look before nodding his understanding, and following Max.

Harry sat down on the grass and pulled Jessica into his lap. It wasn't that he was afraid she'd run away on him, he was afraid Jenny might accidentally grab her in the excitement, and he didn't want to see Jessica get hurt. Even unintentionally.

"Can you tell me what you mean?" Harry asked, and Jenny flopped down next to them.

"I don't know." Jessica shrugged, like this kind of thing happened to her all the time, and she was just going with the flow. "I just know you're afraid, and Max's mom is going to help you. You don't have to be afraid, Uncle Harry."

"But what is he afraid of, honey? How can I help him?" Jenny leaned in closer, just as Harry suspected.

"Back off, Jenny, I don't want you to accidentally touch her." Harry held Jessica protectively, and glared at Jenny. He wanted to find out just as much as Jenny, but he wasn't going to risk Jessica being hurt.

"Jess!" Marlie, holding a plate full of food, called from the patio. "Come eat, honey."

"Okay, Mommy!" Jessica wrapped her arms around Harry's neck, and gave him a kiss on the cheek. "It's going to be okay, Uncle Harry. You'll see."

Harry helped her stand up, and she ran off to join her mother, while Jenny glared daggers at Harry.

"I may be here to help you, but right at the moment, I could slug you. Why did you let her get away?"

"Do you realize you sound like a crazed kidnapper?" Harry chuckled, pulled himself up off the grass, and dusted himself off.

"Well, crap, I kind of did, didn't I." Jenny followed him as he headed to the rest of the group. "I was just hoping she would be able to tell us something more. I really don't want to be stuck here forever if I can't figure out what I'm supposed to do to help you."

"I think she told us all she knew." Harry felt a small sense of peace come over him, and he knew he would be able to get through his talk with George and Luke, one way or another, and it would be okay. Just like Jessica said. "The rest of it, we'll have to figure it out on our own."

CHAPTER NINETEEN

Harry watched the sun set in spectacular shades of pinks and purples across his backyard sky. He loved watching Colorado sunsets as they spread along the horizon in what so many would refer to as Broncos colors, but he always felt the words, "purple mountains majesty" were a much more fitting description.

It had been a great barbecue, in spite of the unwelcome guest, and Max was the happiest Harry had ever seen him. The kid had beamed from all the love and attention from his extended family on Emma's side. Once again, Harry was eternally grateful for the day Emma walked into George's office to apply as his assistant.

Harry was relieved when Max asked if he could spend the night at Spencer's house. It would be easier not to have to worry about Max being a distraction when he talked with Luke and George, and he figured Emma'd had something to do with finagling the invite.

His gaze wandered into the living room where the two most important men in his life were sitting, heads together, talking in low voices. Harry couldn't hear the conversation from where he stood waiting for Max at his bedroom, but he figured George was filling Luke in on some of the history they had with Martin as a father.

He knew it was time to tell George about what he had gone through when he was a kid, but he wasn't looking forward to it. Especially after he'd laid into his older brother for keeping secrets. He was going to have to eat some crow while he bared his miserable childhood secret. And George was not going to like what he had to say about Martin's role in it all.

Luke wasn't going to like it either. But Harry knew that if he wanted a relationship with Luke, and he definitely did, he had to explain why he acted so weird whenever Luke seemed to want to get close. He was a little surprised to realize that, for him, it wasn't a question of *if* he told Luke about his past. It was more a matter of *when* he told him. And there was a certain sense of rightness in his heart about telling Luke at the same time as George. Whatever Luke's reaction was going to be, Harry knew that George would always be there to hold him up.

But it was still going to suck.

"Are you sure it's okay?" Max asked, breaking into Harry's thoughts. This had to be the hundredth time since Martin left that Max asked him that question, but instead of being exasperated by it, Harry thought it was sweet. He liked that Max was concerned about him, and he realized that Max would stay if Harry said the word. Max was a sensitive kid, and the fact that Martin had upset Harry, in turn upset Max.

But there was no way he would ever do that to Max. His job was to protect his son from as much crap in life as he could. That's what a father was supposed to do for his son.

"You and Spencer have a great time." Harry smiled at Max to let him know he was fine. He wanted to hug Max, but figured that wouldn't go over too well, especially in front of Spencer. But when Max hesitated for a second, and lifted his hands slightly, Harry wondered if he was thinking the same thing.

"We will, Uncle Harry. Come on, Max." Spencer grabbed Max's backpack and the two of them raced out the front door.

Harry closed the door then went into the living room to join Luke and George.

Luke had taken Sheldon back to his condo when everyone started to leave. Sheldon had been great with the kids, but Luke wanted to give the dog some down time. Luke had been huddled up with George since the moment he returned to Harry's loft. Apparently, they were both waiting on Harry to get the ball rolling.

Yeah, this was going to require some liquid courage. He'd been too busy during the barbecue to eat or drink anything, which was probably a good thing, because his stomach was struggling enough as it was, and he didn't know how he was going to get through this.

Jenny was waiting for him in the kitchen. "I would have poured you a shot, but..." She seemed to be more nervous than he was, if the fidgeting of her hands was any indication. "Are you going to be okay?"

Why did everyone keep asking him that? Did he look like he was going to lose it at any minute?

"Yeah. I'm okay." He poured himself a healthy shot of whiskey, and threw it down his throat. "That was medicinal," he explained, as he poured himself another shot.

"I'm sure that whatever you have to say is going to be hard for you to relive, but I'm here for you. You know that, right? If there's anything I can do..." Jenny let her words fade off, and she looked at him like she hoped he would give her a job to do.

"Thanks, but I can't imagine what a ghost is going to be able to do to help make this any easier." He smiled at her to let her know he did appreciate the offer. "Let's get this over with."

He took his glass, two empty ones, and the bottle of whiskey out to the living room. George and Luke broke off their conversation when he sat down to join them.

"Did George fill you in on our complicated relationship with Daddy Dearest?" Harry asked, as he set the bottle and glasses on the table. "Help yourselves, gents." He sagged into the couch as if his legs had decided they didn't want to have any part of the conversation, and had gone to bed without him.

"Harry, if you want to speak to your brother alone—" Luke started.

"Nope. You should know what it is you're getting into here, and I'm only going to be able to go through it one time. And it'll help me if George is here to pick up the pieces when you run screaming from my life."

"You don't have to do this at all." George looked like he was as nervous to hear what Harry had to say as Harry was in saying it. "You and I both know what a horrible person Martin is, so you don't have to drag up any—"

"Nope. Gotta get this out. It's poison, and I don't want it interfering in any of my relationships. Not with you, George. And certainly not with you, Luke." Harry smiled warmly at Luke, trying to convey that he hoped he wasn't about to freak out one of the best relationships he had, outside of the one he had with his brother.

"First, George," Harry began, then turned to his brother and laid his hand on his arm. "I have to ask you to please forgive me for keeping this from you. I know I lambasted you for keeping Martin's second family a secret from me, and I'm being hypocritical, but I'm asking you to please give me a pass on this one. If I have to defend myself on this part, I won't be able to tell you the rest. Please, just know that I... I wanted to, but... I couldn't tell you."

"Harry..." George started to say, but he sounded more confused than angry, so Harry continued.

"Please. I need your promise."

"Okay, yes, I promise." George laid his hand on top of Harry's, and Harry took comfort in his bond with his brother. He'd been wrong to feel so nervous. No matter what, George would always have his back, even if he didn't understand why. Just blind loyalty. In spite of, or maybe because of, their shitty father, he and his brother had a deep connection that no one could break.

Harry poured whiskey into the two empty glasses and handed them to Luke and George then said, "You're probably going to need those." He took a healthy sip of his own whiskey, savoring the heat as it slid down his throat and chest, then landed in his stomach where it ignited into a warm glow.

Jenny had followed him into the living room, and sat perched on the arm of the couch next to him, as if for moral support. He thought he would hate having her there – one more person to know his ugly secret – but he was wrong. She was a comfort. She placed her hand on his back, and he felt a fizzle of gentle energy pour through him, similar to the whiskey he'd just sipped.

He shot her a look that said, "Why didn't that hurt?"

She smiled and said, "I have recently discovered that can be nice when I want to be."

Took her long enough to figure that one out, damn it.

Then he began his story...

HARRY HEARD the front door slam, and knew his father was home, but it didn't matter. He almost never came up to Harry's room. Harry was out-of-sight, out-of-mind, as far as his father was concerned.

Jason, his best friend in junior high, talked his older brother into renting the video of *Good Morning Vietnam* for him, and brought it over to hang out in Harry's room so they could watch it together. They were only in eighth grade, so neither of them were supposed to be watching movies that were rated R, but they could get away with it at Harry's house, because his mom was usually too drunk to notice, and his father was never around to care.

Harry liked hanging out with Jason, because they could talk about anything, and he wasn't squeamish about bending the rules once in a while. They both had older brothers, which made it easier to talk about how he sometimes resented that George was always better at everything.

Having an older brother had its advantages, too, though because he couldn't talk to their father. Even on the rare occasions when he was home, Harry would never talk to him about the stuff he and George talked about. His father would probably give him a lecture about what boys his age should, and shouldn't, be thinking, and then Harry'd feel stupid for trying to talk to him in the first place.

He missed having his older brother home all the time. But next year, he would go away to the same high school as George, and they could hang out together more often. George taught him everything important. He even told Harry what it was like kissing a girl, except Harry didn't think it was nearly as exciting as George made it out to be.

Harry took a large gulp from the bottle of rum he'd pilfered from the liquor cabinet downstairs. He almost choked on the cloying sweetness, and the liquid burned as it drizzled down his throat and through his chest, before it landed in his belly. He felt like he'd eaten a whole bunch of jalapeño peppers.

He wasn't worried that his mom would notice the missing bottle, because she didn't usually drink rum. Wine and vodka were her go-to choices, and she made sure she was well stocked in those. She wouldn't notice the missing rum until Christmas when it was time to pour it into her eggnog, and by then she'd probably just figure they'd run out.

"Hey, Jason, have you kissed a girl yet?"

"Yeah. It wasn't all that great." Jason didn't go into any details, and Harry figured he hadn't found the right girl yet either.

The bite from the alcohol was mellowing out, and he was feeling warm inside. He was glad he wasn't the only one who'd been let down by the whole experience around kissing.

"I kissed Margaret Jean," Harry said, as he handed the bottle of rum to Jason. "It wasn't all that great either. George made it sound like it was going to be better than it was. Do you think we're doing it wrong?"

"Beats me." Jason took a swig from the bottle, grimaced, then handed it back to Harry and pushed the video into the VHS player to start the movie.

Harry took another drink from the bottle, and this time it didn't burn as much. He wasn't sure he liked the taste, and decided to pour it into his soda instead of drinking it straight.

Much better. He could understand why people liked rum and

Coke. He poured some into Jason's soda, too, so they could drink them together.

"Here, try this." Harry handed Jason his enhanced soda, and watched as his friend looked dubiously at the beverage, then took a pull from the can.

Jason nodded and smiled, and Harry sat on his bed to get comfortable for the movie. He was feeling warm and pleasant all over, and his toes were tingling. "Do you suppose there's a right way, and a wrong way to kiss a girl? Like, maybe we just aren't doing it right?"

Harry wished George was there to ask him. George had more experience than Jason and Harry combined.

Jason sat down on the bed and looked directly at Harry. "I don't know. Do you want to show me how you did it, and I'll tell you if it was any good or not?"

Harry laughed, and almost choked on his rum-laced soda.

"Very funny. I'm not going to kiss you. That's just... No." Harry lifted his hand in the air to make an emphatic gesture, but it felt so heavy that he let it flop back onto the bed again.

Jason shrugged, but didn't say anything as he continued to stare at Harry, and took another drink from his can. Jason licked the soda from his lips, and Harry's stomach did a flip-flop, while his heart began to beat faster in his chest.

"You want me to kiss you?" Harry's brain tilted, and he wasn't sure it would be so bad. Not if it was with Jason. He and Jason were best friends.

"Yeah. I'll tell you if it was awful, and how to fix it." Jason smiled at him, set his soda on the nightstand, then beckoned with his hands. "Hit me."

Harry wasn't sure what to do. He kind of wanted to kiss his friend. But what if he really was terrible? Did he want his best friend to find out he sucked in the art of kissing? And what if Jason didn't like it? Would it wreck their friendship?

"I don't know if this is such a good idea. Wouldn't it be weird?"

"It'll only be weird if you don't want to do it," Jason replied. "But I kinda think you do. Right?"

Jason was right. Harry did kinda want to see what it would be like to kiss him.

"Okay. But if you laugh, I will punch you."

Harry's heart was beating as fast as when he'd run the hundred-yard dash in gym class. He set down his own can, then leaned in and kissed Jason on the lips. It was nicer than when he'd kissed Margaret Jean. Jason's lips were softer, but harder at the same time, and Harry liked it.

He only meant for it to be a quick kiss, but then Jason kissed him back, and before he knew what was happening, they had their arms around each other.

"Harold!" His father's voice outside his door barely registered as he moved his hand around to Jason's back.

His bedroom door flew open, and his father bounded into the room. "Harold, answer me when I'm cal—-"

His father stopped abruptly, and went stone still.

"MARTIN WENT APE SHIT." Harry felt like he was thirteen-years old again, and reliving the whole experience. His heart dropped into his shoes, and his hands were instantly sweaty. "He picked Jason up by the shirt, as if he was afraid he'd contaminate himself by physically touching him, and frog-marched him out the front door."

"Ohhhh..." Jenny's hands were at her chest as if clutching her heart, and she was smiling. "Your first romantic experience with a boy."

Harry grunted and rolled his eyes at her, because she didn't know the half of it yet. She had no idea what was coming next.

"Jason is your lawyer friend?" Luke asked, and he sounded... Could he be jealous? That gave Harry some hope. He watched Luke rake his hands through his hair and massage his scalp, as if he thought that would help him clear the jealousy out of his head.

"Yeah. That's the same Jason. He told me later that he'd tried to find out what happened when I'd disappeared, but no one would tell him, and I've never filled in the gaps."

"What the hell do you mean, you disappeared?" George had been standing at the window looking outside while Harry had told his story, but he turned around and marched back to the couch. Harry knew George's anger wasn't directed at him, but he still flinched from the boom in his voice.

"What do *you* mean, what does he mean?" Luke asked, apparently confused. "Weren't you there?"

"I was at boarding school."

"Boarding school? For high school?" Luke was definitely confused. "Who still sends their kids to boarding schools?"

"Okay, both of you need to stop interrupting, or I'm not going to be able to get through the really fun part." Harry held up his hands like he was directing kids through traffic at a crosswalk.

He glanced over at Jenny, who was starting to look worried, because she was glowing brighter than normal. Apparently, it had finally registered that this wasn't going to be a sweet first kiss story with a happy ending.

George flopped down on the couch, and put his head in his hands. He looked at Luke, but there was no animosity in his expression. "So, we've established that I was at boarding school. But you? You disappeared?"

"Oh, I hadn't disappeared." Harry was angry on behalf of his thirteen-year-old self. "I knew exactly where I was. I was in hell. Although, it was cleverly referred to as 'therapy' by the nice doctor who told me I was a freak of nature and shot me full of drugs and electricity."

"No." Jenny gasped, and her image flickered.

"That bastard." George was up again, and pacing the floor. His hands were tightly clenched, and he looked like he was going to start swinging any minute. "That rat bastard. I'm going to kill him." He turned around and looked at Harry with so much fury in his eyes, Harry almost felt sorry for Martin. Almost, but not much.

"*No son of mine will grow up to be a flaming faggot,* was what Martin stated after he yelled at Jason to go home and never come back." Harry could see the scene in his mind like it was happening all over again. "Then he hauled me out of my room and threw me into the car. Next thing I knew, I was booked for daily aversion therapy sessions with the happy doctor, and it was several weeks before I was trusted to go back to school and act like a real man. I never did find out how Martin explained my extended absence." Harry took another swig of his whiskey, and felt Luke sit carefully next to him on the couch.

"The minute I turned twenty-one," Harry continued, like he felt compelled to get everything out, all at once, before he lost his nerve, "I went to a gay bar as my rebellious 'up yours' gesture to Martin, and tried to pick up the first guy I saw."

"Aw, shit..." Luke whispered, as if he could sense where Harry was headed.

"I don't know that I actually wanted to pick up a guy specifically, I really just wanted to prove to Martin that I could. That it was my choice. So, I ordered a drink from the bar, looked around, and spotted this really good-looking man watching me. He was maybe in his twenties, a couple of years older than me, and all I could think about was taking him home to meet Martin. The look on Martin's face, when I proved to him that all that money he'd paid on *conditioning* had been wasted on me." Harry could still remember the feel of the anger, as it twisted in his gut.

"I was already feeling queasy, but I'd convinced myself it was just nerves, and the alcohol. I told myself I was in control, and I would decide which way I wanted to go. Not some freak doctor with one hand full of pills, and the other hand holding the equivalent of a cattle prod." He paused to take another sip of his bourbon, and give himself a minute to settle from the experience that still upset him twenty-one years later.

"We chatted, and the queasiness subsided. Then the guy reached down, rubbed his hand over my crotch, and I was instantly so ill, I almost didn't make it to the bathroom in time."

Harry sat quietly, waiting for the pain from the memory to subside enough that he could speak again without the lump in his throat. But still, all he could manage was a croak. "That was the last time I tried anything with a man."

Luke didn't say anything, and didn't try to touch him, but he sat close enough that Harry could feel the warmth from him, seeping into his own body. He could smell Luke's soothing cinnamon and orange scent, and it was enough. Harry wasn't sure how he would react to a touch at this point, but the energy from Luke's presence was a balm, slowly melting the icicles that had begun forming in his soul.

George didn't say anything either. He sat on the coffee table and reached out to take Harry's hands. Harry instinctively flinched, pulling his hands into his chest to avoid the contact. He didn't know what would happen if either of them touched him, and he was afraid to find out.

"Sorry," Harry whispered, and he felt like he'd turned back into that scared kid again.

"No, I'm sorry." George tucked his hands under his legs as if he didn't trust himself not to reach out and touch Harry. "I wasn't there for you. I should have been there."

"What would you have been able to do? You were only fifteen, and had your own issues with Martin." The last thing Harry wanted was for George to feel responsible.

"I love you. You know that, right?" George looked into Harry's eyes, and Harry could see that he was barely holding back tears.

"You're okay with me being gay?"

"Jesus Christ, Harry, you're my brother. You are who you are, and I love you. How would you being attracted to men make any difference to me? I only want you to be happy. You could have told me you wanted a sex change operation, and I would have written out the check, then held your hand through the entire procedure."

"I would prefer that you not get a sex change operation." Luke grinned at Harry, and that was enough to break some of the tension.

Luke tentatively reached out a hand as if he was afraid he might burn Harry by touching him. Harry didn't know what he would feel, because everything was still so close to the surface. He wanted to hold Luke's hand, but he was afraid he would revert back to the kid who'd been conditioned to hate the feel of a man's touch.

He heard George take a deep breath, and looked up to see him staring at Luke with so much hope in his eyes, it was as if he was willing Luke to break through Harry's barriers. Harry felt Luke's hand on his own, and closed his eyes for a moment, but he didn't flinch. Instead, he drew in the warmth from Luke's touch. When heard George let out his breath, he knew he had made a significant step forward.

Harry opened his eyes, and saw that Jenny had started to shimmer. She smiled gently, then laid her hand on Harry's back, sending another fizzle of warm energy through him. Luke slowly stroked Harry's hand, and he felt a sense of peace settle into him.

"Maybe Jessica was right," Jenny whispered in his ear. "I think I am here for you." He felt the warm energy from her touch spread through his body, like she had reached inside and lit candles in every dark space.

Harry slowly reached up and cupped Luke's face, touching it like a blind man trying to memorize every detail.

"You can do this." Luke smiled encouragingly, then lightly cupped Harry's face in return. "We'll take it slow."

George cleared his throat as he stood up and turned away, but not before Harry got a glimpse of him wiping his eyes.

"I'm going home to hold my wife." George turned back to Luke, and Harry could see his eyes were still wet. "Thank you." It came out like a croak, and he cleared his throat again. "Good night, you two." He smiled, then turned and left.

Harry hadn't noticed that Jenny was no longer touching him, until he saw her standing by the window. She was sparkling with energy, as if she'd been supercharged by a nuclear power plant.

"I think I'll go have a word with your father. I'd like to see how he reacts to a little shock therapy of his own." She grinned, then held up her hands to show sparks shooting out of her finger tips. She disappeared, but her laughter lingered a second longer, and Harry was a little bit scared of his friendly ghost.

He had a moment of worry for Jenny — he didn't want her getting into trouble with The Powers That Be on his account. Was there some kind of a rulebook in *Ghostworld*?

But then again, Martin had it coming.

CHAPTER TWENTY

Harry felt like a new man. As he mixed up the batter for waffles to make for breakfast, it occurred to him that it was because he was a new man. He was completely changed from the person he'd been a month ago. He could finally, freely admit that he liked men, or one man in particular.

He had a boyfriend. That sounded great, even if it was just in his head. He and Luke hadn't actually come out and defined anything, but this was the longest he'd ever lasted in a relationship. And he wasn't running for the door.

Boyfriend.

The word made his heart flutter.

Two months ago, he would have thrown up simply thinking that word. Now, it made him feel like a teenager with his first real crush. He'd missed out on so much of that. Sure, he'd had girlfriends as a teenager, but he'd never felt the euphoria that he was feeling now.

Over the last few weeks, he and Luke had spent every waking minute together. True to his word, Luke had been taking everything slowly, one step at a time, and Harry was finally feeling comfortable in his own skin for the first time in his life.

Holding hands with Luke walking down the street together,

slowly led to being comfortable kissing in the back row at the movie theater.

Last night, they stayed up almost the whole night talking, and holding each other. Harry knew he should be exhausted from the lack of sleep, but instead, he was riding the high of his first real love.

Luke had been so careful with him, as if he'd been afraid to break him. Every touch was gentle and steady, like each time he was asking permission to move to the next level. When Luke finally worked up to kissing him, and asking if he could spend the night, Harry'd been more than ready, and it had been perfect. He'd fallen asleep feeling safe in Luke's arms.

He realized that he had a lot to learn with this new relationship, but Luke was going to be a fantastic partner, and Harry trusted him implicitly.

"Don't you look all happy and bright." Jenny, glowing herself, like a Christmas tree on fire, was sitting at the kitchen counter watching him while he prepared breakfast. "Bet I can guess what – or who – you're thinking about right now."

He had been so lost in his own thoughts, he hadn't seen her pop into the kitchen with him. He cracked eggs into the batter as he glanced at her.

"Well, look what the cat dragged in." Harry was genuinely glad to see her. "I thought you'd moved on, or whatever."

"Yeah. Nope. Still here." Her glow dimmed slightly, which put her back into her 'normal' wattage range. "I have no idea why. I thought I'd be gone now that I know Max is settled, and you are in love. Except that I seem to keep coming back to you, like a magnet."

"What does that even mean?"

"Beats me. I just know that I've had stronger feelings lately of when to be with you."

Jenny didn't seem too bothered by being yanked around like a rubber band, and it answered some of the questions he had about her mission, or whatever the hell it was that was keeping her here. But he was still fuzzy on how it all worked.

"Is it that you try going to the other side, but end up back in my kitchen each time instead?"

"Not exactly. It's almost like I seem to know when I need to be... well, here, I guess. In the beginning, it didn't seem to matter as much, I could come and go whenever. But lately, I've been feeling like I need to be here with you more. Like something big is going to happen, and I keep getting drawn back to you."

"Something big already happened, and you were definitely there for me." Harry wished he could hug her. "I'm glad you're here. I wanted to talk to you about the other night."

"I know that was a hard story for you to tell, but I'm glad you finally got it out in the open. I'm glad *you're* out in the open." She smiled at him, and he was touched by her kindness.

"You understand now why I couldn't marry you, don't you? Even if I didn't exactly understand it at the time myself?"

"It's okay, Harry. I think I might have had an inkling, even then, that we weren't meant to be together."

"I'm sorry it took ten years for me to be able to tell you."

"Oh, I know!" Jenny's outburst startled Harry, and he spilled pancake batter on the counter. "Maybe the big thing is you and Luke getting married. Maybe I get to stay here for that as my reward for getting you two together."

Harry decided it was time to change the subject, or she'd start planning the ceremony, and have them walking down the aisle before he and Luke even had the chance to discuss it.

"Where have you been anyway? Last I saw you, you'd winked out to do some ghost justice on my behalf. Is Martin still alive, by the way? Not that I care, I just want to know if you're going to need help disposing of the body." Harry grinned at her, and realized that he owed a lot to this woman.

"Oh, he's fine. Unfortunately." She waved her hand as if shooing a fly. "He didn't know what hit him. Literally."

Harry's phone dinged that he had an incoming call, and he looked at the screen to see it was from Anna. She had been calling and leaving texts every day since the barbecue, and Harry had no desire to connect with her.

"She's got nerve." Jenny was leaning over the counter checking his phone. "Wonder what she has to say for herself."

Harry didn't want to know. As far as he was concerned, Anna could just wait until hell froze over, because he wasn't answering her call. He wanted to keep living in his bubble with Luke and Max, and pretend the outside world didn't exist. At least for a couple more weeks.

Her efforts were escalating. This morning, she'd already called three times. He was still feeling the sting of her betrayal and didn't care what she had to say in her defense. No good could come out of it, and he would much rather think pleasant thoughts about Luke.

Harry heard the clickity-clack of Sheldon's nails on the hardwood floor, and knew that Luke had returned. Harry was even feeling happy thoughts about the dog. "Good morning, Sheldon. How did you slee—"

Harry was interrupted by Luke's lips, which locked onto his in a searing kiss that took his breath away.

"Welp, that's my cue to leave. Think I'll go see what Max is up to." Jenny said, just before she vanished into oblivion.

It crossed Harry's mind that Jenny had become a permanent fixture in his life. He had no clue why she was still around, popping in and out like some kind of happy puppy with Attention Deficit Disorder, but he was getting used to her being there.

"Good morning, Harry," Luke said, and Harry was pleased to hear it come out sounding unsteady, as if it had taken Luke by surprise, too. "How did *you* slee—"

Harry interrupted Luke with a return kiss, and he could feel the smile forming on Luke's lips.

Luke tightened his arms around him, and Harry could feel the rapid thumping of both their hearts. "You're good then," Luke said after several minutes had passed. It wasn't a question, but Harry heard the uncertainty in Luke's voice.

"Yeah, I'm good. I'm really good. Thank you." Harry wasn't sure how to convey just how much those two words meant to him.

Luke smiled like he understood, and ran his fingers through Harry's hair. Sheldon woofed, and Harry looked down to see that the dog had licked all the batter off the spoon he'd had been using to make the waffle mix.

"Maybe you should feed your monster, while I finish making breakfast. Max'll be up any minute, and you know what a grump-pot he is in the mornings. Breakfast is critical." Harry placed the licked spoon in the sink and got a new one to replace it.

"I thought we could take Max to a show at the IMAX today," Luke said, and Harry's heart warmed at the thought of his boyfriend wanting to make plans together with his son.

"That's a great idea. Max will love it."

The doorbell rang and Luke went to answer it on his way out.

"Harold Landon?" A tall man with gray hair and mustache holding a clipboard asked when Luke opened the door.

"No." Luke must have felt it wasn't any of the man's business who he was, because that's all he said until Harry joined them.

"I'm Harold Landon."

"This is for you." The man handed an envelope to Harry, wrote something on his clipboard, and walked away. "You've been served."

The warm and tingly feelings Harry had felt from his exchange with Luke in the kitchen evaporated, and his heart fell out of his chest and landed on the cold slate floor in his entryway. He dreaded seeing whatever was in the envelope. But he knew it was best not to avoid the inevitable, and he ripped it open.

"Curtis Matthews is suing for custody of Max."

"What. The. Hell." Jenny's image exploded into existence at the same time Luke said, "Who's Curtis Matthews?"

"He can't." Jenny started glowing red around the edges. "He can't afford the attorney's fees. And he never cared about Max."

"Curtis Matthews is the guy who was married to Max's mom. He's claiming he's Max's father. The attorneys for the case are Martin's."

Harry thought he might pass out. His father was footing the bill for that bastard Curtis to try to take Max away from him.

Luke looked like he was three sentences behind, and still trying to catch up. "Your father is paying to have Max taken away from you, by a guy who claims to be his real father?"

"That's what these papers say to me."

"That's messed up." Luke still looked lost.

"I'm going to kill him." Jenny's glow was getting redder by the second.

Harry wasn't sure which of the shit-for-fathers behind the lawsuit she was planning to murder, but at this point it didn't really matter.

What had him worried, was whether or not Matthews had a case.

HARRY POUNDED on the door of his childhood home, demanding to be let inside. He wanted to hurt something – or more specifically someone. Beating up on the door was satisfying, because he kept picturing it as Martin's face. He probably shouldn't be here while he was so angry, but he just seemed to show up suddenly without any recollection of how he'd gotten there.

Jenny was next to him, and she was just as furious, if the red that had completely taken over her usual golden glow was any indication. He was glad none of that energy was focused on him, because she did look formidable.

The door finally opened as he was raising his fist to hit it again, and Anna stood on the other side. His anger ratcheted up another notch.

"What the hell are you doing here?" He didn't even try to be nice, letting his anger spread into his words.

"If you'd please just let me explain." Anna spoke in a low voice as if she was afraid someone would hear them. "I've tried calling you several—"

"How could you think I'd want to talk to you after what you did.

None of this would be happening if you hadn't brought Martin, and his attention, to my front door."

"It wasn't like that Harry. Please, you have to understand—-"

"Don't leave my son standing on the front porch, let him in." Martin's voice rolled over Harry like poisoned slime, and he struggled to keep down the bile that rose in his throat.

Anna reluctantly moved aside, and gestured for Harry to enter. Jenny followed, but Harry was only dimly aware of her. All of his focus was centered on not strangling Anna, and not beating Martin to a pulp.

"Hit him, Harry. Either you do it, or I will." Jenny must have read his mind, because she had assumed a boxer's stance, and looked like she would take a swing. "Or we both could. You could hold him down, and I can poke him into a heart attack."

Unfortunately, that would require physical contact with Martin, and that was even more repulsive to Harry than any satisfaction he would get by sending the bastard to the hospital. He still might though, and risk the violent puking that would follow. It might be worth it.

"Call it off, Martin. For once in your life, do the right thing and leave me in peace. Max and I have a life. What you're doing will only hurt your grandson."

"What about the hurt of a father by his son. Why can't you see that I only want what's best for you? I see you heading down the wrong path with this... this *relationship* you think you want to have with your artist friend, but I know you will regret it. Is that really the best decision, the best example you want to set for your son?" Martin held out his arms to Harry like he expected him to come running into them and beg for forgiveness. Harry was reconsidering punching him in the face, just to bring him down a few pegs.

Instead, he decided to try reason. "Matthews doesn't give a shit about Max, he never did. Why are you even involved in this?"

"Because I don't want my son labeled as a faggot."

All of Martin's pretense of kindness vanished, leaving Harry stunned. He couldn't believe his father had actually used that word. It only served as more proof that Martin was so steeped in his bigoted narcissism, it was coming out his pores.

He also couldn't believe the venomous way Martin had said it. "Do you really hate me so much?"

"I don't hate you, Harry. You're my son, and I love you."

Harry was struck by the words, which were almost the same ones George had spoken the night Harry had opened up to him and Luke. But the vast world of difference between the emotions behind those words could have filled the universe.

"You don't love me. You don't even know me."

"I know what you are becoming, and it breaks my heart. I have nothing but unconditional love for you."

"Is he serious right now?" Jenny's voice echoed around the room. "Does he honestly believe the words he's spewing? I never liked your father." Her red glow was getting brighter, and Harry wondered if she would explode.

"Martin, you don't know the meaning of the word love." Harry wondered if his energy was turning red, too, because he was so angry now he could feel the heat pouring out of him. "Love to you is manipulative and distorted. It sure as hell isn't unconditional. Unconditional love means you accept that person for who they are no matter what. You don't ship them off to a loony bin to have some quack pump them full of drugs under the guise of reconditioning because you want to change them."

Anna gasped, and Harry was vaguely aware he'd revealed more to her than he'd intended, but he was too worked up to care anymore. He glanced over to see her reaction, and was surprised by the horror on her face.

"Is that true?" Anna looked at Martin like she'd never met him before, and Harry was glad her blinders were finally slipping. She turned to Harry with a look of pleading in her eyes. "I didn't know. What happened? What did he do to you?"

Was that compassion Harry saw? Had he misjudged her, and she wasn't trying to manipulate him? Was it possible she was as much a victim of Martin's need to control everything as he was?

It didn't matter, and he didn't care.

"I did what was best for my son." Martin held out his hands like a poor imitation of Jesus preaching to his followers, and Harry wanted to smack the sanctimonious look right off the man's face. "He was an abom—"

"Don't use that word with me ever again." Harry shouted so loudly, the neighbors were probably calling the cops by now. Let them. "You did what was best for Martin Landon. Don't turn this back around on me. This is all about the fact that you can't stand me having feelings for another man. Well. Fuck. You."

"You watch your language in this house. I'm still your father, and I deserve your respect."

"No. You don't. You don't deserve anything from me, especially not my respect." Harry was seething now, and everything that he'd kept locked away was finally coming out like a lanced cyst.

"Let's talk about this rationally." Martin gave Harry his patented smile that said, *You see? I'm not the bad guy here*, and Harry wanted to slap it off his face.

"No. I'm done. I am beyond caring about you, and don't give a shit what you do anymore." Harry poked his finger in front of Martin's face. "But this? This vendetta against me because of my sexual preferences has to end. You are only going to hurt Max with this custody case you're paying for. Is a man who beats his wife so much better an option to you than someone who loves another man? Wouldn't you rather your grandson be in a happy, healthy home with two people who can love each other, and put his needs first?"

Anna was crying, and Harry almost felt sorry for her. He knew she had believed whatever vile story Martin had told her in order to use her, and was finally discovering how wrong she had been.

Martin was silent for so long, Harry felt a small glimmer of hope bloom inside his chest. Was it possible he'd finally gotten through the bastard's thick self-centered personality?

"As long as you continue to go against the natural way of things, I will continue to fight to keep my grandson out of that environment."

Jenny went nuclear. She screamed so loudly, Harry had to cover his ears. Then he watched with a sick sense of satisfaction as she poked Martin in the chest causing him to yelp.

"What the—?" Martin rubbed his chest, and looked around the room, as if he'd find someone holding a cattle prod. Jenny exploded into a magnificent red dust, and Harry almost smiled. She was brilliant when she was in her angry momma bear role.

"Harry." Anna reached out to gently touch Harry's arm. "I'm so sorry. I truly had no idea what his ulterior motives were. Can we please talk? We have our own unresolved issues, and I don't want you to hate me because I was an idiot. Please? Can we go somewhere and talk about it?"

Harry ignored her. She was clueless, and she had picked the wrong side. He turned his full attention on Martin. "Old man, you are a sad, pathetic excuse for a human being who will never know real love, because the concept is unfathomable to you. I almost feel sorry for you. But I don't. If it's a fight you want, it's a fight you'll get. And it will be very public. Do you want that? Because I will never let you take my son away from me."

Harry left his childhood home without a backward glance.

CHAPTER TWENTY-ONE

"I'm not going to lie to you, Harry, this is going to be an uphill battle." Jason pinched the bridge of his nose and tossed the papers Harry had given him onto the coffee table between them. He looked over to where Harry and Luke were sitting together, and Harry could see that Jason was in full-on attorney mode.

Jason was the second person Harry had called after receiving the subpoena. George was the first, and he was sitting next to Jason with his elbows on his knees desperately raking his hands through his hair as he listened to their friend explain the situation.

Harry hadn't doubted that George, as his brother, would drop everything and come to Harry's loft in a heartbeat, but he was eternally grateful, and humbled, that his friend had been willing to do the same.

Jenny had to be going through the same feelings as Harry because she wasn't glowing the way she had been earlier. Her... light... aura... whatever, was gone, and she was blurring around the edges.

"Don't let them take Max away from you, Harry." Jenny's image was wavering in and out, as if, in her fear, she couldn't maintain the energy. "Please don't let Curtis take him."

The thought of Max back in the hands of that madman was too

much for Harry to even consider. He would do whatever it took to keep Max safe.

"What are my chances for keeping my son?" Harry needed something he could hang onto in the hope department. He was beginning to feel like he was being punished for allowing himself to be so happy.

How could he have been so stupid as to have let down his guard after Martin showed up at the barbecue? He knew kissing Luke in front of him was a taunt Martin would never forgive, let alone forget.

"The way I see it, we have several things going against us." Jason leaned forward, and ticked them off on his fingers. "First, your father appears to be footing the bill for Matthews, so he can afford the best attorneys."

Harry still couldn't wrap his head around it. Was his father so against him having a relationship with a man that he would fight to send his grandson to live with a wife-beater?

"That's not too big an obstacle, Jason," George stated. He gave Harry a look that told him they would not give up without a fight. "We can afford the best, too, and we have you."

"I appreciate the compliment, but I couldn't possibly charge for my services in this."

"Jason, you can't—" Harry started to protest, but Jason put up a hand to stop him.

"This is important to me, too, on many levels." Jason turned his steely gaze on Harry and continued, "You and George aren't the only ones who hate your father. And I will fight with everything I have to keep that sweet boy from ending up in an abusive situation. I couldn't help you when we were kids, Harry, but I can sure as hell do whatever I can for you now. Please let me do this for you."

"Thank you." Harry felt his throat tighten, and almost couldn't get the words out. He could hear the finality in Jason's voice, and felt a wave of gratitude toward his life-long friend.

Jason nodded his own thanks, and continued. "The other issues, as I see them, are bigger than money. Like everywhere else, Colorado recognizes same-sex marriage. That said, there are still judges in this state who are openly prejudiced against homosexual relationships."

Jason glanced at Luke, and Harry felt him shift uncomfortably beside him.

"So, now that I have finally swung open the closet door, I have to shut it back up again?" Harry felt like someone had poked a tiny hole in his balloon, and it was seeping air so fast he was going to strangle from it.

"I'm not saying that. But we have to be prepared for the fact that there are people who are in the same homophobic camp as your father." Jason rubbed his face before he went on. "But the biggest hurdle we have is biology. Do you know for sure that Max is your son? What did the paternity tests show?"

"I didn't end up getting paternity tests done. Max freaked out in the waiting area, and I didn't have the heart to force him." Harry wasn't sure if it was good or bad that he hadn't gotten around to going back to the clinic. In his mind, and more importantly, in his heart, Max was his son. It didn't matter to him anymore what any test results proved.

"Besides, his birth certificate claims me as the father. Why should I have to get tests to prove it?"

"I'm sure Jenny didn't deliberately lie on the birth certificate. She could have simply been mistaken. But Matthews's attorneys will contest it."

The room went silent, and Harry looked over at Jenny hoping for answers from her. She stared out of vacant eyes, and her image began to waver.

"What are our chances?" George spoke slowly and calmly, as if he was processing a thought that was slowly taking shape in his mind. "If it turns out that Harry isn't Max's biological father, does Jenny's will hold any weight against Curtis taking him away?"

"It depends. Matthews's attorneys have petitioned for a paternity test, which tells me he believes he's Max's biological father. Either way, he has nothing to lose by the results. If he is, the judge will automatically award him custody. If he's not, he will still fight you, and could still win in the end." Jason looked pointedly at Harry. "What are the chances he's not Max's father?"

Harry glanced at Jenny, who was slowly shaking her head. "You're his father, Harry. You have to be." Jenny crumpled onto the floor, wrapped her arms around her chest and rocked back and forth like a mental patient who had completely disconnected from reality. "You have to be. You just have to be. He can't go back to Curtis. He can't."

In that moment, Harry realized that Jenny didn't know the answer for sure either. She'd probably been going on the hope and assumption it was Harry, but still had her own doubts.

"I don't know," Harry whispered. He felt like his world had just tipped over a cliff.

It was a bad case of déjà vu, being parked outside the clinic again. Only this time, Harry wanted the result to prove he was Max's biological father, instead of the other way around.

What would happen if he started the car up again and drove away? What if they just kept driving? Harry had resources. He could probably run with Max indefinitely, and they could just keep moving.

No. That wouldn't be fair to Max. He needed stability in his life, especially now. He was making friends at school, and had a healthy supportive family system – provided Harry could keep Martin far, far away from them.

He turned to Max, who was sitting in the front seat, but hadn't said a word since pulling into the clinic parking lot.

"I know what you're thinking, Max, and it isn't true." Harry wanted to weep watching his son – and he didn't care what anyone said, Max was his son – retreat into his shell. "We aren't here because I want to be, we're here because we have to be."

Max glanced at Harry but still didn't meet his eyes, and Harry knew he didn't believe him.

"It's a very complicated story, but Curtis wants you to come back and live with him."

"I won't go back to him. And he's not my dad." Max's bellow was loud enough to wake the dead. "If you don't want me, then I'll go away." Max unbuckled his seatbelt, and started to open the passenger door before Harry stopped him.

"Whoa there, buddy." Harry grabbed Max's arm to keep him from leaping out of the car. He was angry that Max still had doubts about being wanted. He'd thought they were over this hump. "Don't ever again believe that I don't want you. You have to get that out of your head once and for all."

Harry felt like a jerk for yelling, and he took a deep breath to calm himself down. He had to remember that Max was only a nine-year-old boy, who had all kinds of crap heaped on top of the normal issues of a kid his age. Max couldn't help having suspicions about the men in his life – look who he'd had for examples. Harry took a moment to calm down before he continued.

"I know I didn't give you much to go on with trusting me in the beginning, but I care about you. More than anything. And I'm going to do everything possible to keep you. You are my son, no matter what anyone tries to say. In my heart, you are my son. Do you believe me?"

Max took a long time to answer, and Harry was worried they might never get over this hump. "Yes. I believe you."

Harry was so relieved, he had to stop himself from reaching out and hugging Max. He wasn't out of the woods yet.

"I promise, I will always be honest with you, Max. I wish I could promise that everything will be okay, but sometimes dads are wrong to make that promise when they might have to break it. Do you understand that?"

Max nodded, but Harry could tell by the hope in his eyes that he still wanted Harry to tell him nothing bad was going to happen. But with Martin involved, bad was definitely going to happen eventually.

"Do you remember meeting that man at the barbecue who showed up but wasn't invited?" Harry wasn't sure how he was going to explain a lifetime of complications in a few minutes, but he'd promised to be honest, and that meant at least giving it a try. And he didn't want Max to be sideswiped by anything that might happen because of Martin.

"The mean guy? The one who called you names?" Max's eyes narrowed, and Harry could tell he didn't seem to like Martin any more than Harry did. Smart kid.

"Yeah, that guy." Harry took a deep breath and tried to check his emotions. If he let Martin get him all worked up again, he'd never get through this. "That guy is my father, and you should probably know that he's helping Curtis try to take you away from me."

"He's your father? Then how can he be so mean to you?"

Well, shit. That was a really good question. It was the same question Harry had been asking himself for almost thirty years. How was he supposed to explain something he didn't understand himself?

"See, the thing is—"

"Is he like Curtis? He's just a mean person?"

"I don't really know Curtis, but from what you and your mom have told me about him, yeah, I think they are similar types of people. Except, where Curtis uses his fists to hit, Martin uses his words. Both are really hard to bounce back from."

Max turned away for a moment as if processing that new information in his head, before he asked, "But why are they so mean all the time?"

"I don't really know, Max." Harry sighed, and felt deeply inadequate to be having such a difficult and philosophical discussion with a nine-year-old boy. But if this is what Max needed to talk about, then he would do his best. He just hoped like hell he didn't screw him up for life. He definitely saw counseling in their future. For both of them.

"Sometimes," he continued, carefully navigating his words like walking through a minefield, "a person just believes so much that they are right about something, they don't care how much they hurt people in order to hold onto it. For them, it can be worse to admit they might be wrong. It's about having all the control, having all the power. Maybe Curtis needed to feel like he was bigger than you and your mom, and the only way he could prove that to himself was to make sure he kept your mom smaller by hitting her."

"But that's not right." Max's voice broke, and Harry could tell he was fighting not to give in to the tears.

"No, son, it isn't. And sometimes, there's nothing you can do about it." Harry pulled Max across the console and into his lap. "It's okay to cry, buddy. I've got you."

Max buried his face in Harry's chest and cried while Harry rubbed his back and murmured into his ear. "I couldn't be there to help your mom, but I'm going to do my damnedest to be here for you. You just need to always remember that. It doesn't matter what results come out of that clinic today, I am your father, and I will do everything I can to protect you."

Harry wrapped his arms more tightly around Max, and waited for him to cry himself out.

CHAPTER TWENTY-TWO

"I'm so sorry, Harry." Jason sat in the guest chair on the other side of the desk, but Harry felt like he might as well be sitting in another universe.

Nothing after the words, "conclusive of Curtis Matthew as the biological father" seemed to be registering in Harry's brain. He'd been sitting at his desk, reviewing the new manuscript of a horror author, and wondering why he'd been stuck with it instead of George, when the horror of real life blew into his office in the form of a legal test.

Then blew his beautiful life to smithereens.

He had immediately called Jason, hoping he would be able to save the day with some kind of legal miracle.

"I wish there was something I could do, but legally, Curtis Matthews has all the power." Jason's words made Harry suck in a breath as if he had been physically punched. He didn't even notice that Jason had left his office, and closed the door to give Harry some privacy.

It had all been too good to be true. He had known, somewhere in the back of his mind, that he hadn't deserved this new, blissfully idyllic existence. He'd known he was going to end up standing here in the middle of the carnage of his life because this is what Martin did best.

Martin devastated the people around him with one swift slice through what mattered the most to them.

That wife-beating, miserable excuse of a human being was Max's father. And there wasn't anything Harry could do to keep the bastard from taking away the boy who had become the son of his heart.

The worst part was that Max had started having nightmares again. He'd had them every night since their trip to the clinic four days ago. The kid was no dummy, and he'd obviously put two and two together to come up with what amounted to the end of the world to him.

Harry looked out at the majestic mountains that laid the backdrop of downtown Denver, and tried to feel something – anything – a glimmer of emotion that could prove he was still among the living.

But he felt dead inside.

Except that he couldn't be dead, because he was still breathing, and every breath he took sent sharp pains like icicles to his still-beating heart.

He had let Max down. He had promised him safety and love, and now he was going to be forced to turn him over to a monster. Jason had made it very clear that the courts would side with the biological father, and then Max would be gone from Harry's life forever.

He didn't know how he was going to get through it. Thank god for Luke. And Sheldon. Sheldon kept Max calm during the nightmares, and Luke kept Harry from beating his head into a wall.

"Harry?" Anna opened his office door, and poked her head inside. She looked hesitant, as if she was uncertain of the kind of reception she would receive from him.

Chilly. That's the kind of reception she would receive from him. Hostile was another option. He just wasn't sure he had the energy for either.

"What the hell are you doing here?" Harry wanted to pick her up and throw her from his office window. Maybe falling fifty floors would make her feel even the smallest fraction of the pain he was going through. All because she'd brought Martin back into his life by telling him about Luke.

"I came to help."

Was she serious?

"Little too little. Little too late. Or haven't you heard the good news for Team Shitty Fathers? You won. Matthews is Max's biological father."

Anna gasped, and Harry knew this was the first she'd heard the news. "I'm so sorry," she whispered, but Harry was beyond caring what Anna thought.

He swiveled his chair around, giving her his back. "Get out."

"I know you hate me right now, Harry, but please listen to what I have to say." She moved to the front of his desk, and sat in one of his guest chairs, like she was there for an interview. "We can fix this. I can help you beat Martin, and keep Max. Curtis Matthews doesn't want Max, he only wants the money Martin is offering. If we cut off the money, Curtis Matthews will slither right back under the rock where Martin found him."

"Why should I believe anything you say to me?" Harry whirled around and poured every ounce of hatred into his voice to scare her away. He wanted her out of his office, and out of his life for good. "You brought Martin back into my life. He never would have known about Luke, or Max, if you hadn't told him."

"I was jealous." Anna fiddled with her hands, which were resting in her lap. "I didn't like that you were spending more time with Luke than with me, when I was the one you were supposed to be dating. So, I got pissy, and whined about it to Martin."

"We weren't dating, Anna. That's the problem. You were living in some dating dreamworld that didn't exist, and I couldn't seem to talk you out of it. Even before all the confusion over you being a sibling or not, we were finished. I was done dating you. But you wouldn't let it go." He probably shouldn't have been so harsh about it, but he wanted her to feel pain. He was in pain, so why shouldn't she be, too? He didn't want to forgive her.

"Please." Anna looked up at him with tears and desperation brimming in her eyes. "Please listen to what I have to say first. There is a way you can keep Max, and I can help you."

Harry knew he wasn't going to like whatever it was she had to say, but at this point, he would sell his soul to the devil to keep his son. So, he waited, both fearing and hoping for whatever it was she planned to say.

"I can get Martin to drop everything, and kick Curtis Matthews to the curb in a heartbeat. Matthews is a drunk and a waste of space on this planet. Martin hates Matthews."

"And yet, he's willing to pay the asshole's legal expenses to take away my son, all because I happen to be in love with a man."

Anna flinched, and Harry couldn't tell if it was because of his remark about Martin, or because he'd said he loved a man. Was she just as homophobic as Martin?

"Why are you so willing to help me all of a sudden?" Harry was afraid to get his hopes up, but she had his attention.

"I was wrong." She looked back down at her hands, and Harry could see that she at least seemed contrite. "In the interest of full disclosure, I should tell you that when I first found out about Curtis Matthews, and that it was possible he was Max's father, I didn't feel it was right for Max to stay with you. I've always believed that a child should be with his – or her – biological parents."

"His biological father is a piece of shit. That didn't bother you at all?" Harry stood up from his chair. He couldn't seem to sit still in front of her. He wanted to walk out the door and not listen to anything else she had to say. But he had to at least hear her out if there was a chance she could do what she'd said.

"Yes." She said it so quietly, Harry almost didn't hear it. "But I didn't know that at the time. And I had no idea Martin would react so strongly when I whined about Luke to him. I swear to you, Harry, it was only a stupid, passing comment that I made. But Martin jumped all over it, and started asking all these questions about you and Luke, and I had no idea what he was doing. You have to believe me when I say that I don't want Max going to Curtis Matthews now either. I've tried to talk to Martin, to get him to drop his support. But he refuses."

"Jesus." He started pacing, because he had to continue to move to keep from wrapping his hands around her neck and squeezing the life out of her.

"I'm sorry." She sounded like she had something stuck in her throat, but Harry refused to look at her. If she was crying, he would be conflicted over what to do about it. And she didn't deserve his forgiveness or his sympathy.

"I love you," Anna continued. "I've loved you since the first moment we met when my brother, Dean, and I came to pitch his book to Landon Literary. George wouldn't have anything to do with us, but you were so open and willing. You bravely defied your older brother, and I couldn't help but fall in love with you on the spot. You were my hero."

Harry was flummoxed. All he could do was stare at her in disbelief. Was she crazy? He wasn't a hero. A hero would have been able to find a way to keep Max.

"But you knew from the minute I found out you were my sister that we could never be anything more than just friends."

"We're not related—"

"It doesn't matter." He spat the words at her. She could argue about it until they were both blue in the face, but it wouldn't change anything. He was still in love with Luke. And he was still going to lose his son. Why was she bringing this up?

"I didn't like that Luke was distracting you from our relationship. You spent more time with him than you did with me."

"There was no relationship with us. You and I were never going to be in anything more than a friendship."

"I know that, now." Her words came out in a rush, like she was trying to defuse the bomb that was about to explode from his head. "But at the time... Like I said, I was jealous. I think I knew, even then, that you were interested in Luke. I guess I thought I could change your mind or something, because I knew you were also interested in me. At least, in the beginning." She spoke the words quietly, as if realizing how ridiculous they sounded, and was ashamed of them. "But please believe me, Harry, I never would have said anything to Martin if I had known how he would react. I never wanted it to come to this."

"Well, it did. And I'm going to lose my son because you 'got pissy' and couldn't accept reality." Harry had never felt so betrayed in his life. But he did have to give her some credit for coming here and admitting it all to him.

"I'm sorry. For everything." She turned to look him full in the face. She had gumption, and he'd always admired that about her. "I see how important Max has become to you, and I know now that he was better off with you than with Curtis Matthews, and I tried to get Martin to back off. But he's so freaked out by your relationship with Luke that he can't see Matthews for what he is."

"Why the hell does it matter to him?" Harry couldn't believe how, after all these years without any contact, his father still had to push his point. "Why does he even care? I'm not even in his life."

"Don't you see?" Anna came over and placed her hand on his arm. He flinched, but she didn't seem to notice. "It's all about appearance for him. He believes that what you do – what we all do – reflects back on him, and you are a blemish on his perfect existence by being in love with a man. But we can turn this around on him. We can make him believe he's won. But in reality, we'll be flipping him the bird."

Harry broke away and returned to his chair so that the desk was between them, and she couldn't touch him again. She was starting to freak him out. "We all know already that Martin believes he's God. How does this have anything to do with how I'm going to be able to keep Max?"

"It's simple." She sat back down in her chair and looked him straight in the eyes. "You and I will get married."

CHAPTER TWENTY-THREE

"Are you out of your goddamned mind?" Luke was livid, if the stiff posture and flushed face were any indication.

Harry couldn't blame him for being so angry, but he'd never seen Luke lose his temper before. He was always so calm, and unflappable. But when he did finally let loose, it was spectacular. He looked like some demigod of war, ready to go out and start kicking some enemy ass. He was gorgeous, inside and out, and it broke Harry's heart even more that he was the cause of making Luke lose control.

It had taken Anna three terminally long days to convince Martin that she and Harry were serious. Yesterday, she had given Harry the news that she'd convinced Martin to agree to dump his support of Matthews, but not until "the day I watch you and Harry exchange vows in the eyes of the Church."

That happy day was going to be in six more days.

Matthews officially withdrew his claim for custody after he found out he would no longer have Martin's support. Anna had been right. Apparently, without Martin's money, Matthews decided he didn't want another mouth to feed.

"You're seriously considering marrying that crazy woman?"

"What other choice do I have?" Harry was exhausted, and wanted to give in to his own frustration. Trying to remain stoic was giving him a headache. He didn't want to fight, and he knew Luke didn't either, but they had to work through this. "A judge will order me to hand him over to Matthews. I don't have a fighting chance in court, at least not without some evidence proving he's abusive. Even then, there's not much hope over the fact that he is Max's biological father. If I have a way to keep that bastard from taking away my son, then I have to take it."

"That bastard being your father or Max's?"

Harry felt like he'd just been verbally slapped. "*I'm* Max's father. I don't give a shit what an—-"

"I know. I'm sorry," Luke said softly. "That was a terrible thing to say, and I'm sorry." He laid his hand on Harry's cheek, and continued. "I'm struggling here, and I lashed out. It wasn't nice, and I regret it. But I don't know how to react or even what to say. Since the day I moved into this building, I knew you would be someone significant in my life. I craved your attention, falling in love with you more and more with every minute we spent together, everything we did together."

"You have more than my attention. I love you, too." Harry closed his eyes, and let the feel of Luke's hand on his face seep into his core and his memories. He reached up and closed his hand over Luke's, wishing he could hold it there forever. Luke was the best thing to happen to Harry, and he didn't want to ever lose that.

But the other best thing was Max, and he couldn't abandon him. He was only a nine-year-old boy, and Harry would do anything possible to protect him. Even if that meant losing the man of his heart, and marrying a woman he could never love.

"Do you have feelings for her?" Luke stepped back, looking as though the reality of the situation had finally sunk in, and he wanted to hit something. "Will this be a marriage in name only, or are you going to sleep with her, too?"

Harry wanted to be angry – he felt betrayed that Luke had even asked – but he wasn't entirely surprised by it. He would probably be asking the same question if their roles were reversed. Perhaps, with time, he and Anna would feel a friendship in their marriage, but that would be all. Not that it mattered. Max mattered. Max wouldn't be able to protect himself if he ended up back with Matthews, so Harry would make sure that never happened.

He took a deep breath and tried to stay calm while his world seemed to be imploding around him. "I understand why you're asking. This is all just as confusing to me as it is to you. I have dated women – enjoyed dating women – in the past, but none of those previous relationships came close to what I feel for you." Harry tried to close the distance between them, but Luke took a self-defensive step back. "I don't want to give you up either. After I marry Anna, and am sure that Max is safe with me--"

"What about you and me?" Luke demanded.

"We can figure something out." Harry reached out to pull him into his arms. But Luke pulled back even more, as if he was afraid he'd be scorched, and Harry's anger ignited. "What, exactly, do you expect me to do, Luke? Do you want me to let them take Max from me without lifting a finger to do anything to prevent it?"

"That's not what I'm saying."

"Well, you're sure not making this any easier on me either." Harry's restraint snapped, and he knew he was venting his anger out on the wrong person, but he couldn't help himself. He was frustrated, angry, hurt, and a whole bushel of other negative emotions he couldn't even identify, but that were threatening to send him to bed with the covers over his head for the rest of his life. "It's not like I have a whole ton of options. Anna is my only option. If I want to keep Max, I have to take Anna in the process. What I need to know from you is, where does that leave us?"

Harry held his breath, waiting for Luke to continue – to give him some hope that they weren't permanently broken. But Luke only stood there, staring at Harry as if he was trying to memorize every last detail of his face.

"I don't know." Luke sounded as worn out as Harry felt, and again

Harry reached out to him, wanting nothing more than to hold him and tell him everything was going to be okay.

But Luke took another step back, sadly shook his head like he was in a trance, and repeated, "I don't know."

Then he walked out of the condo, leaving Harry alone and afraid.

"This is all wrong." Jenny's voice had the impact of an air-raid siren, and Harry couldn't stop himself from covering his ears. "Go after him. Tell him you didn't mean it. You can't marry Anna. You have to marry Luke. You love Luke, you idiot!"

"If you'd been paying attention, instead of floating in and out whenever you damned-well felt like it, you would know that this is the only way." Harry threw the full force of his hurt and anger at her, which was coming out of his pores like a poisonous gas. "Did you happen to miss the fact that I'm not Max's biological father? You lied to me, Jenny."

"I didn't lie to you," she yelled. "I didn't know. Not for sure."

"Yeah, well, this is the consequence of that." Harry was too beat up to stand. He collapsed into the couch, and held his head in his hands, trying to hold back the urge to scream. Or cry. Or throw things. "If your plan to transition was based on me adopting Max, *and* living happily ever after with Luke, you came up short. No wonder you're still here."

He was being mean, and vindictive, but he couldn't help himself. If he was hurting, she should have to hurt, too. She's the one who got him into this mess in the first place.

"It's not too late. I can fix this. Just don't do anything stupid until I get back."

"What the hell are you talking about?" Harry looked up, ready to yell at her again, but she was already gone.

CHAPTER TWENTY-FOUR

Harry had agonized over what to tell Max ever since getting back the DNA results. He was afraid if he let him in on their plans, and give him hope, Max would go into a tailspin and never recover if the whole thing fell apart in the end.

Harry was beginning to realize that he might have been too hard on Anna, and he was getting used to having her around, even after a few days. She had let slip in their conversations that her relationship with Martin had been less than stellar, and that there had been times when she'd felt non-existent to him. Harry understood all too well what it was like trying so desperately to please a man who only cared about himself.

It felt kind of like when he and Anna were dating, and he was glad that they were even enjoying each other's company. He believed it would be an easy marriage. Just not an intimate one. But he would live with that.

If he could stop thinking about Luke.

Kind, gentle, strong Luke.

Infinitely patient, compassionate Luke.

He hadn't seen or heard from Luke since he'd walked out, and he was beginning to wonder if he would ever see him again.

Harry knocked on Max's bedroom door, and went into his room. Max was sitting on his bed reading, but he looked up when Harry knocked.

"Hey, buddy. Got a sec? I need to talk to you." Harry sat down on the side of the bed. Max had bruises under his eyes from lack of sleep, and looked almost as hollowed out as he did the first day Harry had met him. If Harry still had any doubts about marrying Anna, this was even more evidence that he was doing the right thing.

"You know how Anna has been coming around a lot lately, and spending time with us?"

"Yeah, she's nice."

"Yeah, she is." Harry smiled at Max to show his agreement. "And I'm glad you like her, because... see... the thing is... Anna and I are getting married in a few days."

"I don't get it." Max scrunched up his face and looked like he was trying to understand some strange and ancient language Harry was speaking. "How can you marry Anna, if you're going to marry Luke? Isn't that against the law or something?"

Harry didn't know whether he wanted to hug Max, or run from the room. All Max saw was that he and Luke loved each other. All Martin saw was two men committing a crime against nature.

Why the whole world couldn't see things through the eyes of this sweet nine-year-old boy, was beyond anything Harry could answer.

"I'm not going to marry Luke." The words threatened to choke him, as the thought drove home the reality of his situation. He hadn't heard from Luke since their argument, and he was afraid he never would again. He coughed to clear his throat and continued. "I'm going to marry Anna. Then you can stay here with us, and you won't have to go live with Matthews."

"I won't have to live with Curtis?" Max looked like he wanted desperately to believe Harry, but was bracing himself for Matthews to show up at any second and haul him off anyway. Then Max threw his arms around Harry, almost knocking them both off the bed. "I get to stay here with you?"

"Yes." Harry squeezed his son, relishing the fact that he would get to continue to hold him for many more years to come. Another reaffirmation to himself of why he had chosen Anna. "You can stay with me for as long as you want."

"Where will Luke and Sheldon live?"

"Luke and Sheldon are going to stay in their own place, but they can still visit whenever they want." Harry sincerely hoped that was the truth.

"What happened? Don't you love Luke anymore?"

Harry fought hard not to cry. He couldn't tell Max the truth. None of it was his fault, but he would believe it was, and Harry would never allow that. He loved this boy with his whole being, and he knew that, given time, he would learn to share his life with Anna for the benefit of Max.

"Luke and I didn't work out like that." Harry had to stop and clear the boulder from his throat again. "We still care about each other, but we weren't meant to be together like Anna and I are."

Harry needed to wrap this up before he started sobbing, and he pasted on a brilliant smile to show Max he was happy. He also hated that he was probably giving his son the wrong impression of what made up a *real family*, but that was a lesson for another day. "So, in a few days, I'm going to marry Anna. Will you be my best man?"

"Sure, I guess. What does a best man do?" Max looked like he wasn't buying the fake smile, so Harry toned it down a bit.

"It's easy, but it's the most important job." The earnest excitement on Max's face gave Harry the conviction he needed. "You have to hang onto the rings until it's time for us to put them on our fingers. Think you can handle that for me? Grooms can be really nervous, and I might lose them if you put me in charge of them."

"Yes!" Max jumped up and down on the bed. "I'll be the best Best Man ever."

"I know you will. That's why I asked you." Harry took a moment to enjoy Max's exuberance before getting up to go. Max settled back down to read his book again, and Harry left his room.

It was time to go ring shopping.

CHAPTER TWENTY-FIVE

Harry was exhausted. He felt like he was coming down with something. Every. Single. Part. Of his body seemed to take a Herculean effort to make move.

He was getting married in four days, and he felt like a shotgun wedding groom. Anna was being great, and he grew more used to her as the days dragged by. He was fond of her.

As a sister.

But he ached for Luke.

He hadn't heard anything from him since they'd argued, and Harry was beginning to despair that he would ever hear from him again. He'd tried to call Luke, but kept getting his voicemail, and couldn't seem to form the right words to leave a message.

He felt like he was facing a death sentence instead of his wedding day.

And where the hell was Jenny? She had disappeared completely. Again. He felt awful that they'd fought before she disappeared. He missed her – which, in and of itself was a startling revelation – and wished she was around to talk to about everything that was going on with him.

He had grown used to having her there all the time, and now he felt her absence like some task he kept forgetting to do. Had she transitioned and not said good-bye? It would serve him right. It had been wrong for him to throw that in her face, but he'd been so messed up at the time.

When the doorbell rang, he was too tired to answer it, hoping whoever it was would go away. But, it might be Max, back from his playdate with Spencer, and he'd probably forgotten his key again.

Harry sighed heavily, then dragged his carcass to the door and opened it.

To Luke.

Harry's heart fluttered in his chest, and he wanted to throw his arms around Luke and kiss him until they both passed out from lack of oxygen. But one look at Luke's face stopped him like a freight train running full-on into a concrete barrier.

Luke looked like he hadn't slept since the day he left Harry's condo. His bloodshot eyes were puffy, and rimmed in dark circles that made him look like he'd gone a few rounds with a prize-fighter, and lost. He had his hands in his jeans pockets, and his stance vibrated the words *don't touch me.*

"No." Luke said the word so quietly, Harry almost didn't hear it.

But he did hear it, and he felt like he'd just been shot.

Luke shook his head, then slowly removed a hand from his pocket and reached out. He stopped just short of cupping Harry's face, as if he didn't trust himself to make contact.

Harry wanted to lean his head the rest of the way into Luke's hand, but instinctively knew that wouldn't go over very well. He stood there, bleeding internally from the virtual blow to his heart, waiting for Luke to continue.

"I understand," Luke finally said, and his voice was hoarse. "I do. My head tells me that you're doing the right thing. For Max."

Luke smiled a sad smile that only emphasized the bleakness in his eyes. "I just wish there was another way to do it without sacrificing our happiness together. But, please believe me when I tell you, I do understand."

Harry wished he'd never opened the door. If he hadn't, he could have kept on pretending there was still hope. But he knew this was not going to end the way he wanted it to, and he had to fight the urge to run screaming.

Instead, he stood there, and let Luke say his piece. Luke deserved that at the very least.

"You had to choose Max," Luke continued, and each word tore another piece out of Harry's soul. "And, I'm glad you did. The way you care about him is only one of the many reasons I love you. He needs you. He's a great kid, and he's damned lucky to have you."

Luke dropped his hand, and stepped back. Harry could see him shutting down all emotion, as if arming himself for battle. He stood ramrod straight and looked blankly back at Harry, like he was reciting lines he'd rehearsed. "But I can't be the other man in a marriage. I won't be. That isn't fair to anyone. It would end up confusing Max, and torturing me. I want all of you. And if I can't have that, then I won't settle for just a piece of you."

"What are you saying?" Harry felt the panic swell in his throat, and threaten to choke him.

"I'm leaving Denver. I can't be here and pretend it isn't killing me not to be with the man I've waited my whole life for." Luke started to leave, but Harry was desperate to stop him.

"No, wait. Please. We'll figure something out." He couldn't lose the man it had taken him so long to find. "How am I supposed to do this without you?"

Luke gave Harry one last longing look, before he turned to leave. "I'm sorry."

And then he was gone.

CHAPTER TWENTY-SIX

Harry wandered aimlessly into the living room, and sprawled onto the couch. He wished he could undergo some type of surgical procedure to remove Luke from his head.

And his heart.

And his soul.

He rubbed his chest, trying to ease the pain that had taken up permanent residence there since the day Luke left. But he knew it wouldn't help. Yesterday, a moving truck arrived and movers packed up Luke's condo. It drove away later in the afternoon, and then there was nothing left of the man who had become so much a part of his life.

"I'm sorry about Luke." Anna sat down next to Harry on the couch, and placed her hand on his leg. She came over to talk about last minute details for tomorrow's service with the Justice of the Peace – because they sure as hell weren't doing this in a church, no matter what Martin wanted -- and had just finished putting Max to bed. Harry was glad she was here, because he was exhausted. Emotionally, physically, spiritually, and psychologically exhausted.

"Can we just... not." Harry leaned his head back, closed his eyes, and willed her to get the hint that he didn't have the energy to talk about Luke. Especially not with his future wife.

"I know you love him." She either missed his not-so-subtle hint, or chose to ignore it. "And I want you to know it's okay if you want to talk about him."

"I don't want to talk about him." Harry knew she meant well, and that she was trying to understand his feelings, but he couldn't discuss this with her. He had finally reached the conclusion that she wasn't the one to blame – he knew who the real culprit was in this whole scenario – but his break with Luke was still too close to the surface. The only evidence he'd once had a heart was the gaping crater left inside his chest, and he couldn't bring himself to talk about any of it. "I'm fine."

"You aren't fine. I can see it." She persisted in spite of him trying to shut her down. "You aren't getting cold feet, are you? I completely understand if you are. But you know that, in order to beat Martin, we do need to get married. You aren't going to leave me at the altar like your last fiancée, are you?"

Harry decided that question was too ridiculous to waste time with an answer. Instead, he gave her an eye roll.

Anna took a deep breath, as if gearing up to drop an emotional bomb, which caused Harry to open one eye and look at her with suspicion. "That said, though... If you and Luke want to continue to have a relationship after we're married, I won't stand in your way."

She had gotten the sentence out as if was one long word, like it had been building up inside of her waiting to break out at any minute.

Harry was astonished. Had she just offered to let him keep Luke on the side? He wasn't sure why he was surprised, he'd thought of it himself for one moment, but he never expected to hear Anna suggest it. He gaped at her, unable to come up with a single thing to say in response.

"Believe it or not, Harry, I do care about you. I've watched you these last few days, and I've seen how much you miss having him around. I don't want a marriage where you will always resent me for being in the way of having a relationship with the man you love. I don't want to be the bad guy here. We can figure something out."

"I don't know what to say."

"Call him." She patted his leg for emphasis. "Martin doesn't ever have to find out. It can be our secret, and we will always know we beat him at his own game." She grinned conspiratorially, and Harry could see that she meant every word.

If only it could be that simple.

"He left Denver." The empty crater in his chest started bleeding all over again. "I've tried to call him, but his number is no longer in service."

He couldn't tell her that he'd already made the same offer to Luke behind her back. She was trying to work something out for him, and he didn't want to diminish her kindness by telling her he'd already planned to do that very thing. Besides, Luke had turned him down, so there wasn't any point in thinking about it.

"Oh, I'm so sorry." She looked like someone who'd just been told there was no tooth fairy, and Harry was again struck by her generosity.

She was a better person than he was.

"Thank you." Harry covered her hand with his, and looked at her for the first time since she sat down. He saw love and compassion in her eyes, and he realized that he could love her. Like he had loved Jenny. As a good friend, someone he could grow old with as a companion. He would never feel the deep physical and emotional connection that he'd shared with Luke, but he could care for her, in time.

Anna had stopped by the loft often over the last several days, claiming she wanted to "get to know Max," and Harry had to admit he was grateful for her gestures. She was putting a lot of effort into making this work. The least he could do was support her, and participate.

"Okay," Anna said, as she rose from the couch and began gathering her things together. "Well, tomorrow's the big day, and I have a few million things left to do, so I'll get out of your hair."

"Anna." She turned from the front door when he called after her. He wanted to tell her how much he appreciated everything she was doing for him, but he didn't know how to navigate through the jumble of emotions he was feeling. "Really. Thank you."

She nodded her head and smiled at him, then gently closed the door when she left.

"Holy crap. I leave you alone for a couple of days, and everything goes to shit from Sheboygan."

Anna wasn't gone two minutes, when Jenny was suddenly standing over him, her finger poised over his chest like she was about to give him one of her signature jolts. And not the nice one, either. It was as if she'd been waiting for Anna to leave before daring to pop in and start harassing him.

And cussing at him.

That was something new that she'd picked up in the afterlife.

"I told you not to do anything stupid. You can't marry her. If you marry her, you won't be happy, and I will end up stuck here forever." Jenny jabbed her finger toward Harry again.

"Poke me with that finger, woman, and I swear to god I'll go get the vacuum and suck you right out of existence." He wasn't sure that would even work, but he was in no mood for her antics. "It's already decided. I'm marrying Anna to keep Max. I have to do what's best for my son."

"You have to marry Luke. Luke is the one who'll make you happy. If you don't marry him, I'll never be able to leave here."

"And if I marry him, I'll lose Max. He'll end up back with that asshole you married, who beat the shit out of you. Do you want that?" Harry was going out of his mind. If what Jessica said was right, then Jenny would never be able to move on, but he couldn't save everyone. He couldn't even save himself. He had to save Max. No one else mattered as much.

"How did this happen?" Jenny looked like she was about four chapters behind in a psychological thriller.

"Where the hell have you been?" Harry was too tired to explain. "You just disappeared."

"I've been busy. I think I have something on Curtis. Some of it you'll have to go get, of course, but I think we might be able to put him away so you can keep Max for good."

"What are you talking about?" Harry didn't want to get his hopes up, but he would love to see Matthews behind bars. Maybe then he wouldn't have to marry Anna, and he could still get custody of Max.

"I left evidence – pictures, doctor's reports, stuff like that – at the women's shelter where we were staying. It's still there, I just checked. I hid it when Max and I moved in, just in case I ever needed it. Like now."

"Why the hell didn't you use it to put him away when you were alive?"

"Where would I take it? To his cronies at the Bear Forest Sheriff's Department?" She fisted her hands on her hips and glared at him like he was too stupid keep up with her in the conversation. "I told you what happened the last time I tried to get the police involved. I would not have survived another 'reminder' of who was in charge at our house. Plus, I think I figured out what Curtis was talking about in the car before I had the accident, when he said I'd gotten him into trouble with his cronies."

"What did you find?" Harry wasn't sure if being a ghost had finally turned her into a stark, raving, lunatic, or if she really had found something they could use on Matthews.

"I stole a stack of bills I found in his duffel before I took Max and ran." She grinned at Harry, as if that explained everything, but he was still in the dark.

"Annnddd...?"

"It turned out to be ten grand! I think he was supposed to use it to pay their dealer." Jenny was so excited, she was bouncing like a balloon. Literally bouncing, because her feet never connected with the floor.

"Dealer? What dealer? What are you talking about?"

"That's what I'm trying to tell you. That's where I've been this whole time. I followed Curtis. I heard him telling his Sheriff's office buddies that he would be able to pay them back soon. They were not happy with him, to say the least."

"He owes them money?" Harry was still confused, but things were starting to settle into place.

"They weren't happy that he'd 'lost' ten thousand dollars, because the suppliers were making demands and bitching about reputation, and how they weren't sure they should be trusting the good people in the Bear Forest Sheriff's Department." Jenny snorted. "Talk about irony."

"So, that's why he wants Max. Or rather, why he wants Martin's money to take Max."

"You have to go get it, and take it to Detective Jackson. Everything is still where I left it at the shelter. It's all there. I was afraid to spend the money, because I thought Curtis might have been able to find me through it."

"How am I supposed to get anywhere near a battered women's shelter? In case you hadn't noticed, I'm not the right sex."

"Stop being so negative. I'll be with you every step of the way. I'll tell you exactly what to say to get them to let you inside my room. But we have to hurry, before another woman moves into it. And before you do something really idiotic, like marry Anna as some kind of vendetta against Martin, instead of marrying Luke. You are such a dumbass."

"Oh, really?" Harry was furious that she could say that to him. "I was willing to do anything to keep Matthews from getting his hands on my son. You were certainly no help. You disappeared."

"I know, and I'm sorry." She reached out and caressed his arm using her soothing energy. "But it was very important, and I'm here now. You can't marry Anna. Not when you love Luke. You know that, right?"

"No, I don't know that. All I know is that Max is the most important person, and he needs my protection."

"You're a good father, Harry Landon. I knew you were the perfect choice, even if it took you a while to figure it out." She smiled at him, and he believed that anything was possible. Somehow, he knew she would make this right for him, and he felt better than he had since the whole Matthews mess got started.

"None of this is hard enough evidence to convince any jury though, Jenny. The pictures and doctor records prove that you were beat up, but the money isn't going to be traceable back to Matthews or the Bear Forest Sheriff's Department."

"Call Detective Jackson. Tell him everything."

"Everything? Like the fact that I've been talking to my dead ex-fiancée's ghost?" Harry would end up being the one arrested if he told him that.

"No, obviously not that part. Let's get the evidence before it disappears, and then you can take it to Detective Jackson."

"Fine. I'm pretty sure I'm going to regret this, but at this point, I'm desperate enough to try anything."

"We're going to have to be careful about how we handle Curtis." Jenny began pacing the room, which Harry found distracting because she wasn't bothering to go around any of the furniture. She simply went through it. "We need him to believe he still has a chance at your father's money, or he'll bolt and go straight back to his cop buddies. Then we'll never get to him no matter how much evidence we have on him or them."

"You know that those cop friends of his don't have nearly the power you keep giving them, don't you?" He spoke as carefully as he could, knowing that even as a ghost, she still had an irrational fear of them. "Even they won't be able to protect Curtis against charges of spousal abuse."

Jenny smiled maniacally. "It would be nice to get him for involuntary manslaughter, because I know he's the one who really killed me, not the car accident. That's a felony crime, and he could get at least four years in prison."

"You've been planning this a while, haven't you? Even before you died."

"Yes, but I didn't know what they were doing until now. I really want to get him, and all his buddies in the sheriff's department at

Bear Forest, and expose them for the dirty rotten drug dealers they are."

"Jesus, Jenny. Why didn't you tell me this before?"

"I didn't know before. I told you how I knew Curtis was into something with those guys, because every now and then he'd come home with a wad of cash. But the one time I asked him about it, he got so angry I ended up in bed for a week. I learned to stop asking questions, and just keep my eyes and ears open."

"If I'd known this, I would have taken Max and run with him." Harry felt sick at the thought of how Max had almost ended up in that life. "I never would have even considered letting Matthews get his hands on him."

"Last night, I found their base camp, or whatever you call it. I was following Curtis around, hoping to get something else on him, and he led me straight there. There are some advantages to being a ghost." Jenny smiled, and her image flared brighter. "So, you need to call Detective Jackson right now."

"I'll call him. And I'm also going to get Blake involved, see what he might be able to dig up. I'll call both of them on the way out to the women's shelter. Let's hit him with everything we can."

CHAPTER TWENTY-SEVEN

"He's not going to show. Someone surely tipped him off, and he's already in the wind." Jenny was walking beside Harry up 16th Street Mall, not paying any attention to the sensations she was causing every time she walked through someone on the sidewalk.

"Would you relax? You're starting to sound like a cheap detective novel." The stress was apparently getting the better of her, which was not a good thing, because it was spreading to Harry and he was already nervous enough on his own.

"I can't believe he wasn't there. I saw him at that house. He was there yucking it up with his ass-wipe friends."

"I know. I believe you. But that was a week ago. We had to wait for confirmation from Blake, since it's a little difficult to prove the eye witness account of a ghost to a bunch of federal agents." He covered the place where the wire was taped inside his shirt, then remembered he wasn't supposed to draw attention to it. He just hoped there were enough other people on the street causing interference, so that they weren't picking up on his side – and only his side – of the conversation.

He had been surprised when Detective Jackson let him know that the Bear Forest Volunteer Sheriff's Department was already under investigation for several crimes, which made everything go more smoothly for him in convincing them to raid the house. He had to do some fancy tap dancing around the truth to get them to believe he knew the location of the house, but Blake was also a help in that.

Blake never even questioned how Harry knew about the house. He simply dropped everything, and went out there to do his own reconnaissance. He ended up being a significant help in aiding the task force.

Unfortunately, they hadn't picked up Matthews in the raid, and weren't getting any information on him from the major players they had in lock-up.

"I just hope we can get Matthews to say something incriminating that can be used against him in court." Harry was feeling determined, and would sit in the coffee shop all afternoon if he had to.

Jenny snorted so forcefully, the hair of the woman beside her flapped, and the woman looked around curiously. "He's not exactly known for his intellectual prowess. He's known for his ego. He *thinks* he's the next Stephen Hawking, so if you insult him, he will go out of his way to tell you how brilliant he is. Just be careful, because that's usually punctuated by his fists."

Harry pushed through the door of the coffee shop, and the bell over the door chimed lightly. The smell of fresh coffee beans blended with the scent of vanilla and cinnamon from the pastries on display, and Harry's stomach rumbled, reminding him that he'd been too distracted to eat lunch.

The shop was set up with several mismatched tables and chairs scattered among sofas and loveseats. Along the back wall of the shop were bookshelves with "Take a book. Leave a book" signs that invited customers to cozy up and stay awhile as they drank their caffeinated potion of choice.

Stan and his partner, David, the owners of the shop, were friends of Emma's, and everyone at Landon Literary bought their coffee here, so it was a simple matter for Harry to arrange for the store to be closed.

He'd offered to pay Stan for the lost business, but Stan was a notorious gossip, and was thrilled to be included in the sting operation. He'd have something to talk about with his customers for months, and he was more excited about that prospect than the potential loss of income. Harry was pretty sure the notoriety would end up boosting his business in the end.

The FBI had already briefed Stan on "just act normal," and he was busy cleaning counters and pretending not to notice anything going on. He waved as Harry entered, and pointed to a table in the middle of the room with four empty chairs grouped around it.

Harry waved back, then went over and sat in the chair facing the door, suddenly understanding first-hand the concept of not sitting with your back to the door.

He glanced over at the only other customers in the cafe. Blake and Detective Jackson sat at separate tables each keeping an eye on the situation. Blake gave Harry a slight nod, which told Harry that he was on alert, then turned back to reading a copy of *The Denver Post*.

Detective Jackson sipped his coffee while pretending to check emails on his cell phone. Harry knew that there were federal agents and police officers outside, ready to arrest Matthews as soon as he got enough information from him, and he was anxious to get this done.

Jenny looked like she was going to explode into a thousand ectoplasmic pieces, and he was worried about her. "Just don't do anything stupid. Okay?" he warned, knowing it was probably a wasted effort.

"Giving yourself a little pep talk?" Anna slid into the chair next to Harry and placed her hand on his arm as if worried he was going to run screaming at any minute. She must have arrived earlier, because she came from the direction of the restrooms. "I don't blame you. I'm so nervous, I just threw up my lunch."

That answered that question.

Harry was glad she was here with him, so that he didn't have to do this alone. Between the two of them, they should be able to get Matthews to tell them what they needed. "Thank you for convincing Martin that you and I aren't getting married."

Anna waved him off as if convincing her father was something she did on a regular basis. "I enjoyed it. You should have seen him shut down. You know how he sticks his nose up in the air, and gets all thin-lipped to show his disapproval?"

Harry snorted. He could see the exact picture of disdain his father would have presented to Anna. "I also appreciate you being here today with me. This was above-and-beyond."

"Are you kidding?" Anna looked genuinely surprised. "Miss a front row seat to see Martin's reaction when he discovers he's been outmaneuvered by us not once, but twice? I only wish I could've invited friends for the show."

"You're sure he contacted Matthews to tell him the deal was back on for him to take Max?"

"I'm positive. I heard the conversation myself." Anna seemed to be almost as nervous as he and Jenny, because she was lightly tapping her fingers on the table. "But you know how Martin is. He wants to maximize the attention he'll get, so I'm sure he's late on purpose. He likes to make an entrance. He probably wants to make sure you're getting sufficient time to wallow in misery over his victory."

The bell over the entrance chimed again as the door opened, and Martin walked in as if he owned the place. He didn't hold the door for the man who followed him inside, and Harry bit back a satisfied grin recognizing the gesture as Martin's way of expressing his displeasure.

"He looks like he's planning to give a presentation to the Board." Anna shook her head in disbelief, and Harry knew she didn't like their father any more than he did. The man had burned many bridges with this latest scheme of his.

"He prefers to gloat with an audience, and looking like a televangelist when he does it." Harry gave his father a once-over, and wanted to throw cow shit all over the perfectly pressed Brooks Brothers suit he was wearing. Jesus Christ, the man was so ostentatious.

"I still can't believe he's wearing a suit. Seriously? To go meet up with his kids at a coffee shop, in Denver, no less, where people wear flip-flops in the winter. The man feels compelled to wear a two-hundred-thousand-dollar suit." Anna's disgust showed not just through the tone of her voice, but also in the sneer on her face.

Harry fought back a smile. He had misjudged her in the beginning, believing she had sold out to Martin, and although he was greatly relieved they weren't getting married, he looked forward to continuing a friendship with her.

He returned his attention to the two men approaching their table. Although he had never met him, he knew the man behind Martin was Matthews, and he was a shock to the system. Harry felt like he was looking into a mirror. A fun-house mirror, where his features showed him several pounds rounder in the face and build.

No wonder Harry had originally thought that Max had his eyes. Matthews's eyes were almost the same color as Harry's, which he could see in spite of the puffy lids and bags. He even had the same dark blond hair. *Dishwater Blond*, his mother had always called it, but Harry's had darkened as he got older. Matthews's color was still dishwater blond. It probably came out of a bottle.

Harry gave Jenny a look that conveyed, "What the hell?"

"Yeah, so he looks a bit like you. What can I say?" Jenny shrugged, and returned her attention to Matthews. "I really want to poke him until he has a seizure." Jenny talked tough, but Harry could see her flickering as if she was scared to be in the same room with him.

Matthews also looked scared, his eyes darting around the room like he was expecting bullets to start flying at any minute. Harry hoped he didn't bolt before they got him to spill his guts.

Great, now *he* was starting to sound like a cheap detective novel.

"Anna. Harry." Martin sat down in one of the empty chairs at their table, in spite of not being invited to join them. He didn't glance at Matthews as he continued to speak, "I was sorry to hear that we wouldn't be having a wedding for the two of you. It's unfortunate that you chose this path, Harry. I would have much rather supported you as the father for Max than this..." Martin gestured toward Matthews with a sneer, "person."

"You still can." Harry didn't know why he bothered trying to argue with Martin. They would never have a father and son relationship – hell, he didn't want any relationship with him – but apparently, he still had work to do on expunging his old habits.

"You're the one who's put me in this difficult position. I wanted nothing more than to love my son and my grandson. But you turned your back on—"

"Blah, blah, blah. He said, she said." Matthews was apparently not interested in the Landon family dynamics. "You two can work out your relationship troubles on your own time. Just give me my money, so I can get the hell out of here." Matthews scowled at Martin, and Harry could tell that there was no small amount of mutual hatred between the two of them.

They deserved each other.

"Interesting, Matthews, how you neglected to mention Max," Harry pointed out. "Some of us might think you don't care about him as much as the money you're getting."

"Whatever. Give me my kid and my money, so I can get out of here."

"I told you he never wanted Max." Anna and Jenny spoke exactly the same words at the same time, which made Harry dizzy for a moment.

"My, my." Harry leaned back in his chair and scowled at Matthews. "What's your hurry? Got someplace you need to be to spend my father's blood money."

Martin glared. "That isn't funny, Harry."

"It wasn't a joke, Martin." Harry mimicked Martin's tone, and glared back at him.

Anna leaned in and laid her hand on Harry's arm, giving him the subtle reminder that they weren't there to get into a pissing match with Martin. "You must be in a hurry to get back to your buddies at the Bear Forest Sheriff's Department."

"What the hell?" Matthews jumped out of his chair, and looked like he was torn between strangling Anna, or running for the door.

"Sit down, Matthews," Martin warned, as he placed a restraining hand on Matthews's arm. "You still don't have your son yet."

"Or Martin's money." Harry couldn't resist the urge to poke the bear. Either one of them. But it seemed to be the decision breaker for Matthews, because he sat back down.

"What did she mean by that?" Matthews turned his glare on Anna. "What the hell do you know about the Bear Forest Sheriff's Department?"

"We know that they were all arrested last night for drug smuggling," Harry said, as he watched Matthews closely, getting ready to pounce on the guy if he so much as looked at the door.

"That's bullshit." Matthews didn't look nervous, as Harry would have expected. The idiot looked smug, and Harry was feeling more confident in Jenny's assessment that he was too stupid for his own good.

"Here we go," Jenny chimed, bouncing like a prize fighter heading into the ring. "See? I told you he was a dunce."

"Believe it," Harry continued. "They're being interrogated because there's still one guy they didn't find there last night." Harry paused to gauge Matthews's reaction. Sure enough, he wasn't as self-assured as he'd been moments ago, and tiny beads of sweat were forming on his upper lip.

Harry looked over at Martin to see how he was taking all the good news. Martin sat rigid in his chair, like he was weighing options in his head and determining how to turn this all around to his own advantage.

"It's only a matter of time before they give him up to the Feds," Anna pointed out, as if she, too, wanted to get in there and twist the knife a bit.

"They'd never do that," Matthews hissed. "I don't know what kind of game you're playing, but—"

"They already did, Matthews," Harry snapped back. "They gave you up last night the minute they were arrested." He was lying, of course, but hopefully Matthews would believe him. "They told the cops you masterminded the entire operation. I knew that wasn't possible, of course. You aren't that bright."

Harry hoped that would be the spark that would light the fire, as Jenny had suggested.

"Oh, really, smartass?" Matthews leaned closer to Harry, and looked like he was about to tell everyone how he'd planned the entire operation from start to finish.

"Stop talking, Matthews," Martin interrupted. "That makes no difference as to why we're here today." Martin acted as if he couldn't care less what Matthews did in his spare time.

Harry was furious, and he turned his focus on his father. "Don't you care that you're fighting to give custody of your grandson to a criminal?"

"Except that he isn't my grandson. Is he?"

"No, he's not. He's my son," Matthews gloated, and Harry wanted to choke him. "Now, give me my goddamned money so I can get the hell out of here. You people are pissing me off."

"You may leave whenever you want, Matthews," Harry said, as calmly as possible, "but you are never getting my son."

"That's not what a judge is going to say, is it Martin?" Matthews sat back in his chair and winked like they were best buds. Harry felt a flicker of satisfaction watching Martin take a deep breath, as if trying to calm himself in order to keep from strangling Matthews.

Matthews had the nerve to look cocky, and Harry wanted to punch him in his perfect, but pudgy, nose. He felt much better when Jenny poked Matthews in the arm, and he jumped out of his chair with a shout and looked around the room.

Everyone looked at him like he'd gone mental, and Harry coughed to cover his laugh, which seemed to make Matthews even more mad. "You people think because you have money, you're above the law. Well, you aren't."

"But you believe you're above the law?" Harry growled. "You and your drug buddies at the Bear Forest Sheriff's Department? Admit it. The only reason you're even pretending to want Max is for Martin's money, so that you can pay back what your buddies discovered missing."

"How do you know about the missing money?" Matthews blanched, as if someone had told him he had less than a week left to live.

"I know a lot about you," Harry continued, infusing as much

menace into his voice as he could manage. "You don't really want Max."

"Of course he wants his son." Martin was either deluding himself, or he was trying to get Matthews back on board with the plan.

"I don't give a shit about the kid." Matthews spat the words out at Martin. "I just want my money, so I can get as far away from here as possible."

"You need to stop talking now," Martin snapped.

"Shut up, old man. You may be footing the bill, but you can't tell me what to do." Matthews looked like he was beginning to fray around the edges, and Harry was hopeful that the guy was going to tell them everything, in spite of Martin's interference.

"But the people you owe the money are all locked up. You don't have to pay them now. You could just walk away." Harry still had to get Matthews to admit his connection to the group.

"Do you think I'm stupid?" Matthews snarled, and Harry was sure the guy had caught on to their scheme. He wasn't sure what to say next.

"Let's see," Anna chimed in, "you're dealing drugs with people who probably want to kill you. So, yes, I think you're stupid. Or was that meant to be a rhetorical question?" She gave Matthews a look of such condescension Harry almost applauded.

Matthews was less than thrilled, and looked as if he was going to reach across the table and slap her. "You don't want to get on my bad side, bitch. It won't go well for you. You have no idea who you're dealing with."

"All I see is a pathetic excuse for a human with delusions of grandeur. In case you missed this part, your muscle has been locked up, and you're on your own."

Matthews was turning fire-engine red, and Harry thought the guy was going to spontaneously combust. He hoped it all landed on Martin.

"They won't be in there forever." Matthews glared at Anna. "When they get out, they're going to want to pick up where things left off. And if I don't have their money, and a thriving business for them to return to, my life won't be worth shit."

"So, you think you're going to continue working their operation by buying drugs while they're in prison?" Harry asked, hoping Matthews was too worked up to notice he was being baited, but he had to get something incriminating on the tape.

"That's exactly what I think, moron. You don't think I can keep things running until they get out? You think you're the only one who can run a business? Buying and selling the drugs is the hardest part, and I was already doing that. The rest of it is just business." Matthews turned to Martin, who had finally gone speechless. "Give me my money, and my son. I'm leaving." Matthews looked around the coffee shop. "Where is my son?"

"He's. *My*. Son." Harry leaned across the table and growled the words into Matthews's face. He wanted Matthews to pay, not just for the drugs, but for all the damage he'd done to the people in his life. "He stopped being your son the moment you started beating his mother."

Harry whipped out the pictures he retrieved from the room at the boarding house, and threw them at Matthews. "You don't have your friends at the Bear Forest Sheriff's department this time. They're all too busy trying to save themselves by turning on each other. And I have proof that you beat Jenny the day she died." He didn't have proof, but Matthews wouldn't know that, and he pushed harder. "She suffered a brain bleed from your beating, which caused her to crash the car. That's murder one."

It wasn't murder one, it was involuntary manslaughter, but Harry decided murder one would sound more frightening to a chicken-shit like Matthews. He knew Matthews wasn't a cop, or a criminal attorney, and he hoped the guy hadn't picked up any knowledge of the law hanging around the sheriff's department.

Judging by the way Matthews slumped back into his chair, Harry could tell the guy was falling for it.

"She had it coming. She was trying to leave me. We made vows together in front of God and witnesses. Til death do us part. But she was going to throw that all away. And then the bitch stole from me." Matthews was looking around, as if trying to find supporters for his cause.

"So, you decided to hit her?" Anna knew the story, but she still seemed shocked by what he was saying. "You thought the best way to control her was to beat her into submission?"

"She needed to know who was boss."

"You beat her to death." Harry couldn't believe the bastard thought he was justified. "Your blood and fingerprints are all over the car she was driving." Harry didn't know if this was true or not – there had to be several hundred fingerprints on the car Jenny had borrowed from the shelter – but she had given Matthews a nose-bleed, so hopefully they could use that against him.

"You're a piece of shit." Anna whispered, as if she couldn't believe such evil could exist.

It seemed like everything happened at once.

Matthews turned on Anna, with a look on his face that said he wanted to teach her the same lesson he'd taught Jenny.

Anna looked like she was getting ready to launch herself across the table at Matthews, but Blake materialized next to her in a heart-beat and shoved her behind him.

Jenny screamed a banshee war cry, and punched Matthews in the face.

Matthews jumped up and howled in pain, just as the Federal agents poured into the coffee shop.

And Detective Jackson had Matthews on the ground and cuffed before Harry even knew he'd left his table.

Anna pointed at the place where Matthews had been sitting. "Did you see that? I swear I saw a shadow, or something, fly by Matthews just before he howled."

When things calmed down, and Matthews was being taken away, Detective Jackson came over to Harry with a smile on his face and said, "Well, that should do it. Nice job." He gave a puzzled look at Blake who was still holding a protesting Anna behind his back.

"Move, you Neanderthal." Anna ineffectively punched Blake in the arm.

Blake chuckled at her punch, and turned to face her while he rubbed his arm in mock injury. "That's the thanks I get for trying to keep you safe?"

"Yeah, yeah, poor little wimpy female can't take care of herself." Anna was jabbing her finger into Blake's chest to punctuate each word, but he only seemed amused by her. "For your information, bub, I didn't need your help."

"Not today. But you will." Blake flipped his business card into his hand like a magician, then tucked it into the back pocket of Anna's jeans. Harry was impressed that the guy had managed the whole maneuver without copping a feel in the process.

Anna seemed to grow even more angry when Blake stood there grinning at her. Harry knew from past experience that this was like catnip to Blake. Anna was toast, and that made Harry happy. She deserved to have a good guy like Blake, even if she didn't realize it yet.

"Call me when you change your mind." Blake continued. "I'll help you find your father."

Anna gasped like she'd been doused with a pitcher full of ice-cold beer.

Harry understood her reaction. But if Blake thought he could find her real father, then he would. Blake never committed to anything unless he knew he'd succeed.

"Should I go break that up?" Jackson seemed concerned by the interaction between Blake and Anna.

"No, that's just foreplay for Blake." Harry started to chuckle, until he realized that Jackson was glaring at Blake. Holy shit, Jackson was interested in Anna, too? Well, she was certainly going to have her hands full. Harry hoped he'd get front row seats to the show.

"Catch ya later, Harry." Blake spoke to Harry, but he never took his eyes off the stunned-to-a-statue Anna as he gave her one more of his trademark grins, then left the shop.

"Hey, it just occurred to me." Harry turned back to Jackson, who was scowling at the door Blake had just closed. "No one read him his

Miranda Rights." He had heard about people being released because they weren't properly Mirandized, and he didn't want that to be a possibility with Matthews. Too much was at stake for a technicality.

"That only happens in the movies for effect." Jackson chuckled, shaking his head as if coming out of a trance. "In real life, we have them read their Miranda Rights in interrogation, then sign them, so that there's validated documentation and no question in court. And in case you're thinking about criminals being released because they weren't properly Mirandized, that also only happens in the movies."

Holy shit, was everyone a mind reader? Or was Harry just that easy to predict?

"Sorry, I didn't mean to sound like I was telling you how to do your job." Harry smiled back at Jackson. "I just don't want anything to go wrong that might lead to him getting out."

"I get it. I know what's on the line for you." Jackson held out his hand, and Harry shook it.

"Thank you, Detective Jackson. For everything."

"Please call me, Ryan." Jackson glanced at Anna and smiled. "Something tells me we'll be talking a lot over the next couple of months."

"Thanks, Ryan," Harry said, even though he knew Jackson was no longer paying any attention to him.

Jackson took one last look at Anna, who didn't seem to know where to look, then he left the shop.

"Anna?"

"Hmmmm?"

Harry chuckled, because he knew she wasn't focused. He could tell her that the pope just walked in and ordered a double caramel macchiato with whipped cream, and she would have answered the same way.

Then he realized that Martin was gone.

No one had even seen him leave.

CHAPTER TWENTY-EIGHT

Harry was in his kitchen feeling a little absurd to be dressed as a pirate, while stirring a pot of chili.

After dinner, he and Anna were taking Max trick-or-treating in the neighborhood. Max was almost over the age of caring about begging for candy on Halloween, but Harry wanted at least one memory of trick-or-treating with his son.

"Do you think I'll go to hell if I sneak into Curtis's cell and torture him a bit?" Jenny sat on a stool at the kitchen counter keeping him company.

They were celebrating. Matthew's trial wouldn't happen for a very long time, but the judge at the preliminary hearing had denied bail, so he was successfully out of their lives. Harry was so relieved, he wanted to post an ad in the *Denver Business Journal* to tell the whole world.

What he really wanted was to share the news with Luke.

He shook a small amount of cinnamon into the chili, and his knees buckled from the evocative scent. Would he ever be able to cook with the spice again without being overwhelmed by memories of the man who smelled of cinnamon and oranges? The man who tasted of love and home.

Christ, he still missed Luke so much it was like a piece of his soul had been sliced away. Whoever coined the phrase *time heals all wounds* was an idiot, and had obviously never been in love, because that was a load of shit. Harry still felt as miserable as he'd been the day Luke left.

The nights were the hardest, when he was alone in his cold and enormously empty bed. The sorrow seemed to seep out of him, and he'd wake with a tear-soaked pillow.

He had failed Luke, and he had failed Jenny. She was going to be stuck here forever, and it was his fault. Would she be set free if he found someone else to love? If he went out onto one of those dating sites, and hooked up with someone else, would it count?

He'd talk to Jason about it, and see if he'd be able to help him with his profile, or whatever the hell it was called. Even though Jason was happily married to Michael, and had been out of the dating pool for a long time, he should still be able to help point Harry in the right direction to the best sites, and keep Harry from making a complete ass of himself.

He had to try. For Jenny's sake, at least, if not for his own.

The thought of trying to love someone who wasn't Luke sent sharp needles stabbing into his heart, and he almost knocked over the pot of chili.

Would it even work? Or would Jenny still be trapped here because he'd lost his only real chance at love with Luke? Maybe he should go talk to Jessica, and see if she knew the rules before he subjected himself to the torture of dating.

"You need to go find him." He didn't have to ask who Jenny was talking about. He'd long since gotten used to her being able to read his mind. Even if she kept denying it.

"That's not as easy as it sounds." Harry added more chili powder to the pot, and stirred it in, hoping the mundane task would take his mind off the man he loved. The man he missed so much it caused physical pain.

"Have you tried looking for him as Sebastian Lucas?" Jenny continued to badger him, not allowing him his own thoughts. "Did you check to see if he's doing any new art shows, or interviews lately?"

"Please, just stop." Harry rubbed his chest in a vain effort to dislodge the burn in his heart that had nothing to do with any food he'd eaten. "I've called his cell. It's no longer in service. I've checked the papers, run Internet searches until my head hurt, and left messages at the galleries showing his art. I even thought about asking Detective Jackson to put out an APB. But the bottom line is this: The guy doesn't want me. Just because I can't find him, doesn't mean he can't find me. He knows where I am. And he isn't here."

"He does want you. He just couldn't stand being here and watching you marry Anna."

"I'm so sorry, Jenny. I'm sorry you're stuck here, and it's all my fault. I'll find someone to make me happy. Someday. I promise. And then you'll be free." He wasn't sure he could keep that promise, but he would do his best. "In the meantime, please, please, *please* stop talking about what can't be. You're just making it harder for me."

"Are you talking to Mom?" Max, dressed in a smaller version of the exact same pirate costume as Harry's, came into the kitchen, grabbed an apple and sat down on the same stool Jenny occupied. She moved quickly and shifted to the stool next to him.

Harry swallowed several times to clear his throat, and welcomed the opportunity to change the subject. "She wants to know if she'd be in trouble if she gave Curtis a few ghostly jolts. I'd say she's justified. Wouldn't you?"

"Give him a good jolt for me, too." Max squinted in the direction he'd seen Harry looking, as though trying very hard to see her.

Harry chuckled, not in the least worried that his son might have inherited some kind of blood-thirsty revenge gene from his mother. She was really getting into the whole, jolt-the-enemy thing.

"Dad?" Max sounded hesitant.

"Yeah, bud?" He stopped stirring the chili, and turned to give his son his full attention. He wondered if he would ever get tired of the small thrill he got every time Max called him "Dad." Whatever collateral damage he and Jenny suffered was worth the price of keeping Max safe and happy.

"Is there something wrong with my mom?"

"Sure. There are tons of things wrong with her. Can you be more specific?" Harry winked at Jenny, to let her know they were going to be fine.

"I mean, why is she still here? Shouldn't she be happy now, and move on? Or whatever?" Max scrunched his face, looking like he did when he was trying to solve one of his math problems. "It's not that I'm not glad she's here, but I'm worried that she'll... like... get stuck here or something."

"I don't know." Harry glanced over at Jenny for help, but she merely shrugged. He had promised Max he'd never lie to him, but he wasn't sure how he was going to explain the complicated mess of Jenny's now permanent existence. The last thing he wanted was for Max to believe it was somehow his own fault.

"You know what I think?" Max took a bite of his apple, and spoke while chewing it. Harry knew he'd have to break him of that habit, but that was for another time. "I think it's like what Jessica said, that Mom's here for you. And I don't think she can go until you and Luke get back together. You should tell him that you and Anna aren't getting married, and I bet he and Sheldon'll come back."

To Max, it was just that simple: Go find Luke, and everyone lives happily ever after.

Harry wasn't sure how much more of this he could take.

"It's not that easy. Luke moved away, and didn't tell me where he was going, so I don't know how to let him know that." His eyes started to water again, and he turned back around to stir the chili.

"Can't Mom help? I bet she knows where he is, and can get him to come back."

Harry heard Jenny sigh. "If I could, I would."

The doorbell rang, and Max jumped up leaving his half-eaten apple on the counter. "Anna's here. Finally."

Harry smiled, glad that he and Anna would be able to give Max the full family experience of trick-or-treating. He turned off the stove, and placed the lid on the pot to keep the chili warm. He wiped his hands on a kitchen towel, then threw away the half-eaten apple, and followed Max to greet Anna.

Sheldon barreled inside.

"Sheldon!" Max shouted, and Harry was pretty sure that everyone all the way to Castle Rock could hear him. Harry's stomach fluttered and flipped, as dog and boy wrestled on the floor, obviously glad to see each other.

Harry figured he had to be hallucinating, because if Sheldon was here, that meant...

"Hey, Luke!" Max waved in the direction of the entryway. "Can I take Sheldon to my room?" He must have received an affirmative nod, because he ran to his room, Sheldon following, as if it had only been a few hours since they'd seen each other, instead of almost six months.

Harry slowly walked to the front door, and couldn't believe his eyes. Even though his head knew what he would find, his heart still stuttered with unexpected joy.

Luke stood there, hands in his jeans pockets, looking like he'd been through hell and back. His hair was longer, and tucked behind his ears. His face looked like he hadn't shaved since he'd left. And there were dark circles under his eyes, making him look like he'd slept even less than Harry.

He was the most beautiful thing Harry had ever seen. He wanted to wrap his arms around him, and never let go again. But Luke hadn't said a word yet, and Harry wasn't sure what to do.

"Is the Zombie look supposed to be your costume for Halloween?" Harry knew it was a lame thing to say, since he was wearing a costume himself, but he couldn't think clearly with all the racket his heart was making.

"I got your messages." Luke's voice sounded scratchy, like he hadn't used it in years. "Thank you."

"*Thank you?* Are you serious?" Just like that, Harry's joy turned to anger. "Six months of me leaving you messages at every gallery across the continental U.S., not to mention several in Europe, and all you can say is *thank you*? What the hell, Luke?"

"Don't get mad, you dope," Jenny screamed. "He's here. Tell him you love him."

She was right, and Harry immediately felt panic take control. What was he saying? He was so confused. It was as if finally seeing Luke again had broken the dam on his emotions, and they all came crashing out at once. He needed to get control, or he was going to lose him again. "I'm sorry. I—"

"No." Luke interrupted.

Harry's heart plummeted to the floor. He'd blown it. Six months of pure hell being apart, and he'd let his anger get the better of him.

"Don't be sorry," Luke continued. "You aren't the one who should be sorry. I am. I left you. Alone. I should have been here. No matter what." He looked hopeful, but also scared, and Harry could see his hand shake when he reached out. "I can't live without you. I don't care that you married her, you were right to make that decision. But I made the wrong decision. Because I can't live without you."

That was the longest string of words Harry had ever heard Luke put together. And they were wonderful.

Harry couldn't hold back any longer. He held Luke's face in his hands, and kissed him. He didn't know if he tasted Luke's tears or his own, but it didn't matter. He'd spent the last several months trying to get used to the fact that he would never get to kiss Luke again.

"I'll do it," Luke said, as he kissed Harry's eyes, his cheeks, and then kissed him again on the mouth. "I'll take whatever I can get with you. I love you. We'll figure something out with Anna. We can make it work. Tell me we can make it work."

"We don't have to." Harry wiped away Luke's tears, then kissed each cheek, slowly, savoring the taste and smell of the man he never thought he'd see again. "It's a long story, but Anna and I aren't married. And, we aren't *getting* married."

Luke froze. "But Max...?"

"He's mine. It's all legal. Anna and I didn't have to get married for me to keep him." When Luke still didn't move, Harry started to worry.

"It's okay. He's safe. Anna and I are friends, but we aren't married. I promise, I'll tell you everything."

Harry was so happy, he almost couldn't get the words out through the lump in his throat.

"I never should have left." Luke let out a breath of relief so long, Harry was surprised he hadn't passed out from lack of oxygen. Then he was kissing him again, and nothing else mattered.

"Oh, Harry." He heard Jenny's blissful sigh, but didn't break the kiss with Luke. "Sorry I'll miss the wedding, but know that I wish you all the best. Take care of our boys."

Harry opened his eyes just in time to see showers of tiny sparkling lights raining down over him and Luke.

EPILOGUE

"**M**ax, please take Sheldon outside. He keeps getting into the paint."

Max set down his paintbrush and hustled Sheldon outside a little too eagerly, and Harry almost laughed. Apparently, painting a bedroom, even your own, wasn't high on the wish list of a ten-year-old boy.

Harry gave Luke a look of fake pity. "Your dog's a menace. You know that, right? He likes to eat paint for chrissake. How healthy can that be?"

"*Our* dog is perfect. And he's crazy about our son, so what more could we want?" Luke leaned down from the ladder and kissed Harry, who dropped his brush and pulled Luke down for a better angle. "He wasn't eating the paint. You only wanted them both out of the way so that we could make out. Admit it."

"You know me so well." Harry ran his hands down Luke's back so that he could run them back up again underneath his T-shirt. They'd been married a year already, and he was still amazed that he had this man in his life forever.

The sound of another man clearing his throat brought Harry out of his trance, and he looked up to see Jason standing in the doorway to the bedroom.

"You can both afford to hire a painter. Each. You'd think a world-renowned artist would be above such menial labor." Jason looked serious, but Harry knew he was enjoying ribbing Luke.

"No task is too menial when it's important. Besides, it brings back happy memories." Luke winked at Harry before letting him go. "Buy you a beer, Jason?"

Eight months ago, Harry had talked Luke into doing a complete remodel of their lofts. They knocked down the wall between the two condos, turning the two kitchens into a state-of-the-art one that would make a master chef weep with envy.

Most of the rest of Luke's condo was converted into a studio with floor-to-ceiling windows that gave him abundant natural light. Harry loved to watch Luke in his element, and even posed for private sessions when Max was at sleep-overs.

The other half of Luke's condo had been converted into a library. The mahogany bookshelves covered the entire length of the two walls surrounding the fireplace, which had been re-done to look like something out of an old English castle. The plush sofa in warm earth tones, accented with wing chairs in deep reds and sapphire blues, had taken Harry many frustrating months to find, but they were worth it. He loved their new library.

They had hired contractors to do all the remodeling work, including the painting, but they had both wanted to paint Max's bedroom themselves as a reminiscence of the first time they'd painted together, and as a way to show Max that they were a family. A whole family.

Luke pulled three beers from the Sub-Zero wine cabinet next to the fridge and handed one each to Harry and Jason. In spite of being considered a wine snob by his husband, Harry got a kick out of seeing Luke's Coors Banquet and Blue Moon mixed in with his Chateau Margaux and his Louis Roederer Cristal Brut.

"What's the word?" Harry sipped from his beer bottle, pretending a nonchalance he didn't feel. Today was Curtis Matthews's sentencing, and Harry wanted it to be for a very long time.

"Five years for involuntary manslaughter." Harry held his breath and waited hoping Jason would continue. Jason looked from Luke to Harry, drawing out the final moment. "Five years for spousal abuse, and five years for drug trafficking and distribution."

Harry was so relieved, his legs went weak, and he almost lost his balance.

"Five years is good." Luke held up his bottle to toast.

"Fifteen years is better." Jason grinned, then took a drink from his bottle, fully aware that he was making Harry wait, again, for a more dramatic effect. "The judge sentenced Matthews to consecutive sentences, not concurrent. He's going to be there for fifteen years, serving each sentence out to the end before the next one starts. Even if he gets out early on parole for good behavior – and we all know what the odds are of that happening – Max will be an adult."

"Now that is worth drinking to." Harry set down his beer, then pulled a bottle of Dom Perignon out of the wine cabinet. "I was saving this for just this occasion."

Harry popped the cork, as Luke pulled glasses out of the cupboard.

"Well, that's a happy sound if I've ever heard one." Anna wandered into the kitchen with a smile on her face. "What are we celebrating, gents?"

"Hey, Anna. Just in time," Luke said with a smile, He pulled another glass down, and Harry handed him the bottle.

Harry went around the counter to Anna, then lifted her up, and twirled her around. He kissed her loudly on the mouth for special effect. "Fifteen years, Anna! They gave him fifteen blessed years."

Anna whooped and clapped her hands, then kissed Jason and Luke on their cheeks, as they both hugged her in turn. "I'll drink to that."

They all raised their glasses in a toast. "To Max!"

Then, while everyone talked at once, Harry quietly raised his glass again in another toast.

"To Jenny."

If you enjoyed reading *Family Spirit*, you will also like George and Emma's story, book one of the Landon Legacy series, *Christmas Spirit*.
http://juliecameron.net/buy-the-book/

Please also consider posting a review on Amazon or Goodreads.
Amazon Author Page
Goodreads Author Page

ABOUT THE AUTHOR

Julie Cameron is an award-winning author and screenwriter of humorous women's fiction and romantic comedy. She has been a member of RWA and CRW since before her first book was published in 2015, and a member of Lighthouse Writers Workshop since 2012. Julie is a long-time resident of Denver, Colorado where she enjoys spending time with her family and friends. When she isn't writing, she's thinking up excuses to take her nieces and nephews out in search of a chocolate fix.

Julie invites her readers to check in with her on her website and other social media.

For more information, please visit:

juliecameron.net/

info@landonliterary.com